FRACTURED

FRACTURED

JB ROTH

AUTHOR OF **BLUNT FORCE**

Fractured

© 2026 by JB Roth

Editors: Deborah Froese, Josh Owens
Cover and Interior Design: Emma Elzinga

Indigo River Publishing
3 West Garden Street, Ste. 718
Pensacola, FL 32502

www.indigoriverpublishing.com

Ordering Information:

Quantity Sales: Special discounts are available on quantity purchases by corporations, associations, and others. For details, contact the publisher at the address above.

Orders by US trade bookstores and wholesalers: Please contact the publisher at the address above.

Printed in the United States of America
Library of Congress Control Number: 2025920481

ISBN: 978-1-964686-81-3 (paperback) 978-1-964686-82-0 (ebook)

First Edition

With Indigo River Publishing, you can always expect great books, strong voices, and meaningful messages. Most importantly, you'll always find . . . *words worth reading.*

To Penny:
You are my love, my life, my inspiration.

PROLOGUE

"**Something hit me!" Pam said,** wheezing her words.

No one said anything in response. Maybe no one heard her over the fireworks, though they were finally petering out. Five minutes earlier, they'd sounded like flak in a World War II movie.

Bodies shuffled when Pam slumped, head down, then fell sideways onto the ground from her position sitting on the retaining wall, legs dangling freely, the beach and ocean below. Someone tried to catch her. Someone else asked what was going on. A shriek pierced the air. Pam's body crumbled, eyes rolling back into her head. A red spot spread across her tank top.

Someone else screamed.

People ran but went nowhere.

In the distance, a voice called out, "Have you seen three girls? Three college girls? Have you seen three girls?"

No one listened. They watched in horror as Pam Howard died on the Fourth of July.

CHAPTER 1

The call came at 7:07 a.m. on the seventh day of the seventh month.

I stared at the phone for a couple of rings with a mixture of anticipation and irritation. Private investigators are not like DUI lawyers. Those guys hired extra staff to take in the flood of calls after a major holiday like the Fourth of July. Still, shit happened when people drank too much or blew off a little too much steam. Sometimes, they hired us to sort the mess.

Not every call became a case. There was plenty of nonsense. People wanted us to get to the bottom of credit card fraud when they didn't remember drunk shopping online. Others called because their car was stolen, only to realize their friends had put them in an Uber and their car was safe on the other side of town. But there were legit calls too. We'd lined up a couple of new cases already after this Fourth of July, and today the office line was forwarded to my cell.

I picked up the call. "Malone."

A pause followed, a short one, then a clear, strong baritone came through. "Yes. Good morning. I'm sorry. I was prepared to leave a voicemail at this hour."

The voice sounded familiar. I stood there trying to place it as I squinted at my tiny backyard through the breakfast nook's window, coffee in hand.

"Well," I said, "you've got me, caffeinated and everything."

"Yes, I shouldn't be surprised. This is *Cooper* Malone?"

"Yes, how can I help you?"

"The same Cooper Malone who served in the First Infantry Division?"

With those last three words, it clicked, like a key rotating a lock's tumblers. My back straightened as I recognized the caller. "General Overby?"

"Long retired, son. Call me John."

"I'll make no promises on that. Old habits die hard." I didn't tell my former commander they died so hard I was still standing damn near at attention. I shook my head, pulled out a chair, and sat down.

"Fair enough," Overby said.

I was more than a little surprised to hear his voice. I masked my reaction the way I usually did when caught off guard. I went straight to business. "Sir—I mean John—I'm guessing you did not call me at 0700 just to hear an old grunt's voice."

"No, I didn't. I need your help. When I say 'I' it's not just me, though. I mean me, my daughter, and two other families."

I took a second or two to digest that information. Three families were an awful lot of people to need a PI's help all at once. My head started hurting, a pressure between my temples that even coffee could not keep at bay.

General Overby was a smart guy. He guessed the string of thoughts marching behind my silence.

"Yes, it's a bit complicated," he said. "The situation is better explained in person. We're all in Key Largo. I realize it's not exactly next door to your office, but we will pay for your time, and I'd consider it a personal favor."

"Paying me is not a favor, it's business. And I do not charge for consultations. I either take the consult or I don't."

"Will you take this one?"

It wasn't really a question, no matter how he phrased it. It was a plea, one I'd known the response to the moment I'd recognized Overby's voice.

"Tell me where to find you. I can be there in ninety minutes."

"We'll be at a breakfast place called the Secret Passage." He gave me the address.

"I'll see you there."

We fell back on our old army habits and hung up. Exchange information, over and out. There'd be time for thanks and goodbyes another time.

I put the restaurant's name and address in my phone and finished getting ready. I walked past the mudroom that led to the garage and left through the front door. The garage was there for the old Indian motorcycle and to store my stuff. This was Florida, after all. The company CR-V slept outside.

It was early enough that getting in the car did not suffocate me with heat. I drove out of my neighborhood and pointed the Ham Sandwich south on US 1. I still got eye rolls at the office for nicknaming the company car, but the moniker fit. The Honda was like a ham sandwich for lunch: it wasn't exciting, but it got the job done, and you could find it anywhere. That was the point. Trailing a suspect in an Escalade only got you noticed—fast.

Once settled on the highway, I placed a call on the hands-free. The office wouldn't be open yet, so I called CJ, my partner, on her cell. I smiled as the expected cacophony reached my ears the moment she picked up.

I knew CJ's morning routine from our long-ago dating days—before we'd decided we were both better off sticking to running a business together. That was hard enough. We'd broken off our romance early and on good terms, and we stayed friends as well as business partners. We always had each other's back, no matter what, at work and everywhere else. I trusted CJ as much as anyone I'd shared a foxhole with.

I checked my watch. She'd be done with her run and showered by now, flying around at Mach ten between getting dressed, assembling some kind of breakfast, checking overnight emails, and that was just to start. She'd have clicked the answer button once she saw my name on the screen and put me on speaker within half a second. She would not slow down for my benefit.

"What's going on?" she asked. "It's early."

"I always wake up early."

"You wake up early to spend quality time with your coffee. But it sounds like you're in the car."

"That's because I am." I gave her the 411 on my call with General Overby.

"Okay," she said, "I'll open a new case file when I get to the office. Let me know when you might make it in. I won't expect you for a while."

"That's probably wise."

"I think you've mentioned Overby before. That was during your MP days, wasn't it?" Her voice fluctuated between loud and barely audible as she moved about. CJ could walk up and down the little corridor from her bedroom to her family room and kitchen fifty times a morning, her phone resting on the counter—getting dressed, eating breakfast, and checking emails all at the same time.

"You recognize the name because you have a mind like a steel trap. I hadn't heard from him in years. I probably did mention him on occasion, though. I caught his eye for some reason when I was a young officer and he already had a star on his shoulder.

"I never really knew why or how. Generals don't normally notice lieutenants—too many people in between, too many links in the chain of command. But he did. When my MP commitment ended, he put his thumb on the scale to help get me into Military Intelligence."

"So, you owe him and you're going to help him," CJ said. "It's the right thing to do."

That was typical CJ. She had a strong sense of right and wrong. I had a strong sense of getting things done. We made a good team.

"Glad you think so," I said. "I'll call you when I know more."

"Very well. Talk to you later."

I said goodbye and cranked up the radio for the drive. Classic rock filled the car, and I was once again grateful we'd splurged on a good sound system. I thought of it as extra pickles on the Ham Sandwich. That'd earned me plenty of eyerolls at the office too, but I wasn't going to let anyone's lack of a sense of humor stop me.

I made good time by South Florida standards—which did not stop me from griping about too many cars on the road—and found the Secret Passage where the GPS said it would be. It was a squat building with a fenced dog-friendly patio, if the signs nailed to slats and the young couple walking in with a golden retriever were any indication. The pooch wagged its tail at the scent of waffles. I took a deep breath. I did not have a canine sense of smell, but the sweet, buttery scent made my mouth water.

I had yet to lock the car when General Overby came out of the restaurant and headed straight for me. I would have recognized him anywhere, even in the shorts and golf shirt that had replaced his uniform. He was tall, thin, fit, with a strong jaw and bright eyes framed by smile lines at the corners. As he walked toward me, his head swiveled toward every parked car and every palm tree as if he expected someone with an AK-47 to be crouching in wait. I'd seen many a soldier who could never shake that habit.

When he reached me, Overby's grin mirrored mine as he extended his hand. "Thanks for coming, Malone."

I suppressed the urge to chuckle and widened my grin into a smile. "I told you old habits die hard. Generals call me Malone. Friends call me Coop."

He smiled back briefly, but the emotion was fleeting. His face was lined with concern—something I'd rarely seen on him. He'd always been a rock.

"I won't make any promises either," Overby said, "but I'll try and remember that, Coop. Walk with me, will you? I'll brief you on the basics before we walk in there."

I nodded, and we started off in lockstep, heading out of the parking lot and onto the sidewalk. Overby pulled his sunglasses down from the top of his head as we walked side by side into the sun. We were close enough to the ocean for a little breeze to offer relief from the rising heat.

Overby started talking in a brisk, precise tone. "You may remember I have a daughter."

"Yes, I remember seeing her picture on your desk—a beautiful young woman, I recall."

"I figured you'd remember. She's still a beautiful woman and still looks younger than she is. Her own daughter, my granddaughter, is grown now, about to start her junior year of college in Gainesville."

I let out a slow whistle in appreciation for the passage of time. My former boss's daughter's daughter attending college made me feel old.

Overby went on. "My daughter and granddaughter have spent every Fourth of July with two other families for the past four or five years—just the moms and daughters, actually, a girls' bonding time. The three younger women met in high school. They are the same age and thick as thieves.

"The past couple of years, they've taken to staying at the Overseas RV Resort, just up US-1 from here. For context, the place deserves the name 'resort.' Facilities are top-notch, and service is good. Most of the land juts into the ocean, so nearly all the sites face the beach. Half the RVs there on any given day cost more than my house. They're luxury dwellings on wheels."

I nodded.

"It probably won't surprise you," he continued, "that there's a lot of money spent on fireworks the night of the Fourth. What the guests at Overseas set off on the beach rivals a small town's commercial display."

We turned the corner, walking around the block as Overby talked.

He took a deep breath. "This year, things went horribly wrong. A woman was shot and killed. Bullet to the chest."

I stopped in my tracks. General Overby stopped too but stayed silent. Maybe he was letting me digest that piece of information. Maybe he was gathering his thoughts as he was about to explain why I was here. I didn't think it was because of a random murder on the beach.

We resumed walking and turned another corner. The sun was now beating on the back of my neck.

"That same evening, my granddaughter and her two friends disappeared," Overby said, his speech clipped as though each word was carved with a knife. He looked directly at me for the first time since he started, his eyes narrow and hard. "No one has seen or heard from them since. Three days, Coop."

He let a second pass, then went on. "The parents reported them missing and provided a host of information, but . . . you know how it is, Malone. It may not be like the bad ol' days when cops wouldn't bother investigating missing persons until forty-eight hours passed, if at all. But right now, the Monroe County Sheriff's Office is more worried about a murder they know happened then three college girls who, for all they know, got bored and hitched a ride to go party in Key West."

"Could they have? Gone to Key West or up to South Beach to be young and stupid?"

Overby showed no surprise at the question. "Chloe—that's my granddaughter—is no angel. Neither was her mother at her age if you want to know the truth. They've both been a pain in my ass from their first steps. It would not surprise me if Chloe had ditched her mom to go party. But not for three days. She's the kind of kid who'll sneak out, drink too much, and do whatever else I don't want to know about, but she'll call an Uber at the end of the night or even call her mother to pick her up. So yes, she and the other girls could have found something more fun than watching fireworks with their moms. But she'd have called since then."

I took in the information. Overby's concerns were valid—not that I'd have expected anything else. And his concerns about law enforcement not being concerned enough were valid too. I knew a little bit about the Monroe County Sherriff's Office—MCSO to county residents and those of us in the biz. For one thing, it was divided into geographical districts. Everyone in each district pitched in, and right now, they'd all be pitching in to solve a murder, not to look for college kids.

"No sign of violence?" I asked, though I suspected I knew the answer. "No ransom call?"

"Nothing of the sort. And I'm sure that informed the sheriff's office's decision about . . ." Overby trailed off, choosing his words. His voice softened with resignation. "How to allocate their resources."

"You said you got in yesterday?" I asked. Talking to General Overby made for an easy consult. Most clients needed coaxing and positive reinforcement along the way. The stories they had to tell were often daunting to them. There was no need for that with Overby. I just asked questions, and I got answers.

Overby stopped still at that last one, though, and I stopped a half step later, turning to him. He pulled his sunglasses off to look me in the eye.

"I did," he said. "Jill, my daughter, called me for advice the night before last. I jumped on a plane yesterday morning. I was the last one to arrive among the people you'll meet. I should probably tell you it wasn't pretty when I got here. The three families get along well enough, but they're all very different. They're friends because their daughters are. In a situation this messy, tempers flare and emotions run high.

"I tried to make sense of what happened, and once I heard everything, I suggested hiring a private investigator. Not everyone's on board, but after some googling, I recognized your name. Everyone agreed to at least talk to you."

"Who's 'everyone'?"

"The three moms are still here of course. Jill's not married. Never was. Chloe's dad was never in the picture. The other two husbands are here."

"Dads or stepdads?" I asked. In and of itself, it made no difference to me. I just needed to know if someone else was going to drop in on us.

Overby caught my drift. "They're the biological dads. No other voice calling shots from the wilderness."

I grunted. We resumed our walk back to the restaurant. "Anyone upset at our private chat?"

"No. They know our history, and they understand it's easier for me to lay out the facts before we all talk. Best I can tell, everyone accepted that."

"Make sure you introduce me to Jill last," I said, "make the others feel important."

Overby looked at me with half a grin on his face. "Generals usually learn a little diplomacy along the way."

"And you more than most. Sorry, General. You're not my typical client." It wasn't like I had a typical client, but it sounded like the right thing to say.

"Don't sweat it. We're thinking along the same lines, anyway. In fact, I'll introduce you to Jennifer and Bill Berger first. They're the most hesitant about asking for outside help."

By that time, we'd made it back to the parking lot.

"Ready?" Overby asked.

"I should have stayed in the army," I said in response. "I have an easier time with terrorists than pissed-off moms."

Overby slapped me on the back as I walked into an emotional lion's den.

CHAPTER 2

We walked into the building to find the others. Only dog lovers and their pups braved Florida's morning heat for breakfast on the patio. I took a look at them over my shoulder before crossing the threshold. Something about a dog wagging its tail lifts one's spirits. The Golden I'd seen come in earlier was in rare form, sitting with its tail swishing on the deck, nose straining toward the bacon on the table.

All of a sudden, I felt a little lighter on my feet. My breathing slowed. You're living the good life when what you desire most is a strip of bacon. I lingered on the happy sight and let my hand trail the fence as I slowly walked on. I was about to have a hard conversation, and the excited pup had soothed my soul.

General Overby led me to a table in the back—several tables pulled together, in fact—and five people with worried faces on the other side. They rose to greet me. My arrival didn't interrupt their chatter because there'd been none. The tension was so thick you could reach out and touch it.

I recognized Jill Overby from the picture on her father's desk all those years ago. She looked to be about my age. Obviously, she always was my age, but I'd never had a reason to think about it. She was lean and tanned with a round face and a tomboy haircut. She managed to put warmth in her smile despite the circumstances.

Next to me, General Overby motioned to the couple on our left. "This is Bill Berger and his wife Jennifer. They're Ann's parents."

I reached across the table. Bill was tall and slightly stooped, with glasses that were too big for his face. His buzz cut may have been meant to cover a receding hairline, but it looked out of place on his thin frame, all skin and bones. He was so pale that I wondered if he ever stepped outside. He reached around his wife to give me a weak handshake.

His wife Jennifer shared the pallid skin of the chronically indoor. She was a mousy-looking woman and as thin as her husband. Her hair was graying, but she had not seen the need to color it. She'd reached for the cross pendant around her neck when the general and I walked in, and she was holding on to it for dear life now. She voiced a weak "hi" without letting go of the necklace.

That earned her a look from the woman next to her, a large black woman with smooth, unblemished skin, who pushed forward, bumping against the table, and thrust her hand toward me.

"I'm Cassie Raymond," she said behind a professional smile, the kind people put on their faces in those networking events CJ tolerated and I couldn't stand. She had tasteful makeup on, even now, though she didn't need it. Cassie barely had a hint of laugh lines. She dressed her voluptuous frame elegantly in a floral top and a long skirt that fitted her well, even if the clothes were a touch formal for the locale.

Cassie's husband, Reggie, introduced himself with a handshake that matched his wife's grip. But his voice was weak, as if pushing out his words required too much effort. He looked older than the other parents, with receding gray hair that contrasted with his brown scalp. He dressed casually in shorts and a plain T-shirt stretched thin over a prominent beer gut.

"They're Christine's parents," General Overby said. "And this is Jill, Chloe's mom."

Ann. Christine. Chloe. Three missing women. Families wrecked by anxiety. The case was getting to me already. The voice inside my head screamed *it shouldn't be this way. You're not supposed to go to the beach for Fourth of July fireworks and not see your daughters again, not know where they are.*

Jill and I leaned over the table and shook hands. If she'd changed in the many years since I'd last been in her dad's office, I couldn't tell. She looked strong, all angles and muscles, at ease in her tank top and shorts, moving with grace. She was all of five feet two, but she looked like she towered over the others.

We all sat down, which made the whole scene look more like an interview and less like an execution squad.

Jill Overby spoke first. "Can you find our daughters?" she asked. It seemed she enjoyed small talk as much as I did. She also expected a direct answer to a direct question.

I couldn't give her one. "Probably," I replied, "but only probably. And it's 'probably' because I'm good at what I do. We don't know what happened, though I agree something did. If they got hurt, someone would have found them by now. If somebody took them, we don't know who, how, or why, and we don't know where they went. Taking someone off the streets is not as easy as Hollywood makes it look. Taking three healthy young women out in the open—and on a night when half the island is out shooting off fireworks—is improbable. All this to that say that I agree MCSO is not paying enough attention, but not because they don't pay attention to missing persons. Intuitively, they don't think anything happened."

"What do you think?" Jill asked.

"I think they're wrong, but I understand their perspective. I'd better, in case you should hire me, and I end up talking to them. They're more likely to help out if I can show them I understand their position."

"So, you have a better chance of finding them than the cops?" Jill asked, rephrasing her question, pushing for an answer.

Before I could respond, Jennifer Berger interrupted, her hand still clutching her cross, red splotches creeping up her neck. "He's not going to tell you no," she said. "It's money to him. I'm sure the police will find them. They've been gone three days now so the police must start investigating. It's the law. Hiring him means spending money for someone to get in the way. I don't understand what good that could possibly do."

Her husband Bill was already nodding his agreement. I raised my hands. I needed a little silence before the parents started arguing with each other.

"Look," I said, "three hours or three days makes no difference. That's a common misconception. If you report someone missing, law enforcement investigates." My instincts were to use stronger language, but antagonizing Jennifer would only make things worse. I left my comments at that, with one addition. "And if I didn't think I could help, I would not offer to."

Jennifer's pinched lips told me that correcting her mistake had been bad enough. She shrunk in her seat and glared at me.

I offered a thin smile, figuratively reaching out to her as I kept talking. "In most cases, you wouldn't be wrong trusting MCSO. I know some deputies on the force. They're good people. They're also three days into an unsolved murder on top of the slew of crimes that always add up over the summer, particularly after a holiday. You know your daughters. You know they'd have called. The deputies in the sheriff's office don't know them. They don't see what you do. Bottom line: outside help makes sense if you want it."

"I just don't agree," Jennifer said. Her husband Bill shuffled in his chair, wringing his hands. He was sitting away from the table, half hidden behind his wife.

Jill slapped her hand on the table and leaned in, looking at Jennifer. She started to open her mouth, but Cassie Raymond spoke first. Unless I missed my guess, she did so much more softly than Jill had been about to.

"It doesn't hurt to listen," Cassie offered. "And Mr. Malone came down here at no charge, which is very courteous of him. We really should listen." She turned to me without waiting for an answer from Jennifer. Reggie, her husband, nodded next to her, though I wasn't sure if he was agreeing or dozing off. He looked like a man who had not slept much in the last couple of days.

"How would you go about it, Mr. Malone?" Cassie asked. "The investigation, I mean." She maintained that professional demeanor, sounding like she was moderating a panel at some conference in a hotel ballroom, not asking how to find her missing daughter in the back of a tourist breakfast joint.

"Have you called the hospitals?" I asked.

"Ann always carries my and Bill's contact information," Jennifer said. "Any hospital would have found it and called. See, you don't know what you're talking about."

Jill Overby could not contain herself any longer. "Right," she said, her tone dripping with irony. "I'm sure your twenty-year-old daughter stuffs a laminated card in her bikini with mommy's number on it."

Cassie pushed her large frame forward in a symbolic attempt to separate the other two women. "We called," she said, speaking loudly enough to snuff out whatever Jennifer had been about to say and end the bickering, at least for now. "We called," she said again, softer this time. "No Christine Raymond, Chloe Overby, or Ann Berger has been admitted to any clinic or hospital in Monroe or Miami-Dade with an ER department."

Jennifer turned her body away from the other parents, tears forming in her eyes. Bill put a hand on her shoulder and whispered in her ear. Jennifer shrugged him off without looking at him.

The parents had done the right thing. They'd started to, anyway. They had not asked about Jane Does, and not all people who get hurt ended up at an ER, though that conclusion was logical enough. I didn't mention any of that and changed the topic. We could extend the search at the office if need be.

"What about one of those find-my-phone apps?" I asked. "Can you locate any of the girls' phones this way?"

"I trust my daughter," Jennifer said, still looking away.

"We trust her completely," Bill added, his voice shaky. "I hate to be a negative person, but you do not know us or our daughters any better than the police do."

Jennifer would not like anything I had to say, and Bill was backing her up. I repressed the urge to snap at her and tell her that I trusted my partner too, and CJ and I still had access to each other's phones. Our trust extended to not abusing that access when we did not need to.

Instead, I turned my attention back to Cassie. Her eyes were glistening now. Reggie grasped her shoulder and addressed me, his voice stronger than when we shook hands. "Cassie and I both decided that Christine should be more independent in college. She got her own phone and plan, and we didn't ask her to install a location app."

Jill reached for Cassie's hand with both of hers. "I did exactly the same thing for Chloe. Our girls don't need to wonder whether we know when they skip class or stay up too late or go see a boy. It's biting us in the ass now, but it wasn't wrong."

Cassie nodded, wiping a tear with her thumb, and I moved the conversation along.

"I'm guessing you called their friends?"

Answers came in nods and a croaked "yes." Emotions rose from question to question. I shifted uncomfortably in my seat. I wished CJ were here. She was better at this kind of stuff. She would probably grill me about how much damage I'd inflicted on these poor parents when I got back to the office.

"Friends, and friends of friends," General Overby added. "Nothing."

I reached for the carafe and one of the upside-down mugs on the table and poured myself a cup of coffee. I sat back, the precious liquid in hand. I was starting to understand the group dynamic. Stress causes one of three basic reactions: fight, flight, or freeze. Right now, Jennifer was frozen, and Jill looked ready to fight—something, someone, anything. The Raymonds had taken on peace-keeping roles, but struck me as doers, which isolated the Bergers. I'd try to bring Jennifer in, but it might be too late.

I pushed my chair back to make it easier to address all of them together. I wasn't used to this. I did not like making speeches. I didn't usually pitch my services. I either took a case or I didn't. Then again, I didn't usually have a half dozen people in front of me who couldn't decide among themselves if they wanted me to work their case or not.

"You did all the right things," I said. "Those were only first steps, though. If you want me to work this, I'll take the next steps. I'll go to MCSO, let them know they have help, not an interloper busting their chops. If they have not gotten a warrant to ping the phones yet, I'll nudge them to do it. I'll also walk the resort with a fresh pair of eyes. I'll see if the Overseas owner will share the list of people who were there that night. Or maybe MCSO's murder team will give me that information. They'll have asked for it. Someone from my team or I will go to Gainesville and check the girls' places. It's not the highest return on investment, but you never know what might turn up. I'll do some good, old-fashioned gumshoeing—knocking on doors and all that. There's more, but you get the idea."

"I'm sure the police did all that," Jennifer said, defiance in her voice.

"Some of it, but their attention is somewhere else," I said.

"What about going to the press?" Reggie asked.

"That could either help or make things even uglier. If it gets tabloid-style coverage, and it could, every crackpot will call in, and a possible kidnapper could panic. Involving the press could make finding them harder, even put them in danger. I'd rather not take that gamble yet, but it's on the table."

Reggie seemed satisfied by the answer. He sat back, his hands resting on his belly. No one asked anything else. The silence was oppressive. A couple of people shifted in their chairs.

"I can step out if you need to talk among yourselves," I said.

"Thank you, that's probably best," Cassie said, taking on her panel-moderator persona once more.

Two thoughts crossed my mind as I nodded my understanding. First, the discussion they were about to have was sure to be a clusterfuck, and I didn't need to be part of it. Second, I'd take the case regardless, for the general's sake, unless they all told me not to.

"I'll leave you to it," I said. "So long as you all agree and stick to it, I'll agree to take the case. I'll do it on my friends-and-family rate. I owe General Overby that much and more."

"How generous!" Jennifer said, spitting all the viciousness she could muster into her words.

I ignored the dig and made one last point. "If you can't all agree, I can still take the case on behalf of only one family or two, but that doesn't work as well. Let's just say I'd rather have a united front if possible."

A voice that had barely made itself heard until now rose from the table's corner. "You will," Bill Berger said. Jennifer turned around with a murderous look. Bill looked past his wife and spoke directly to me. "Six people cannot always agree on every last detail. But if hiring you is what we decide, I'll want to know what you find out. We're in this together."

I pulled an engagement letter from my back pocket, unfolded the paper, and left it with them. Then I raised my mug in thanks and turned to leave the building. I kept the coffee, the heat outside be damned.

I walked out unhurriedly, taking the time to look around. A waitress was chalking lunch specials on an old-fashioned blackboard. Advertisements from 1950s diners decorated the walls. It was nothing original, but it fit the place. And with the dog patio and the ocean a few hundred feet away, the Secret Passage did not need to be original.

Using the mug to shield my eyes, I pushed past the front door and into the Florida sunshine. I took a deep breath and exhaled slowly. I had left the lion's den alive.

For now.

CHAPTER 3

I leaned on the patio fence, watching people and dogs eat a leisurely breakfast. The aroma of waffles, eggs, and sweets mingled with the scent rising from my coffee cup. I was not usually much of a breakfast guy, but the scene made my stomach gurgle.

Tourists outnumbered the locals—not as badly as in Key West, but they still did. They were the ones with angry-looking sunburns, either from sheer carelessness or from having been taken by surprise by the relentless southern sun. You could tell the locals by their bronzed, prematurely wrinkled skin. That made me the whitest guy for miles. My Irish roots ran deep.

I soaked in a sense of normalcy. That luxury didn't last long. The door to the restaurant opened, and six somber people filed out. They had come to a decision sooner than I would have thought. I reached over the fence, left my empty cup on a patio table along with a couple of bucks in tip, and went to meet them.

Cassie Raymond stepped to the front of the group with her practiced smile. She had a beach bag over her shoulder that I hadn't noticed earlier. She held it by the straps as she started talking. "We'd like to . . ."

Jennifer Berger interrupted her, blurting out her words. "Are you entertaining the thought that my Ann left voluntarily to go to some kind of party?" she asked, looking past Cassie and straight at me.

"I'm not discounting anything," I said. "Not that she did, and not that she didn't."

"You just don't know my Ann," Jennifer said, decibels rising. "You're wasting your time, and you'll only make a mess of things. I won't be a party to this."

"Oh, grow up, Jennifer!" Jill Overby snapped before anyone could intervene. "Our daughters are twenty. They're in college. They're young women, not children. They party. They party and they drink and they smoke and they fuck!"

Tears flowed freely down Jennifer's cheeks. "I wish my Ann had never met your daughter," she yelled.

That was all she had in her to say. Then, she ran. She wasn't running anywhere in particular. She ran away in the direction she'd been facing, wherever that led, and before long, she had left the Secret Passage's parking lot. She left Bill standing there, his shoulders a bit more stooped than they'd been a moment earlier.

I watched Jennifer run, agape. When I returned my attention to the group, Jill was crouched down, head between her knees and hands on her head. "I'm sorry," she said to no one in particular. "I'm sorry, I'm sorry, I'm sorry. I just couldn't take the my-daughter-is-an-angel bullshit anymore."

Reggie put a hand on her shoulder. "That's okay," he said. He had a gentle voice and manner. "We understand."

"How do you stay so calm?" Jill asked, looking around at the rest of us as she stood back up.

"Lots of practice with irate bank customers in a downtown branch," Cassie said, shrugging. "And Reggie, well, he's just Reggie." She took two steps, stood right in front of Jill, and took hold of her hands. "We'll find them, Jill. We will. Have faith."

I let the moment play out. When Cassie let go, she turned back to me, back in business mode, with what I now knew was a banker's smile. "And we would like to hire you to do just that," she said. "Find our girls." She reached into her beach bag and handed me a six-by-nine manila envelope.

I took it, then looked at Bill Berger before checking its content. "Do you need to go find Jennifer?" I asked.

"It would do no good," he said. He looked down and shook his head. He may have been talking to me, but he never met my eyes. He was miles away. He knew his wife better than the rest of us, though, and I had no choice but to trust his judgment. Not only that, I wasn't exactly the world's leading authority on dealing with emotions.

I opened the envelope and removed the contents. There was a personal check on top of several photographs. The check, drawn on Reggie's and Cassie's bank account, covered a twenty-hour advance. I held it up and shot her a questioning look.

"I've made arrangements with the other families," she said. "The Bergers too. It's just simpler this way, but we're all on board." Bill slowly nodded as Cassie talked.

That sounded good, but they were *nearly* all on board. Jennifer worried me.

I slid the check to the bottom of the pile. The top photograph showed all three girls together, arm in arm in a happy moment. They were young women, really, not girls, and looked remarkably alike for all their differences. Chloe had blond hair down to the middle of her back and her mother's button nose. Ann was a curly brunette who was looking at her friends in the picture. Christine sported an impressive Afro and the widest grin of them all. But they were all smiling, all pretty, all bursting with youth and health, all showing a little cleavage—or more than a little—with the carefree daring of college days. I took a long look at that picture. No one said a word. We were all thinking the same thing: *where were they?*

The other pictures showed the girls individually, in various poses and outfits—and in Christine Raymond's case, a wild array of hairdos. I went through them all. I tried to get to know each girl through their clothing and the way they seemed to move as I flipped from one picture to the next.

I looked up to find five expectant faces staring back at me. Jennifer had not returned. I had not expected her to. I would have to deal with that later. Now, it was time to start working the case. I had clients right in front of me who expected me to say and do something.

"Let's go to the RV resort," I said. "I'd like to take a look at the place. We can talk some more there."

A cacophony of yeses and okays echoed back as everyone headed to their vehicles for the short drive.

I called out to the younger Overby. "Ride with me, Jill, will you?" It sounded more like an order than I had meant to, especially with her father right next to her, the man who had happened to be my boss's boss a few times over, no matter how long ago that was. Neither of them seemed to mind.

"Sure," Jill said. She tossed a set of keys to her dad and headed to the CR-V's passenger side.

I was already seated, having unlocked the glove compartment to slide the envelope below the holstered .45 automatic that lived inside. I locked the compartment as Jill settled down in her seat, and we followed the rest of the group onto the Key Largo streets, heading toward US 1.

I allowed a few moments of silence as we hopped from block to block, one stop sign at a time. Summers in the Florida Keys came in three colors: a bright blue sky, bright green trees, and bright white houses. When the window on a plumber's van reflected the sun back to me like a laser, I gave up and reached into the center console for the sunglasses I rarely wore.

I glanced at Jill. "Tell me about your daughter."

A sweet smile filled her face. She turned to look out the window. "She's a wild child," she said, then sighed. "So was I, mind you. I guess that's part of why I can't stand still. It's guilt, I suppose. If the girls got in trouble because they went somewhere to party it up, the odds are Chloe was the gang leader."

So, there was more to the dynamic I'd witnessed than Jill becoming a fighter under stress. She felt responsible. She felt the need to fix this mess. Cassie knew that. That's why she gave assurances she may not have felt.

I glanced at Jill without saying anything. I was giving her space to keep talking. She was thinking it through. It was probably the first time she was doing that out loud in three days, putting the words together and stringing her thoughts in a semblance of order.

"Christine is a strong young woman too, mind you," she said. "Ann's the follower. She's not meek, maybe a bit naive. She'll follow anyone anywhere just to experience what they have to offer and get away from her mom. She's rebelling against . . . the kind of helicopter parenting Jennifer does, I guess.

"Jennifer's not a bad person, but she lives scared. She basically lives between her house and her church. She'd never come to our Fourth of July weekends if Ann would not go with us anyway to be with her friends, come hell or high water."

"Chloe may be wild," I said, "but she's got street smarts. From what the general tells me, she's the kind of kid who'll go drinking but get a ride home, even if that ride has to be from you."

"And she's also the kind of kid who watches her drink and never takes an open one from a stranger. Chloe is smart, period, streets, and books. She's an engineering major and in the Naval Reserve Officers Training Corps. She's so proud of being NROTC. She has it in her mind she'll fly jets from an aircraft carrier in a few years. It terrifies me because I know she'll make it. Nothing stops that girl."

I glanced at Jill again as I turned onto US 1, a gas station sitting on one corner and a strip mall on the other. At least, somebody had had the good sense of making it a four-lane highway here.

"How did your dad take to his granddaughter going Navy?" I asked.

"He said it beats spending the night in a foxhole and shitting in a ditch and that Navy showers are still showers." She turned to me. "Do you know him well? My dad?"

I shook my head. "He was a mentor to me and everything I could have asked of one. I admire him, look up to him. But I only know him within the confines of the United States Army."

"He always loved mentoring younger officers. I think that's what made him so successful. He always had his people front of mind. He's the same with his family. You'll never meet anyone more supportive—of Chloe, of me, of anyone he cares about, really. He'll be tough when he needs to be, and I gave him plenty of reasons in my younger days, but I never, ever, doubted his love or his support. I always knew he had my back."

I nodded. That sounded like the man I knew. "What about you?" I asked.

"What about me?"

"Give me a two-minute Jill tour. I have a feeling not much stands in your way either."

She leaned back in the seat and stared at some distant place that reflected her inner thoughts. "Maybe not these days, though it wasn't always the case. And I feel pretty helpless right now. I was twenty-three when I had Chloe. I thought my life was over. All I wanted was to party every day with my friends. I tolerated what I thought of as a dead-end job with one of the airlines because you're supposed to have some kind of job. I guess I shaped up over time. I even gave the job my all, and then it turned into a better job. Imagine that. So, I kept going. Now I run the airline's operations at MCO."

So, the general was not the only Overby with success thrust upon him. Managing a major airline's hub at MCO, the main Orlando airport, would be a feather in anyone's cap.

Jill pivoted in her seat and turned to me again. "And Chloe, well, Chloe somehow turned into an amazing person. Sometimes, I think it's more in spite of me than because of me. I just tried to teach her right, you know? Maybe that's all a child really needs—that and love—and damn, I love that kid. I gave her a lot of freedom. I think because that's something I needed at her age. Maybe I gave her a little too much." Her body tensed at those last words.

I took my sunglasses off and gave her a look. I sensed her eyes were clouding over behind her shades. "You need to let go of that guilt shit," I said.

"Not that easy."

"I didn't say it was."

That drew a chuckle. "Clearly, Dad had good material to work with. You sound just like him."

"Highest compliment," I said.

We pulled into the resort before I had time to ask Jill for her impression of the other families. I followed the other vehicles into the parking lot. Two RVs were parked side by side: a fifth wheel, and one of those luxury homes on wheels General Overby had talked about.

Overby parked a pickup I figured to be Jill's next to the fifth wheel. I parked close behind him, and the Raymonds pulled up behind the other RV in a black Lexus. Bill rode with them.

I got out of the car and mumbled to the others to give me a minute as I walked away to take a look around. I wanted to take in the lay of the land with a clear head. That required the absence of chatter.

The general had not overstated the luxury. A pool with bar service sat on one side for guests who preferred not to have sand between their toes. It was nearly empty now, the South Florida sun sparkling on still waters, save for a sole woman on her belly on a pool chair, soaking in the sun.

A marina—a few piers jutting out like gray fingers scratching at the blue ocean— hosted boats belonging to those who liked their second homes to float. Cabins at the back were available for those who wanted something without an engine. They bracketed a large clubhouse with its own bar and snack service, judging by the tables on the patio.

The Fourth of July crowd had cleared away. Two-thirds of the sites were empty, maybe more. Overseas was quiet now, but it did not take a lot of imagination to conjure up the constant hubbub of a holiday crowd: steaks grilling, beer flowing, and kids running back and forth from the beach or the pool. The image made the corners of my mouth perk up. Overseas was a happy place. Or it should be, especially on the Fourth of July. This year, well, this year was another story.

I wondered if there were a lot of college-age kids there that night. Home for the summer or not, was this fun enough, cool enough for a twenty-something? I made a mental note to ask Courtney, our very own twenty-something front-desk person, cyber sleuth, PI trainee, and jane-of-all-trades. She acted beyond her years, but she'd know.

I kept walking around. The more I did, the more questions popped into my mind. Did the same people return year after year, like Jill and the others? Would a stranger be noticed, especially on the night of the Fourth, when guests may have guests of their own, crowds gather on the beach, and people drink a little too much? How much were mothers or daughters imbibing, for that matter? When was the girls' absence first noticed? Had they told anyone where they were going? And how far and wide did the parents look that night? Did they see anything out of place—anything at all—assuming they were sober enough to notice?

I took a long look around. There were no cameras I could see. A couple of people in matching black shorts and guayaberas were on hand, offering drinks and snacks to the depleted clientele, but there was no security guard. A three-foot retaining wall bordered the parking area, with four sets of stairs cut into it leading to the beach. I walked in that direction until my boots touched the stone and gazed out at the ocean. Everything around me was so perfectly peaceful, nothing but the sound of the waves and a gentle breeze.

I allowed myself another minute with the ocean before walking back toward the families who had hired me. I felt their eyes on me, and I had to make a conscious effort to keep from clenching my fists. I cleared my throat while still out of earshot, so my voice would not come out rough when I reached them. They needed me to appear confident. I felt the familiar shakes of a new case wash over me. There were too many questions and not enough answers.

CHAPTER 4

I rejoined the group and kept my first question at banter level, easing them into the conversation. "One RV for the girls, one for the moms?" I asked, pointing at the two RVs.

The parents all exchanged uncomfortable looks. Well, shit, that was supposed to be the easy question.

"Jennifer and Ann stay in one of the cabins," Bill Berger said, hooking his thumb over his shoulder at the one where they were staying, with two white Fords, an Explorer and an Edge, parked in front of it. "Jennifer . . . Jennifer prefers that they stay together as a family."

Bitterness seemed to coat his words. Something about the way he spoke made me wince inside. I looked at the cabin he'd pointed to. It was one of the smaller models and sat at an odd angle to fit in the back of the resort. It had a better view of the houses fronting the ocean than the ocean itself.

I looked back at Bill, who was looking down, avoiding my eyes. Maybe he didn't like that isolation, the way Jennifer kept them apart. Maybe he didn't like having to admit to his wife's behavior. Or was something else going on? More questions. Always questions. I filed them away as Jill spoke up.

"You're right, though," she said. "The girls take my fifth wheel, and the Raymonds put me up in their RV."

"Plenty of room," Reggie said, his voice full of pride. That RV was his baby—one of those vehicles General Overby guessed cost more than his house—more than mine, for damn sure.

"Ann's supposed to be back in the cabin by her mother's curfew," Jill added, "but she usually sneaks back out to join Chloe and Christine. Sorry, Bill."

"I'm not surprised," Bill said, eyes downcast. "Par for the course."

I nodded my acknowledgment, and then I started asking real questions. They seemed relieved I had some. I guessed the cops had not delved too deeply into the women's disappearance.

Yes, they said, some of the same people came every year around Independence Day, but there were always new faces around too. A stranger could easily get lost in the crowd, especially on the night of the Fourth, when throngs gathered on the beach. This was the spot, the place to be on the island—or at least one of them.

No, not many college-age kids hung out at Overseas. Most people came as families, but typically with younger children. And no, Chloe and her friends did not seem to mind. All that mattered, the parents thought, was that they were together. And Cassie Raymond seemed to remember other older kids on the beach that night, maybe teenagers, maybe their daughters' age, but no one she recognized.

"When did you start worrying you had not seen the girls in a while?" I asked.

"Jennifer worried first," Cassie said, nodding as she spoke. "Jennifer worries a lot. That's who she is."

Jill's exasperation seeped through as she filled in some details. "Let's face it, Jennifer does more than worry. She can be irrational, panicking every hour on the hour like something horrible is about to happen. This time, her questions started early. Every five minutes, she asked where the girls had gone. I tuned her out. You kind of have to with Jennifer. Eventually, she started wandering around, asking everyone in sight if they'd 'seen three girls, three college girls.' I guess maybe this one time, I didn't worry enough."

Jill's guilt crept up in her voice. The others heard it too. Behind his daughter, the general looked down and shook his head. Cassie stepped in and said she hadn't been worried either. She used that smooth, motherly voice that seemed to come naturally to her no matter whom she spoke to.

Jill took a deep breath and kept talking. "When the fireworks started to slow down, the rest of us started worrying too. For one thing, if the girls had not stayed around our RVs in previous years, they reappeared by the time the bulk of the pyrotechnics were over. For another, with the din of the fireworks receding, we became aware of some commotion across the lot. People were shouting. I couldn't hear what they were saying, but it sounded bad. You know how people sound different when something really serious is going on? I thought I heard someone scream about someone else getting shot. By that point, I was downright panicking."

Cassie took over the story. "I went right over to the ruckus. I'm fat and I'm black, Mr. Malone, and clearly outspoken, so you can imagine the kind of bigotry I have to deal with in my life. That night, I turned it to my advantage, played it up without shame. Cassie, loud, large, and in charge." She snapped her fingers twice for effect. "I started bellowing that my daughter was missing and to let me through, and people parted like the Red Sea for Moses. The moment I saw this poor woman with blood soaking her front, I knew she was dead. May the Lord forgive me, but I felt as relieved as I was horrified because it wasn't my daughter or one of her friends lying there.

"Like Jill said, panic set in. Someone had been shot, and our daughters were nowhere to be seen. It seemed a good time for them to show up, you know? We mostly looked here, around the resort, thinking they were lost in the crowd of people. Overseas was in pandemonium. Some people were oblivious to what was happening, cleaning up and bringing spent fireworks from the beach like nothing had happened. Others were gawking at the gathering police presence because of the shooting."

"I had my head in my phone, to be honest," Jill said. "Things were still loud enough that it was possible they weren't hearing their phones, but still . . . they didn't pick up or text back. They're Gen-Z! They're surgically attached to their phones. Even when Chloe's out, she'll send an exasperated text saying she's fine if I ask her. Between a death a hundred yards from me and Chloe not answering her phone, I was frantic, and I don't get frantic too easily.

"After about my zillionth text, I went down to the beach since Cassie and Jennifer had the lot covered. It's not the largest beach, just enough for the resort's guests. Of course, it was packed that night, but the crowd had thinned out, and the cops had arrived and were cordoning off a big chunk of it.

"I saw quite a few people filing out at the sight of flashing lights." Jill managed a weak smile at the memory. "Others stuck around to watch. You know how it is. Anyway, I didn't see our daughters anywhere."

"Around what time was that?"

Silence filled the air while they all tried to remember. Jill scrolled through her phone. "I sent so many desperate texts it's hard to tell, but I'd say around 10:30 or so," she said.

"That or a little later, but close," Cassie said. "And I'd say it was closer to midnight by the time Jennifer and I gave up searching the lot and joined you on the beach. The police were out in force by then."

Cassie had looked at Jill as they compared mental notes. Now, she turned her attention back to me and resumed her story. "We walked that little beach late into the night, the parts the police had not taped off. It's not like there were unseen hiding places and our daughters would suddenly appear, but we kept looking. We went up and down the beach, back up to the resort, and did it all over again. I don't know how many times we did that."

Cassie lowered her head, chest heaving as if exhausted at the memory. Jill put a hand on her friend's arm.

"Hundreds," Jill said. Cassie put a hand over Jill's. The two women exchanged a weak smile. As painful as the memory was, it was a shared memory. They had each other.

Jill went on. "It was mostly Cassie and me. Jennifer was busy pestering the cops. She sounded just about hysterical, so you'd think they might have given her some attention, but all they did was keep her behind the tape and tell her to report the girls missing in the morning if they did not show up by then. You know the rest. We did not find them, and they did not suddenly reappear out of thin air. The next morning, we went to file the missing-person reports."

"Jennifer called me in the wee hours of the morning," Bill said. "I left before dawn. I had a five-hour drive ahead of me. They were all at the sheriff's office by the time I arrived. I helped with the paperwork. Jennifer was a mess in all kinds of ways. The others are too kind to tell you, but it's what it is: a mess. I've had to deal with a lot over the past few years. I guess you're not surprised at that by now. But anyway, the information we provided in those reports was thorough, and we gave them everything we could. But there was not much follow-up from MCSO once they took in the paperwork."

"I arrived that afternoon," Reggie said, taking Cassie's hand.

I was glad the parents were talking. I stood there, looking at each of them in turn as they spoke, taking in the information. None of their answers came as a shock. I still had follow-up questions for them.

"Did the girls say where they were going before they headed away from your RVs?"

"Most years," Cassie said, "they would go down to the beach, where the fireworks were being set up. I can't remember if they said anything that night or not. I assumed that's where they'd gone."

"Did you see anything out of the ordinary, aside from law enforcement swarming the place once people realized someone had been shot?"

Cassie and Jill both shook their heads. I had yet to ask them the hard question—whether they would have been too drunk to notice. I put it more nicely than that, but I still asked.

"It's a fair question," Jill said quickly. I guessed I'd been delicate enough that she could tell I didn't like asking. "I won't deny I still have my drinking legs. I wasn't in the bag, though, and sobered up pretty damn quick once I started panicking over someone getting shot and Chloe not answering her phone for the first time ever. And I'm the drinker among the moms. Jennifer never drinks, and Cassie barely does."

"I'll have a glass of wine or three," Cassie protested, looking at Jill next to her, a real smile on her face for a moment. "But admittedly, by Fourth of July standards, I was stone-cold sober."

None of that helped me, but it didn't *not* help either. The moms weren't distracted by the murder scene. They were looking for their daughters and were sober enough to notice something out of place. They didn't see anything weird. Sometimes, the absence of evidence is evidence. Only just now, I didn't know evidence of what.

"Do you have a card from anyone at MCSO?" I asked.

Cassie and Jill each produced one from the same officer. I pulled out my phone, took a picture of it, then made sure it was clear enough to read. The name on the front read *Detective Sergeant Brian Michaels*.

"Alright. I'll get out of your hair and get some work done, starting with MCSO."

I turned to General Overby, who'd retreated to the background while I asked questions of those who'd been there. "General, I'll route all information back through you to save time and keep communications simple."

My old boss stepped forward with a short nod. "And I'll pass that information along to everyone," he said. His voice was firm, matter of fact, and did not suffer any doubt. No one objected.

"I still may need to ask some of you additional questions," I said, "so I'll need everyone's number, just in case, and your daughters' as well."

I wrote my cell number on a business card and gave it to General Overby while the parents did what I'd asked. I emphasized again that everyone should go through him if they had questions outside of my regular updates. I explained the temptation to ask for news may feel overwhelming, but if they wanted me to work the case, I could not spend my time answering the phone. I doubted they particularly cared for that, but either they didn't show their irritation, or they got the point.

I turned to General Overby and asked if there was anything else I should know, anything I hadn't asked. He scanned the others' faces. No one spoke up.

"Nothing," Overby said. "Thank you, Malone—I mean, thanks, Coop."

I gave the group some general reassurance about doing everything in my power. Cassie took my hands and said, "God bless you, Mr. Malone."

I wasn't sure where God had been that Fourth of July, but Cassie meant every word, and I could use all the help I could get. If Cassie could get a little divine intervention, I wouldn't complain. I squeezed her hands, thanked her, and got in my car.

I drove as far as the next strip mall, about a minute away, just far enough to make a couple of calls without a dozen eyes burning a hole in the back of my head. I started with the office.

"Hi, Coop." Courtney picked up the call at the front desk with her usual cheerfulness. If she had not sounded cheerful, something would have been wrong—wrong enough to send me back to Miami, breaking land speed records and asking questions later. Her voice was a breath of fresh air.

"Have we opened a file on Overby yet?" I asked. Courtney would think nothing of my lack of manners—not even a hello. It told her I was in work mode.

"Yes. I take it we're hired? This case sounds like a mess."

"We are, and it is. I have additional info. You have time?"

"Yeah. Go ahead."

I gave her the names of everyone involved, including MCSO's detective sergeant, and briefed her on the case as General Overby had done for me. I added everything I'd learned since and saved time by not having a pesky PI interrupting me with questions. The only sound on the other end of the line was Courtney's fingers flying over her keyboard.

"What can I do?" she asked when I was done.

I scratched my head and glared at the car's speaker as if I were giving Courtney a look. I'd better think of something, or else she would. No one ever accused Courtney of lacking initiative. And while she'd only gone rogue on me once, once was enough.

"Start with the girls' social media," I said. That was right down her alley and about as far from mine as anything could be. "And call Cindy Kassner. Ask her to meet me this afternoon, tomorrow morning at the latest. I doubt you'll need to tell her time's critical, but if you need to, give her a push."

"Got it."

"Thanks. Oh, and one more thing."

"Shoot."

"You ever been to Key Largo for the Fourth of July or another party-friendly holiday?"

"No." She sounded like she was pouting over the phone. "And I wouldn't call the Fourth party-friendly in a college, spring-break sort of way. It's more of a family-time thing. You'll have some beach parties, I guess, but that's just the South Florida thing if you don't have a club or mansion around. Any excuse will do. What kind of parties those are depends on who you're going with, you know?"

"Yeah, I get the picture. Thanks."

I killed the connection and stared through the windshield. Did the girls party hop? If so, did they stumble into one they shouldn't have? And just what would that be, anyway?

I took a breath and pulled up the photo of Sergeant Michaels' card. I memorized the number well enough to punch it into my contacts and called him. He answered after two rings, identifying himself by rank and name. I gave him a second in case he wanted to add his badge number. He didn't.

I launched into an explanation of who I was, why I called, and how I was there to help, not to make a mess or get in his way. It was a well-rehearsed speech, one I'd made many times. Practice makes perfect.

Traffic flowed in my peripheral vision as I listened to what sounded like a canned answer. "Yes, sir. Absolutely. I'll be happy to assist in any way I can." The detective sergeant's voice had a flat, professional tone. He could have made a radio commercial for the sheriff's office, sounding the way he did. Problem was, I could not tell whether he meant what he said or was feeding me bullshit.

"Can we meet?" I asked.

"Yes, sir. Absolutely." I thought I heard an echo. Then a pause. "There's this sandwich shop I like if you don't mind meeting over lunch, say in an hour or so."

If his lunch spot was on the island, I could probably get there in five minutes. An hour was a long time to wait. But I didn't have much choice, and I could put the hour to good use. I took him up on the offer, he gave me the address, and we hung up.

With the strip mall that served as my temporary headquarters conveniently close to where I'd started, I got out of the car, locked it, and walked back toward the Overseas RV Resort to speak with the owner. Turned out, he was happy to see me. I didn't flatter myself. The resort had already been hit with cancelations. He'd be happy to meet anyone trying to solve these cases.

Unfortunately, he didn't have any useful information. Like everyone else that night, he'd been watching fireworks. From his seat on the patio, his first clue of mayhem had been people yelling for someone to call 911. He gave me a list of everyone who stayed at the resort that night. I thanked him, sent a picture of the printout to Courtney with instructions to start digging, and took my leave to talk with the cops.

CHAPTER 5

I got to the sandwich shop before Sergeant Brian Michaels, ordered a Coke while I waited, and sat down, fidgeting with the cup. Michaels was late—not very late, not yet—but late. I put the cup down, pulled out my phone, and distracted myself by catching up with the rest of the world. It was all bad news there too, and I quickly put the phone away.

I sat back, closed my eyes, and recalled my Fourth of July, a much quieter and happier one I spent with Amy. We'd only been dating for three weeks or so. Still, we weren't hormonal teenagers. We were two career people who knew what we wanted and respected the other's space. It was still new between us, but we felt right.

We felt so right that it earned me some raised eyebrows from those who knew me best. There I was, Mr. Skeptic, always questioning everything—but not Amy or the way we were together. That was the whole point, raised eyebrows and all. Amy was the one person with whom I didn't get stuck inside my head. I could just *be*. I had no intention of changing anything between us.

We'd stayed in for Independence Day, sitting on her back porch overlooking a stretch of nature, just the two of us and our favorite drinks, a rye for me and white wine for her. Neither of us needed more. We didn't even follow the siren song of fireworks—unless you counted those we put on in the bedroom.

The officer who entered the shop and ended my daydream a minute later was young—terribly young. He had a buzz cut and a smooth face, the kind that made me wonder if he was old enough to shave. He had the practiced smile of a law enforcement officer, a cop's smile that was calculated to put you at ease but meant nothing else.

I was surprised he was in uniform. Most detectives wore plain clothes. It was an interesting choice. I was even more surprised the uniform was still crisp halfway through a South Florida summer day. Was he trying out for the recruitment poster?

I stood up and approached him, extending my hand, and he shook it. Uniform and prepubescence aside, I felt good about the kid, maybe because he reminded me of some people his age who'd served under me in the Military Police. Most of them had been eager. They wanted to do the job right. Many were smarter than they were given credit for. They tended to seesaw between rebellion and an unspoken gratitude for the structure the army gave them. Either way, those kids all felt invincible with the uniform on their shoulders and a gun on their hip. Maybe that's why Brian Michaels wore his.

We said our hellos and walked to the counter to order. Michaels had the advantage of youth and asked for a gigantic po'boy. I made do with a chicken salad wrap. I got to business as soon as we'd carried our trays across the room and sat across from each other, chairs dragging on the wooden floor.

"What can you tell me about the investigation into the missing girls?" I asked.

"Do you believe there was foul play?" he asked. That was not an answer. I didn't mind—yet. I could indulge him, choosing to trust he'd tell me what I needed to know soon enough.

"I take what parents tell me about their kids with a grain of salt," I said, "but even so, yes, I think something happened. They've been gone the better part of three days. They haven't so much as answered a text. Even accounting for parental bias, the girls' behavior is out of character for them—or for anyone in their generation, frankly."

"But three women gone at once? Our office believes this is more likely a case of playing hooky than something nefarious. I tend to agree."

"If you look at this case as a statistic, maybe. Three women missing at once because of something nefarious is unlikely. Thing is, I'm not looking at statistics. I'm not looking at anything theoretical." I put my hands flat on the table on either side of my tray and leaned in. I fixed him with a stare, commanded his attention. "I'm looking at people. I'm looking at the people involved here. One of them wore a star on his shoulder in my old unit. He's not a man to panic or not face reality. He knows the difference between partying-it-up behavior and something fishy. He thinks something fishy is going on. I don't 'tend to agree' with him—I flat out agree."

My little speech sent Michaels into good-soldier mode. He rattled out the official line like he was reciting a press release. "The Monroe County Sheriff's Office is taking this and every missing-person case very seriously. We are following our investigation techniques, which have been proven to work. We started with the information the families provided. We are checking with the missing persons' friends, contacting hospitals, and following up with potential witnesses at their last seen location."

Speech over, Michaels picked up his sandwich.

I managed not to roll my eyes, but I kept pushing. I was not trying to antagonize him. It was just that pushing was what I did best, so I kept at it. "Those are calls the families already made. And there are no witnesses because everyone was busy watching fireworks or gawking at the bunch of you working a murder scene."

"I'm afraid so, yes," Michales said. He put his sandwich back down without taking a bite. His shoulders deflated a little.

"Did you pull a warrant to ping the phones?" I asked.

"Legal was supposed to have one drafted and filed." He pulled his notebook from his uniform's chest pocket, flipped the pad open, and scribbled a few words. "I'll follow up on that. If they ping, I'll let you know."

"Thanks." My own shoulders relaxed, but I maintained eye contact. I was sending I-mean-it vibes his way. He may tend to agree that the daughters were up to no good and that they were fine, but he still wanted to do the job right. At least I thought so. I hoped my instincts about him were right.

I gave it a second and leaned back into my chair, hands in my lap. I started on another, softer tack. "Look, Sarge. This is your beat. It's your island. You probably know half the people here. Let's say, for a moment, you thought a crime was committed. Maybe it was just one girl gone missing, or you found signs of a struggle. Something. Where would you look, then? Where would you start?"

Detective Sergeant Brian Michaels thought about my question for a long time through mouthfuls of po'boy. The sandwich was never far from his lips. That was okay. The wheels kept turning. Eventually, he put the mostly eaten, overloaded, once-foot-long monster back on its paper plate, straightened his posture, and looked at me. When he spoke, his words were as crisp as his uniform.

"Two things," he said. "First, I think Captain Tornero is right to focus on the homicide. If something took place that night, and if the death was more than the result of a reckless act, then the two events may very well be related. Solving one case would resolve the other.

"Second, I'd walk along the shore with the missing person's disappearance front of mind. That's where most of the action is on the island, whatever kind of action we're talking about, legal or otherwise. The closer to shore, the likelier you are to encounter trouble."

I had not thought the murder and the disappearances as connected. The odds of either one happening were low enough. The odds of them being part of some kind of big conspiracy were minuscule at best. It made no sense. Then again, this early in a case, nothing ever made sense, so I filed the idea in the back of my mind.

I put my chicken wrap down after a bite. "Is that the working theory for the woman's death? A reckless homicide? A drunk shot off his gun when he ran out of bottle rockets, and the bullet lodged itself in some poor woman's chest?"

Michaels took a slow sip of water. Half-melted crushed ice sloshed in the cup. He took the time to put his drink back on the table before returning his attention to me. "I wouldn't call it a working theory. But it's like doctors say: horses before zebras."

"What can you tell me about the murder?"

He paused again, briefly. "Off the record, we're chasing our tails. Nobody saw anything, or if someone did, they're not talking. The victim's name is Pamela Howard. She was on the island with friends and neighbors for your typical vacation weekend. She worked in HR for an insurance company. She has no known enemies or drug problems, and her record is clean, besides a couple of speeding tickets. So, the reckless homicide theory fits."

I thought to myself that it *could* fit, that maybe the murder was random, and no one admitted to seeing anything because it would mean admitting they saw someone brandishing a gun and did nothing about it. But maybe no one saw anything because there was more to the story. Maybe there was nothing to see because there was a killer out there, one who meant to end a life, and he or she made sure not to be seen taking the fatal shot.

I did not verbalize any of that. I'd contradicted Michaels enough for one lunch, and he'd been reasonably helpful. I was content fishing for a few more details while he ate, things like the time of death (probably a bit after 10:30 p.m.) or the murder weapon (a nine-millimeter firing standard round-nosed bullets). I had his attention until Michaels finished his meal, then he stood up to head back wherever duty called. I stood up with him, and we shook hands again. I promised to keep him posted if only to remind him he'd made that promise already, and we parted ways.

I checked my phone on the way to the CR-V. Courtney had texted. Cindy would arrive at three. That was a long time away, even for one with my legendary patience.

On impulse, I quickened my pace, started the car, and pulled away in time to follow the dirty old Impala in which Michaels had just left. Tailing a cop was not particularly smart, but I never claimed to be particularly smart.

There were mitigating circumstances for my bad choices. Michaels had arrived after I did and left before me, so he did not know what I drove. I would keep my distance and count on the CR-V blending in to disappear in traffic—and on Michaels' relative inexperience. I had no doubt he was trained in counter-surveillance, well-trained, even. But he was still a young cop. It's one thing to spot a tail when you expect one in an exercise. It's another to expect one all the time, no matter what, no matter where.

And I was curious. It's not like Michaels did not have other cases, but if our conversation lit a light bulb and sent him checking on something, well, I wanted to be the first to know.

I got a little nervous a couple of times and thought about putting an end to my little experiment. For once in my life, traffic was too light for my liking, but I managed to stay a few cars behind Michaels. He kept driving in straight lines, not making any sudden moves, so I stuck to it until he pulled into an empty parking lot behind a boarded-up business, weeds sprouting out of the cement. I drove around the block and found a parking spot within view of the lot.

By that time, a new player had appeared. Michaels had left his vehicle and was talking to someone in an official MCSO Explorer, gleaming white, with its ribbon down the side, a star on the front door, and the word *sheriff* in gold letters running the length of the truck. I squinted, trying to make out the driver through the open window. He had a dark complexion, maybe Latino, with slick black hair and a walrus mustache. I would have put money down that was Captain Tornero. Their conversation lasted less than five minutes until Michaels nodded, stepped back, and the official vehicle departed.

Michaels stayed standing there for a moment. By the time he made it back to the unmarked, he was just about stomping his feet. It was hard to tell from where I was, but I thought his face looked angry, jaw set, lips pulled in a tight line.

He opened the door, then paused, turned around, and leaned against the Impala. He reached for something in his pants pocket and started sucking on some e-cigarette or vape pod or something —fuck if I knew. He took a few puffs, breathing in the vapor, then got back in the car and pulled out of the parking lot a little too fast.

Discretion was the better part of valor. Screeching my tires to pull behind Michaels would have been ill-advised, even for me. So, I waited five minutes and headed back to the strip mall I'd stopped at after talking to the families. Courtney had pulled its exact location from the find-my-phone app we all shared at the office, and that was where I would be meeting Cindy Kassner and her toys.

CHAPTER 6

I hate waiting. Everyone who knows me knows this because I know it and make no secret about it. Luckily for me, the blue Suburban I was expecting showed up early. A woman stepped out of the truck wearing sneakers, jeans, and a black polo with a patch on the chest that read "AUU Drones" written across the silhouette of a slick-looking quadcopter.

I'd gotten out of the CR-V before she closed her door.

"You Cindy?" I asked. It was a pretty safe bet, but while I'd worked with her outfit before, I'd never actually met her.

"Yep. You must be Coop. Good to finally meet you in person."

She had a firm handshake and made direct eye contact as we said hello. She swatted her hair away from her face as the ocean breeze got a hold of her loose, dark locks. Her hair was as black as CJ's and as curly as CJ's was straight. My partner had inherited hers from Grandma Vinh. I put Cindy's ancestors closer to the Mediterranean.

"Let's do this," she said as she pulled a scrunchy from around her wrist and pulled her hair into a loose ponytail. "I'm glad you're here. I couldn't get an assistant on short notice, so you're it."

"Sure," I said. She was telling, not asking, and I didn't mind one bit. It was more my style.

She opened the Suburban's hatch, and I took a spot behind her, peering inside the truck's cargo compartment. A square metal plate leaned against one side, as long as the SUV's cargo space was tall. A large quadcopter drone on spindly legs took up the rest of the area, even with its rotor arms folded back along its body. The machine was slicker—and larger—than I'd expected, with a lens at the front and a camera mounted in a kind of turret under the nose. And here I thought we'd hang a GoPro under the belly or something. That made me the amateur around here.

Cindy surveyed the lot around us. It was empty but for our two cars. We'd parked at the end of the lot by two out-of-business store-fronts. One still had *Body by Bobby* stenciled on the door with a barbell over the name and half a slogan about being the best something or oth-er on the Northernmost Key. The other door was blank. The buildings sat there, walls bleached by the implacable Florida sun, impervious to the heat that was making me sweat and came close enough to melting the pavement that it smelled like a tar pit.

"This will work," Cindy said. "Plenty of room." She started pulling the metal plate out of the truck. "I've got traffic cones in the back seat," she added.

I figured she was giving instructions, not making idle conversa-tion. I opened the door and pulled the cones out. By the time I'd done that, Cindy had laid the plate on the ground. It had her logo on top, and it looked like a proper miniature helipad. My job was obvious enough, even for my thick skull. I dropped the cones around the plate at regular intervals to keep away any unlikely traffic.

We stepped back to the Suburban. Cindy pointed to where the drone's landing skids joined the body and another spot behind the nose section. "Hands here and here. On my signal, pull up two inches. Then back out of the SUV and onto the helipad. The drone's not partic-ularly heavy—just bulky enough to make this job easier for two."

"Got it," I said.

Bulky seemed like the wrong word for the sleek drone, but it was big, several times larger than backyard models, so two people meant better control. As advertised, it was also surprisingly light. We had it on its helipad in a matter of seconds, and Cindy got to work. She un-folded the arms and the rotor blades, leaned close to her bird, and in-spected every nook, cranny, and panel.

"What's AUU? I asked as she worked. "Clearly not your initials."

"It's a nod to my grandfather," she said without looking up, intent on her task. "He was the first Kassner to operate a flying machine with a camera. His was an Air Force recon jet in Vietnam. He and his people were fearless. Their moto was 'Alone, Unarmed, and Unafraid.'"

"Alone, Unarmed, Unafraid," I repeated, seeing the words in my mind. "A-U-U." I liked it—both the sentiment for her grandfather and the spirit she was honoring. I told her as much as she rejoined me be-hind the Suburban.

She reached behind the seat, pulled a large case toward us, and opened it on the edge of the SUV's cargo compartment. Two screens mounted into the lid now faced us, flickering on at the touch of a but-ton. The bottom of the case held the controls: two joysticks—tiny, skin-ny ones like those on handheld controllers—and a bunch of buttons under the left screen. There was a single trackball with a small knob next to it under the righthand screen.

"This bird has two cameras," Cindy said. She pointed to the screen above the joysticks. "This is my flight screen. It will always point straight ahead in the drone's direction of flight." She pointed to the screen on the right and continued her explanation. "That's the screen for the gimbal camera under the nose. You control it with the track ball. That will be your job. Just be careful not to interfere with my control."

"Understood."

Cindy held up a finger. She turned toward me and went on. "If for some unfathomable reason I am incapacitated or pulled away from the controls, this green button here"—she put her index finger next to it—"that's the 'return home' command. Push the button down and hold for three seconds. The autopilot will take the drone back to the helipad."

"Understood on that too," I said.

"Good. Once in the air, the island's air space is largely open to us, but not the space to the north, nor the maritime space north and west toward the Everglades. There's a no-fly space starting pretty close to the shore in that direction. I can take the 'copter everywhere else within reach, which is a decent ways out for this model."

"That will work," I said. "It's more than I need."

"Great. Can you give me an idea of the flight plan you're looking for?"

"What did Courtney tell you?"

"That three college girls went missing and I should hustle to Key Largo and find you."

"That's about right," I said. "I don't expect us to find them on a boat waving at us with daiquiris in their hands. If we do, their parents will kill them before they get back to dry land. They went missing at the RV resort a couple of blocks from here. I'd like to start there and go up and down the beaches. I'm looking for anything out of place: a sign of struggle, some piece of clothing, trampled vegetation, anything. I'm hoping we can get close enough with your bird not to miss anything and still do in an hour or two what would otherwise take me all day."

Cindy had been looking up at me while I talked. She kept still a little longer, but I was pretty sure she was building flight plans in her head, not looking for the secret to the universe in my pupils.

"You got it," she said. "I can do that." She turned to the controller, double-clicked, and held a button between the joysticks. The drone came to life. By the time I looked at it over my shoulder, the rotors were turning so fast that all I could see were blurry disks, their edges marked by the blades' red tips.

Cindy gently pushed the left joystick with her thumb and turned around to watch the drone rise. She centered the controller and kept her gaze fixed on the machine hovering about five feet off the ground. "No wobble or vibrations," she said.

I turned my shoulders and took a look of my own. It looked steady as a flying rock. "None to these untrained eyes either."

"Let's get started," Cindy said.

She pushed both joysticks. Her movements were small and smooth. She moved the one on the right this way and that. Her fingers danced, and the drone zipped between and above buildings on its way to Overseas. A minute later, it was hovering over the resort's beach. Cindy's eyes were glued to her screen now. It was the window to her bird's life. She pushed the left joystick sideways and gave me a slow, 360-degree panorama of the area as the drone pivoted on its axis.

"What beaches?" I grumbled, seeing none of the sandy expanses I'd expected.

"What was that?"

"Can you go higher, give us a broader view?" I asked. The answer to her question would have to wait.

Cindy nodded and maneuvered the controls, making constant, tiny adjustments as she brought the bird up. The view on the screen showed more coastline by the second as it gained altitude.

"That's about as high as I can go and keep us stable," she said.

"Can you give me another 360 degrees?" I asked.

"Better use the gimbal camera."

I'd forgotten all about it. I reached for the trackball and rolled it to the side, nice and smooth. Cindy's screen stayed rock solid, the horizon a perfect horizontal line between blue sky and darker blue sea. The evenness was deceptive. Cindy was constantly nudging the controls.

Meanwhile, the picture on my screen rotated, starting along the coastline to the northeast and all around and back. The shore was a mix of swamps and built-up property with docks reaching into the ocean like skinny fingers. Everyone had talked about beaches. What fucking beaches? I was hard-pressed to find a few patches of open sand anywhere along the island's coast.

I cursed myself. If I'd paid more attention, I'd have realized that Courtney had talked about beach parties being a South Florida thing in general. She'd never stayed around Key Largo. And Sergeant Michaels talked about staying close to shore for a better chance of finding something—*shore*, not beach.

I should have known better regardless. South Florida, wetlands, and real estate might as well be one long word. I may hate driving through the Keys and rarely leave US 1 until I reach Mile Zero, but I should have expected exactly what I was seeing. I'd let my imagination get the better of me. I'd pictured a long white beach from one end of the island to the other. That didn't exist. It was all wetlands and houses around here.

"I stand corrected," I said, taking slow, steady breaths. "It would have taken me days without your drone."

"Glad to be of service," she said. Her mouth barely moved as she spoke. She hadn't blinked either, not since she took us higher up. She had total focus on the screen before her. Electrical signals went directly from her eyeballs to her fingertips. No other muscle moved.

"You can take us down," I said.

"It will take a hot minute. I don't want a rotor to lose its bite and send us crashing."

I stayed as motionless as she was after that. It would have been bad form to hire her drone only to make it crash.

"You have a better idea of a search plan now that you know the lay of the land?" Cindy asked as she steadied the drone back at a more reasonable altitude.

"Can't say I do," I said. The change in topography didn't impact what I had in mind. "I'm thinking we fly both ways, up and down the island. We overfly the surf line, and I use the gimbal camera to look inland. We'll be lucky if we find anything, but you need a little luck sometimes. That's unless you have a better idea. You're the pro here."

Cindy thought for a moment. She brought up a pop-up on her screen. It looked like a bunch of squiggly lines. "I have pre-programmed search grids," she said, scrolling, speaking slowly while her eyes scanned the graphs before her. "But I don't see one that will work any better to find what you're looking for. Your plan sounds fine to me."

She edged the righthand joystick forward, moving her machine roughly northeast along the shoreline. It moved slowly, but not slowly enough for my liking.

"Back up and start over slower. The closer to the resort, the slower you go. We're more likely to find something closer to where they were last seen. I want a crawl. A slow crawl."

"You got it," Cindy said. She was as on-the-job as I was and took my request in stride, even though I made it with my usual charm.

It turned out that it did not matter how slow we went. We hopped from house to swamp to house to the odd, tiny beach. We found nothing. Cindy turned the drone back to the Overseas' beach, then slowed it down again for our search on the southwestern side of the resort.

We were pulling alongside the third house past the beach when I caught a glint of light off something. "Get me closer," I asked, pointing to the spot that had caught my eye.

Cindy's eyes moved from screen to screen as she maneuvered the drone where I wanted it. "There's limited zoom on your camera," Cindy said. "You control it with the knob next to the trackball."

I kept one hand on the trackball and placed a couple of fingers on the knob, careful not to get in Cindy's way. Zooming in, the sun was reflecting off broken glass from the shattered sliding door to the house's back patio. Broken glass was all I found. There was no patio furniture, no sign of life. I moved the camera around. No furniture on the dock either. No boat nor boat equipment. I turned the camera back to the broken sliding door.

"You want me to get closer?" Cindy asked.

I glanced at her screen. The drone was over the dock. "No," I said. "We've attracted enough attention. Give me a quick overview from further out, though."

She did, and I took in the property. It was a two-story house. Both floors had more glass than stucco on the ocean side. That was the point. You buy a house like this for the view, and you want that view from wherever you are.

"You want to look at the front?"

"No. We've buzzed around this place long enough."

Cindy nodded, reoriented the drone, and restarted the crawl along the shore. "It's probably some rowdy kids looking for a good time in an empty house," she said as we left the house behind.

"Could be. Could be rowdy kids is how this whole mess started. Or could be someone other than rowdy kids broke that door."

CHAPTER 7

A few minutes before five, Cindy and I finished loading the drone back in her Suburban, and I waved goodbye. We hadn't found anything else down the shore, but that was okay. We had more than we'd started with.

Phone in hand, I leaned against the side of the CR-V. It could have been past five, and it would have made no difference. CJ and Courtney would still be at it. It was that kind of time at the office, and they were that kind of people. It was about time I pulled my weight and caught up on the rest of our work, all the stuff not taking place on Key Largo and not involving my old commanding general.

"Hi, Coop," Courtney said. Her tone was no different toward the end of a long day than at any other time.

"Hi," I said, trying my version of small talk on for size. "Is CJ somewhere she can be reached?"

"She's in her office."

"Put her on, will you? And stay on the line."

Courtney's voice was swallowed into a telephonic void and replaced by on-hold music. Ours was no better than anyone else's—I just never had to listen to it. I made a mental note to see if we could change the somnolent elevator music just as the tune stopped mid-chord and Courtney's voice came on again.

"We're both here," she said.

"Thanks. And sorry I haven't been there all day."

"Nor should you have been," CJ said. "You owe the general, and this case is a mess. Messes take time."

"All the same. It's not all that we have going on. Catch me up on the rest of business."

CJ and Courtney tag-teamed through our other cases. They'd made progress on several fronts. It was no surprise, but it was still good to hear our clients were well taken care of.

"Anything I can help with?" I asked.

"We haven't made it to Barrels yet. Can you meet Courtney there at seven? I can do it, but it's on your way back, and technically, it's your client."

Barrels was a South Miami beer-and-wine joint serving locals off the beaten path. It was a typical kind of case for us: it had been vandalized. Badly. The damage was expensive enough to justify hiring us but not violent enough to rely on law enforcement's limited resources. The owner was friends with people behind the bar at one of my haunts, and we ended up with the case.

"I'll be there," I said. "Anything else?"

"No, that covers it," CJ said.

"For me too," Courtney said.

"Let's have a short meeting in the morning all the same—7:45 at the office. I want to talk over one more thing, but not on the phone." Our phones were secure, both the cells and the land line, which told them this had nothing to do with the information itself, but with having them in front of me for that discussion. They also knew there was no point debating it and said they'd be there.

"I'll see you in a bit, Courtney," I said. "CJ, stay on for a minute."

CJ was my partner. Courtney was an employee. The difference did not matter much in the day-to-day, not the way we all worked together, so I knew I'd triggered warning bells in CJ's head. I could picture her sitting a bit straighter in her chair, staring at one of the art pieces on her wall as if she were giving me a look. I'd made her suspicious.

"What is it?" she asked. It sounded more like instructions to start talking—and start talking now—than a friendly question.

"I'll be coming back here after going to Barrels. I wanted to tell you so we don't have a repeat of our fight over the whole Mardi Gras warehouse thing."

"You're not breaking into anywhere," CJ said. Her tone had all the finality she could muster, enough to end most conversations—just not this one.

"Look, you only told me not to do anything stupid without talking to you first. I'm talking to you. But there's no time to dick around, and there's no other way."

That first part was technically true. When I'd broken into the Mardi Gras Cruise Line warehouse during our investigation of a murder on one of their ships, I hadn't told CJ, and we had a fight over it. We'd agreed on one point. Not telling her had been disrespectful, and that was bullshit. I doubted our agreement was quite that limited in her mind. I was right.

"I didn't think I needed to spell out that you also needed to refrain from breaking and entering," CJ said. "And there's no other way because you don't want there to be."

Any other time, she might have been right, but not this time. I gripped the phone harder, trying to keep an even tone. "There's this house that was broken into, three doors down from where the girls were last seen. And sure, it could be nothing—a couple of kids breaking in looking for a place to party or two teenagers sneaking in to make out. Or it could be related to the girls' disappearance. I need to find out."

"Or you could tell the police and let them find out," CJ said. That was one of the many reasons CJ cleared so many cases. She did not have a congenital need to do everything herself. I liked to think that while she cleared more cases, I cleared the hard ones, the bloody ones. There was a kernel of truth to it, though in the end, neither of us could do our part without the other's help.

"I could tell the cops and wait," I told her, phone hard against my ear, looking down at the asphalt. "I could, but I won't. I don't deny your way of doing things works best sometimes. But this is a kidnapping, and it's already been three days. If we don't find the girls now, we'll start finding bodies. Or we'll never find them at all. Even hours could make a difference, and I'm not taking that risk."

CJ was silent for a while, leaving me alone with the sound of distant waves interrupted by speeding traffic. I was happy to give her time. Just as I knew her methods were sometimes best, she knew mine had their place too.

"Okay," she said. "Just don't do anything stupid—more stupid than you already are."

"You got it. I'll see you tomorrow."

"Yes, you will."

I hung up and started driving. I tried driving slowly so I wouldn't get to Barrels too early. I still pulled up to the bar with time to spare and knew I'd be waiting a bit. Even though Courtney was early getting to the office nearly every day, punctuality was not one of her many qualities. She was never very late, but let's just say she was never early.

A vehicle held together by chewing gum and wire hangers, which had been a Civic in another life, parked behind me twenty minutes later. I got out of the CR-V just as Courtney killed her engine, a dying motor that had somehow managed to run long enough to get her here.

Courtney looked the way Courtney always did—a young, pretty, fresh-faced blonde fashionably dressed in skinny jeans and an off-the-shoulders top showing plenty of cleavage. I felt sorry for the fool who ever underestimated her.

I joined her as she wiggled the back door open, retrieved the first of two cases, and handed it to me. "Didn't we just give you a raise?" I asked, raising an eyebrow at her rust bucket.

Courtney put the second case down, closed the door, turned to me, and swept her hands over her body, emphasizing her fashion choices. Even her tactical boots had two inches of heels in consideration of appearances.

"Money is for outfits, Coop," she said. "Outfits. And tech. It's not for . . . for . . ." She waved her hand at the car. "For cogs and cams and wires and stuff. And anyway, don't you diss the Betty."

I rolled my eyes. "Why Betty?"

"For Betty White! Even when she was old, she was glamorous and kept kicking."

"I'm surprised this Betty is taking you from point A to point B."

"It's all about love and good juju," Courtney said, picking up her case.

As we walked to Barrels' front door, I pulled my phone out of my pocket and dialed Todd, the owner, to let him know we were here. The bar had not yet reopened. That was slated for tomorrow night.

"So, is this part of my field training?" Courtney asked as we waited by the door.

When she had crossed a line trying to be a little too helpful last month, I had made a deal with her: no more coloring outside the lines, the lines were wherever CJ and I said they were, and in return, we'd train her for the field. Adding PI trainee to her long list of unofficial titles had not been a big sacrifice. Courtney was smart and had guts. We could use her in all kinds of jobs. She was the future.

"Are you behind your desk?" I asked.

"Hell, no!"

"There you have it."

Courtney was too good at the cyber stuff to never be at her desk, and she enjoyed that kind of work anyway. Not to mention that we still needed someone up front at the office as often as not. But now that we'd started field training, she lived for time on the streets.

Todd opened a few seconds later, his dark hair matted with sweat. He wiped a hand on his jean shorts and waved hello rather than shake hands.

"Sorry," he said. "Still a bit of work to do before I can reopen tomorrow. Come in and take a look at the place the way it was meant to be."

"All good," I said before introducing Courtney, and the two exchanged a friendly wave.

I liked my bars dark and broody. It didn't matter if I was broody myself or not—the bar should be. This one was the opposite of that. Comfortable leather chairs surrounded low aluminum-and-chrome tables. The whole place was light and airy. It was the friendly neighborhood watering hole, the kind that invited patrons to sit down and stay a while.

The last time I was here, the seats had been slashed and covered in spray paint. Most tables were upended. Glass tops had shattered the way only glass can, sharp edges and invisible shards all over the floor.

"No glass on the new tables?" I asked.

"Since I needed to get new ones," Todd said, "I did away with glass. You end up spending half the day cleaning them."

"Amen," Courtney said. "I hate glass tops."

Courtney and I put our cases down and made our way through the back door and into the beer garden. The picnic tables and benches looked like new. They, too, had been covered in spray paint—not graffiti or anything remotely artistic, but splotches and obscenities with no other purpose than to deface.

"I was able to save the tables by stripping them and applying a few coats of fresh paint," Todd said. "Hell of a lot of work—maybe too much for these old benches. It might have been cheaper to replace them, but I got stubborn and needed to work out some frustration."

I could relate to that and put an understanding hand on his shoulder. Then we went back inside and got down to business.

"Okay," I said. "The plan is to put up some webcams to cover the entry points and look through windows so we can cover getaways. I know you don't want cameras because you don't want your patrons feeling like they're under surveillance. This is not that kind of joint, and I get it. No one will see these. They're tiny, and the casings are pre-painted to blend with walls. We're not talking about the kind of shit included with your average security-company package.

"That's the reactive part of what we're doing. Webcams put eyes on the perps if they try again, and maybe, just maybe, someone recognizes them. We're still going after the proactive part—scouring social media, police blotters, and a few other places for clues about this vandalization or similar crimes."

"Thanks," Todd said. He spread his arms wide. "I can't imagine who did this. We're a popular spot in town."

"You are," Courtney confirmed. "At least on social media. Well-liked, and the 'locals' vibe comes out nicely."

"Thanks," Todd said. "We get some tourists. They're welcome. We accept all dollars. They're typically the kind of people looking for that local hole-in-the-wall, though, and they respect that when they're here."

"There's no telling what kind of people do this," I said. "But Courtney and CJ can find a needle in a haystack before most of us know there's a haystack. If there's something to find, they'll find it."

Todd nodded, out of things to say. For many business owners, the business is like another child—or their only child. It was like that for him, and his child had been attacked. This had not been an easy time.

"May we proceed with the cameras?" I asked. Even if I were the kind of person who knew what else to say in moments like this, I wasn't sure there was anything to be said.

"Yes, of course," he answered. He sounded like he had lapsed into another world, and I'd just jarred him back into this one. "I . . . I'll be in the back if you need me. Thanks again. I appreciate all you're doing."

Todd headed to the storeroom for his chores, and we got started on our task, which I used as part of Courtney's training. Instead of telling her where I wanted the cameras, I engaged her, helped her develop a sense of place, and taught her to look at a room with a different part of her brain, the part wired to the needs of surveillance. She had a good eye and picked good spots. If she missed one or I suggested one that could be better, she got it.

We were done in under an hour. I popped my head through the storeroom door and wished Todd a good night. Then Courtney and Betty headed north, and I headed in the other direction to do something stupid—or so said CJ, but what did she know?

CHAPTER 8

I drove straight back to Key Largo. It was 9:30 by the time I got there, and that was too early to put my plan into action, not to mention that I hadn't eaten since lunch. I hunted for a place that still served food and would stay open for a while. I wanted the night to get darker and the tourists on the Overseas beach to thin out.

Unlike Courtney and her wily ways with the dark secrets of the tech world, there was little work I could do with just my phone. I tapped out after three emails. And since I had to wait, I decided there were worse ways to kill time than chatting with Amy, so I used the phone as a phone. I do that sometimes.

"Hey, stranger," she answered.

"Hey, yourself. How's your evening?"

"I'm chilling out at my favorite spot with one of my favorite wines but without my favorite guy. Tsk, tsk."

Her favorite spot was her back patio, which overlooked more nature than I'd thought possible within commuting distance of downtown Miami. I could guess at a couple of her favorite wines. I hoped I was right about her favorite guy. I leaned back, and for the first time today, the muscles in my face relaxed without having to be told.

"Couldn't be helped," I said. "I'm at a touristy spot in Key Largo, stuck between vandals and a kidnapping case."

"Kidnapping sounds like a heavy load."

There was just a bit of an edge to her voice. Amy knew what I did for a living. She was cool with it. Most of the time, she thought it was hot. Still, there was no escaping that we met on a murder case that ended with guns fired. She did not worry, not really, but she had put on a protective layer since we started dating.

"CJ already told me not to do anything stupid," I offered.

"Good. Now let me tell you. Don't do anything stupid! If both your partner and your girlfriend tell you, maybe you'll actually listen."

I shrugged even though she could not see. I couldn't help it. "You know me and listening . . . but I'll do my best. And I can take care of myself, remember?"

"I do remember. I'd rather you didn't have to."

"Me too, babe," I said. I meant it, and I thought Amy knew I did.

With that piece of conversation out of the way, it seemed safe to change topics. "May I take you out tomorrow night, this case permitting, somewhere new I think you'll like?"

"I'll have to check my calendar," Amy said. She spoke slowly, letting the words hang in the air somewhere between the Upper Keys and the western edge of Dade County.

"Some hot advertising exec trying to seduce you?" I asked. Writing ads may be the least objectionable corporate job for my writer girlfriend, but it was still a corporate grind.

"Several, actually," she replied, trying to sound pleased with herself and disguise her knee-jerk repulsion at the idea.

"They can't handle you," I said.

"Maybe it'd be fun to see them try."

I laughed out loud in the middle of the restaurant, teetering on the back legs of my chair. "It probably would be. But if you end up trading the amusement for a night out together, fair warning that the locale will be work-related. I still think it will be your style, mind you, and the work won't interfere with a good time."

"Work, how?"

"It's the place that was vandalized, a local wine bar. I want to keep an eye on the people there for a while when it reopens. I'd rather do it in good company."

Amy was silent for a moment, just long enough for me to wonder if I'd pissed her off somehow, though it wasn't easy to do. Amy didn't offend easily.

"You'd be bringing me into your world," she eventually said.

So, it had been a good silence. I mulled the concept for a second or two myself. I hadn't thought of it the way she put it, but she was right. And I was happy about it. That sounded crazy, even to me, but I wanted her to be as much a part of my world as she could be.

"I guess so," I said. "If you don't mind. Maybe I'll let you drag me to some awful company picnic in return—watch all those suits crash and burn."

Amy laughed. "I'm pretty sure I'm getting the better end of that deal. And tomorrow sounds good. I'd love to, actually. I'll disappoint my suitors."

We talked a while longer, but everything moved in slow motion after that. We'd already had the conversation we were meant to have, the one that built up our connection, that was part of who we were—or who we were becoming.

By the time we hung up, Cindy had emailed me the footage from the drone. I forwarded it to CJ and Courtney in case fresh eyes caught anything we'd missed, and I reviewed the part that mattered for tonight. I didn't see more than low retaining walls between each house. Neighbors did each other the courtesy of not blocking ocean views with high fences. That was good for me.

I checked my watch. Neither dinner nor chatting with Amy nor reviewing the footage had taken me far enough into the night. By the time I was comfortable getting going, I was bored out of my skull and had gulped enough Coke to have a sugar high to match a five-year-old on Halloween night. I left a tip big enough to say sorry for monopolizing the table for so long and finally drove off.

Five minutes later, I street-parked just past the Overseas at a spot I figured put me even with the edge of their beach. I walked across a strip of land to the sand and took stock of my surroundings. Even past eleven o'clock, conversation dribbled down from the few RVs at the resort. I was not entirely alone on the beach, either. I'd expected that. In fact, I'd counted on it.

I had a delicate balance to strike. A lone person in the middle of the night, with no other soul in sight, would have been conspicuous. Too much of a crowd meant too many eyes were likely to see me. I looked around, and I liked what I saw. Time to get to work.

Both houses ahead of the one I wanted to visit were dark. Either the occupants were asleep, or nobody was home. That was a welcome development but not overly surprising either. There were plenty of snowbirds and weekend dwellers in the Keys.

The darkness was no foolproof cover. I could easily get picked up by some alarm system, especially if the houses were unoccupied. I took a second to decide between walking the shore or keeping close to the houses where it was darker, but I was more likely to trigger some electronic gizmo. In the end, I walked along the shore, playing the wandering tourist with little care or awareness of private property. It worked well enough, best I could tell. Nobody yelled after me, and no screaming alarm started wailing in the night.

When I reached the third house, I strode to it at a good clip and stopped at the edge of the broken glass. It was everywhere, inside and outside the house, like it shattered with great violence. There was no way I could avoid it altogether, and I needed to move quickly. Lingering would eventually attract someone's attention. I took long, careful steps on tiptoes to minimize contact with crushed glass until I reached the opening where the glass door had once been. Then I stepped into the house.

I'd expected to find myself in the living room. Instead, I'd walked into an expansive, empty room as wide as the house itself, though not as deep. It had a tile floor and low ceiling. Only a couple of doors were on the other side, and a set of stairs across from me, near the lefthand wall, headed up toward the front of the house. This looked more like a sunroom, with the main level upstairs. It was unusual, but I guessed you could build it any way you liked.

Even in the darkness, I could tell the room was as devoid of furniture as the patio. Salty air and mildew competed to irritate my nostrils. The air felt heavy even this late at night.

I checked the doors, walking carefully, mindful not to trip on some unseen debris. I opened each door slowly, snuck an arm inside, and flashed my phone's light for a fraction of a second. That was enough to recognize a storage closet and a bathroom, both of which were as empty as everything else I'd seen so far.

As far as searches went, this one sucked. It was horrible work. I collected no trace evidence. In this darkness, I could only see clues in plain sight if they happened to be big enough. Items like strips of clothing or anything of the sort would be lost on me. But as an early recon, it would do. I could at least make sure no one was tied up somewhere. Anything more would have to be done in daylight, or with technical equipment, or both, and I would need more than a maybe-hunch to go on.

I turned my back to the windows and walked along the left wall toward the stairs, which climbed up from a doorway ten feet from the wall. Eight steps led to a landing that seemed halfway to between the ground and the main level. I peeked around the corner when I reached the landing, and sure enough, the stairs did a one-eighty to the left. Eight more steps went the other way to the main floor.

To my right, I faced a padlocked door. If the picture of the house that was building up in my mind was correct, there would be a set of stairs behind it, going down to another lower-level room or rooms facing the front of the house.

I pulled at the padlock. It didn't give. I didn't have anything with me to bust it. I swore under my breath. I'd revisit the padlock problem on my way back down. Better check the rest of the house first—take the low-hanging fruit.

I climbed on and emerged at the top of the stairs. What I saw confirmed my suspicion: the upstairs was the main level. Most of it was one big room with a kitchen, a dining area, and what served as a living room. The back wall had floor-to-ceiling windows for an uninterrupted view of the ocean. I walked as quickly as I dared, taking a cursory look and slowing down every time my steps reverberated on the tile floor. I didn't need much time here. The house was empty and spotless. Anything of interest to me would have stood out or been too tiny for me to find, even if I stayed until daybreak.

A short corridor led to two bedrooms. Both had dark walls. I couldn't make out exactly what color. The larger one faced the ocean. I walked through both suites, bathrooms included. They were as pristine as the rest of the place. There was little to see, and I had trouble focusing on it. My thoughts kept pulling me back to the damn padlock.

I lingered by the front windows on the way back to the stairs, shaking my head in appreciation. Luxury was all about the little things. In this case, that included a long driveway and a house set far enough back from the street to avoid traffic noise. One wouldn't want to be bothered by revving engines. I didn't need any light to know that the front lawn would be perfectly manicured, South Florida heat and all.

Stone steps led from the driveway to a large patio in a way that reminded me more of a Georgia mansion than a house in the Keys. I caught sight of a sign on the lawn, close to the steps, discreet but still visible if you knew to look.

Is the house for sale? I wondered. That was a likely explanation for why it was so empty. I didn't welcome the idea. If the house was listed, too many people would know about it, and the chances that the break-in was linked to my case diminished.

Except for that padlock.

I could be making too much of it. Wanting something too badly came with a risk. You ended up seeing things that weren't there. Maybe the padlock didn't mean anything. Maybe no one had been kidnapped and dragged into this house. Maybe the broken door was just the result of college kids partying too hard. And yet . . .

I returned to the landing in the middle of the stairs and stared at the padlock. I stood there, brooding. A knot tightened between my shoulder blades. I had not quite decided what to do about it when I heard the sound of crunched glass. Then I heard it again: footsteps on the patio covered with broken shards.

A loud voice rang out from the lower level—one I'd heard just a few hours earlier.

"This is the Monroe County Sheriff's Office. Come out now with your hands behind your head. This is your only warning." Detective Sergeant Brian Michaels sounded just as official in the middle of the night as he had over lunch.

"You can relax, Sergeant," I called out. "It's me, Malone. I'm not armed." I started down the stairs. "And I did not bust that door." It seemed like good information for him to have.

"Show me your hands," he said.

I spread my arms apart and smiled at him. He stood inside the house, in jeans and a polo, with his badge around his neck and a hand on his holstered gun. He had been sweeping the room with the flashlight in his other hand and now focused the beam on me.

I squinted at the light, but my smile widened. Sergeant Michaels looked ready to act, but he was not about to make things worse by brandishing a weapon. Maybe I'd been right about the kid.

"I'm not playing you," I said, moving a hand to shield my eyes from his flashlight.

Michaels let his gun hand drop to his side and lowered the flashlight's beam, but he did not relax. He kept his shoulders back and his voice stern. "What are you doing here?"

I gave him the bullet points—the drone, the broken glass, wanting to check the house out. It just so happened the truth was the most innocuous explanation for my presence.

"I could arrest you for criminal trespass," he said. "You should have called me."

"You could," I said, "but that would be an awful waste of time and paperwork just to teach me some manners."

"Yes, sir, it would be." His face was perfectly still. Either he had not made up his mind, or he was one hell of a poker player.

"And you'd have to tell your captain you're spending your off-duty hours walking the shore in the middle of the night on a missing-person case he already dismissed as a couple of kids playing hooky."

Michaels kept staring at me. He rubbed his chest just below the spot where the badge hung. "Is that what I'm doing? Maybe someone saw you come in."

"Then MCSO would have sent a patrol, and I would not have the pleasure of your company."

Michaels let his shoulders go south and allowed himself a thin smile. "Yes, sir, if I was doing that, I would have to let Captain Tornero know about it."

As far as I was concerned, that closed the matter. "Let me show you something," I said, turning around and leading him up the stairs to the padlocked door.

Michaels directed his light to the padlock. He shrugged. "What about it? This house is for sale. Maybe the sellers still have some valuables in here they want kept under lock and key."

"All due respect, Sarge, I don't think this padlock is as innocent as you think. Why would sellers keep valuable here—not just valuables, but precious enough they wouldn't let potential buyers look at the space, even with a realtor present?"

He shrugged again, but not as convincingly. "I've never bought a house, so I don't know, but could be."

"In twelve years of army life, what I did not buy and sell, friends of mine did. This doesn't pass the smell test."

Michaels lifted his flashlight beam from the padlock to the door it kept tightly shut. "What, then?" he asked. "You think three kidnapped females are sleeping behind this door while we're talking here?"

Unconcerned with noise at this point, I put that theory to the test. I pounded on the door with my fist, hard, four times. "Law enforcement personnel," I yelled in my best MP voice. "Anyone down there, let yourselves be known. We are here to help."

I waited a minute, then repeated the exercise. I got no response either time.

"Probably not," I said as Michaels looked on. "But that does not mean they weren't. Do you have anything with you to break the lock?"

"I'm not authorized to do that—not without a warrant."

"Are you forgetting a crime was committed?" I asked, pointing in the direction of the patio door.

"No, sir. But no warrant exception applies."

"How quickly can you get a warrant?" I asked, irritation mounting.

Michaels turned his head away from me and stared at the padlock, focusing his flashlight on it again. He chewed his cheek. This guy liked to take his time thinking things through. That wasn't necessarily a bad thing, so long as he came out with answers I liked. So far, he had.

"I guess I'll have to talk to Captain Tornero after all," he said. He turned back toward me. "I'll contact him and keep you posted."

"Or you could pretend this door was busted in when we got here," I said, rapping my finger against the wood. I didn't think he'd go for it, but that was no reason not to try. This was turning into what I'd wanted to avoid in the first place—waiting for a fucking warrant.

"No, I couldn't," Michaels said, making my prediction come true. "Now, walk out with me before I change my mind and put the cuffs on you."

CHAPTER 9

After Michaels dropped me off at my car and made sure I drove away, I went far enough that he might believe I was gone. Then I waited another ten minutes and turned around, back to the house for sale.

I had no intention of going back in. That would have been pushing my luck. Instead, I parked up front and walked down the driveway to the for-sale sign. I took a picture with the flash on. I didn't care if someone saw me. I looked perfectly innocent, someone interested in a house for sale.

I gave the photo a closer look after getting back in the car. It had the agent's name—Tiffany Skidmore—with her phone number and picture above the words *FOR SALE* in letters as big as code allowed. The image was overly touched up, the way many realtors preferred. Tiffany presented herself as a glamorous blonde with perfect hair that wouldn't fly out of place in a hurricane and skin so smooth you couldn't blemish it with a hammer and chisel.

Then, and only then, did I drive home. I allowed myself a little shuteye, woke up before the sun, got ready for my morning plans, and checked out the house online. It was uglier in daylight, maybe some Chicagoan's or New Yorker's idea of a tropical look, with too much wood paneling in an attempt to make it look rustic and an unhappy mix of blue-green and blue-gray walls.

So long as you had blue in there somewhere, it looked like the sea?

The kicker? That sad little thing was going for seven digits, and the number didn't start with a one, either. Oceanfront in Florida carried a big price tag. Oceanfront in the Keys rose into the fucking stratosphere.

It seemed appropriate to make my call at 7:07 that morning. I dialed Tiffany Skidmore, realtor, twenty-four hours to the minute after General Overby's call. It wasn't lost on me this was the fourth day since Chloe and her friends went missing.

Tiffany answered—no answering machine. Unlike Overby the day before, I wasn't the least bit surprised. Say what you will about realtors, they hustle. I leaned back on my couch and imagined myself with a fatter bank account than I actually had. I told her I was interested in a house, in that house.

"Of course," she said. She dragged out each syllable and managed to put just the right amount of Southern to it, keen to sound like her picture looked. "Now, I usually work with the buyer's agent?"

She made it sound like a question, all delicate and polite. She was probing me all the same. I was ready for it. My persona was not nearly as delicate as hers.

"I've done enough real estate deals in my life. I can do the leg work myself. Will that be a problem?"

She sounded more reticent than I'd expected. Half an hour of her time, driving included, would be well worth even a small chance at that kind of commission. She knew it, and I knew it.

I sweetened the pot. "Is Homestead the closest general aviation airport?" I asked, dangling the prospect of a buyer rich enough to fly his own plane.

"I believe so, yes," she said. "There's a private airport about twenty miles north too. I think you have to become a member." I felt the lure of a sale slowly overcoming whatever kept her talking so long.

"Then I'm interested," I said. "I'm in Miami for the week of the Fourth. Can we do this today?"

She agreed and suggested we meet at ten o'clock. Three hours gave me enough time for a second cup of coffee and my meeting with CJ and Courtney, so I told her I'd see her then and hung up.

I made it to the office early. "Early," in this case, only meant I got there before the agreed-upon time of 7:45. That did not mean I was the first one there or even the second.

"Hi, Coop," Courtney said, looking up at me from behind her desk.

"You've got to stop making me look like some lazy asshole," I said by way of a "hi" back.

She sat back in her chair, looked at me with horror, and twirled a finger at me. "What is this?"

I'd fished a pair of slacks and a golf shirt from the back of my closet to impersonate the high-flying millionaire about to look at a house in Key Largo. "Think of it as going undercover," I said, walking away.

CJ's office door was open, which meant we could start the meeting early. Or so I thought. Before we even sat down, my own partner piled on. "What's with the junior salesman outfit?" she asked.

"Undercover," I grumbled.

"As what?"

I told her. She rolled her eyes and asked, "Do you still have that sports coat in your office closet?"

"Yes."

"Put on a T-shirt and that blazer over it. That's more in line with who you're trying to be. And ask Amy to go shopping with you. Or Courtney. Someone, anyone. This is bad." She shook her head at me.

"Sure," Courtney said. "I'd be ha—"

"Alright, that's just about enough," I said. "We can talk about my fashion sense another time, or maybe never." It's not like I didn't listen to those more knowledgeable than me. I just didn't need it laid on quite that thick, and those two knew it.

I started the meeting by summarizing the previous night's events, then I turned to Courtney, who'd taken it all down on her tablet.

"I presume there's nothing of note on the girls' social media?" I asked. It was a fair assumption. Courtney would have told me about it already if there was. I still asked.

"Correct-o," Courtney said. "All three ladies are active on social media. Chloe is a bit more than the others, but not by much. They're posting less since school let out—still posting, mind you, just less frequently. They posted a couple pics on the Fourth, a triple selfie here, fireworks there. Nothing since."

"Alright." I had the urge to tell her to keep an eye out for anything relevant, but I held my tongue. Courtney knew her job. I moved on to the reason why I'd called this meeting in the first place.

"I'd like to have Courtney out to do some work on Overby tomorrow. I know we're busy, and I'll try to pitch in on other cases. We can always subcontract some small stuff too."

"Out, meaning in the field?" Courtney asked, sounding a little too excited.

"Yes, I suppose it would be."

CJ leveled a glare at me. It was not one of her bad ones, the kind that would tell me I'm in trouble, but it was enough to tell me she had something serious on her mind. It felt like a gun pointed at my temple, only with the safety still on.

"Some reading material and a couple of tag-alongs hardly make adequate training to fly solo," CJ said. "But you know this, so I'm guessing you have a good reason."

"I need someone to check the girls' places in Gainesville. You never know. The odds of finding something relevant are low, but low does not mean zero. I don't want to ignore it. Courtney will fit in on a college campus. You and I—"

"We're too old," CJ said, finishing my sentence.

I might have put it more delicately for once, but age was my good reason. "A hard truth," I said.

CJ thought it over for a moment. "It's a low-threat assignment," she said. She turned to Courtney. "It would be a good one for you."

"Take my CR-V," I said as Courtney beamed. "I don't want you driving to Gainesville in whatever it is you drive that passes for an automobile."

"Again with dissing Betty!" Courtney said.

I ignored her. "CJ will give you her spare key. You can pick up the Ham Sandwich at my house. I'll ride the bike tomorrow."

"That's a good idea," CJ said, sealing the deal, and ending the meeting in the process. It had been short and sweet, just the way I liked it.

I changed clothes and headed south. Unlike our meeting, there was nothing short or sweet about traffic. It was so bad that I got to the house in Key Largo a few minutes late. I parked out of the way so Skidmore wouldn't notice the absence of a rental-car sticker on the CR-V and walked the last half block. A shiny black Mercedes SUV already sat in the driveway.

Tiffany Skidmore got out of her ride the moment I appeared. She looked remarkably like her picture. The makeup was a little more obvious, and her hair had enough product to bounce a quarter off it. But match her image she did, and she still looked mostly human.

I walked to her, hand outstretched. "Alan Dunn," I said, using the name I'd used on the phone. "Sorry I'm late." The real Alan Dunn had gotten a good man killed last month and escaped before I could prove it or MDPD could arrest him. Now, he was my new favorite alias for liars and scumbags.

"Not at all, not at all," she said behind a broad, well-practiced smile. Whatever had kept her from jumping at the chance of a sale this morning was gone. She projected professional eagerness and greeted me with a firm handshake. "Let me show you this beautiful home," she said with a sweeping wave of her arm.

We climbed the front steps to the vast porch. She worked the two-factor authentication to retrieve the key from the lockbox, and we walked in. I kept up the buyer charade with the questions she'd expect about the sellers' willingness to repaint, the roof's age—all that real-estate jazz.

I did my best to avoid small talk. Playing a grumpy buyer was not exactly an Oscar-worthy stretch.

What did I do for a living? Trust management. No one knows quite what that means, so unless she had family in that line of work, it was a safe answer.

Where did I live? DC. I'd spent enough time around the Pentagon to fake it.

What kind of plane did I fly? Cessna. I remembered it was a plane company and not much more. Thankfully, Tiffany did not appear to know any more about planes than I did.

My monosyllables had the desired dampening effect on conversation, and I soon followed Tiffany down the stairs. That was the part I cared about. She walked right past the padlocked door without so much as a glance. I did not.

"What's in here?" I asked, rattling the handle.

"A wine cellar," Tiffany said over her shoulder. She had slowed down but had not stopped, her foot reaching for the next step down.

"Can I see it?" I asked.

"The sellers still have wine in there. I guess it's quite the collection because they asked for the door to stay locked."

"I don't want to drink their wine. I only want to see the space."

"I can ask if they'll arrange that," she said. "I don't have a key with me, though."

I dropped it and started back down after her. I kept a close eye on her. Anyone claiming they can tell when someone is lying that they've known a whole five minutes is the real liar. Still, it's human nature to try, and my profession did not help. You always want to get an edge, pick up something from how someone reacts, guess if their reaction is honest or fake. I was not immune to it, and I kept a bead on Skidmore as we came in view of the busted sliding door.

"Oh my God!" she said a little too loudly. Or at least I thought she had been too loud. Maybe that was normal for her. That's why you can never tell for sure in a few minutes. You have no baseline. Did she move stiffly when she brought her hand to her mouth, like it was a planned response? Choreographed? Or is it how she always reacted to something shocking? I had no way to know, at least not yet, so I filed the information in a corner of my brain and reminded myself not to draw any conclusions.

But I did not respond either. For one thing, I was curious to see what else she would say unprompted. For another, I took the opportunity to get a better daylight look at the sunroom. It looked just as bare as the night before.

"What happened here?" I asked when Skidmore did not volunteer anything.

"I . . . I really don't know. Probably some young people up to no good. This is . . . this is very distressing."

"The owners don't have an alarm?" I asked.

"They . . . hmm . . . I . . . I mean . . . this is a very safe neighborhood. Maybe they did not keep up the service after they moved. It's easier for showings, you know."

"Where did they move to?"

"I'm not a hundred percent sure. They're very private people. But this is normally such a safe area."

"Bad timing, I guess."

"I'm so sorry you had to see this."

"I've seen worse," I said. "But I didn't buy those places either."

"I completely understand," she said in that sorry-not-sorry voice reserved for annoying people. "I'll walk you out. Again, I'm so sorry about all this."

I had an itch to be a lot less nice to her. There was something about this showing that seemed made up, scripted—something more than her hair looking like a helmet. I just didn't know if it was her normal personality, if she was hiding something—whatever that would be—or if it had anything to do with my case. I did not have enough to give her the third degree. That made me irritable.

We quickly traced our steps in reverse—stairs, living room, front porch, steps down to the driveway. She left. I did too, then turned back around after a few blocks. Going in circles was becoming a habit on this island.

I parked a few houses back from where I'd been and started knocking on doors. The empty houses that had played into my hand the night before were not helping now. It took fifteen minutes and a walk to the end of the block and across the street before someone answered—a young man with a beach body and long hair, wearing stars-and-stripes board shorts. He had no shoes, no shirt, and a no-problem smile.

"What's up?" he asked. He took a step forward so he could lean against the doorjamb.

"Sorry to bug you, man," I said. "I'm looking at the house for sale down the street." I pointed in the general direction. "I figured maybe you could give it to me straight. Realtors only tell you what the sellers want you to hear."

"Yeah," he said. "Right. Rachel and Joe are pretty cool, though. Good people if you know what I mean."

"They're the owners?"

"Rachel and Joe? Yeah. Pullton. I know them a bit because they lived here, like, for good, you know? Not just weekends or in the winter."

I wondered why they kept the house so ugly then, but beauty was in the eye of the beholder, and in the end, I couldn't care less. "Where'd they go?" I asked.

"Back to Miami. From what they told me, they thought the island life would be cool to retire to, but they missed their friends. Miami's not that far, but still far enough to kill their social life, I guess."

"Did they entertain a lot down here? Or were they more private?"

"They didn't have too many people over, which I guess was the point, why they moved back and all. They aren't shy or anything, though. Joe's a builder, and he'll talk your ear off about houses and shit. Rachel said they were retired, but I think Joe was only half-retired. Anyway, he loved to hang out. And he loved his beer too."

"Oh, yeah?"

"Yeah. He could pack away a few for an old guy."

"Doesn't he have a wine cellar at the house?"

"Maybe, I don't know. Hell, Joe probably wouldn't know either. Like I said. He's a beer guy." He laughed at his own joke.

I joined with a courtesy chuckle. "What about the neighborhood? The back door was busted when the realtor showed me around."

"That's weird, man. This is a sweet corner of the planet. No joke. Good peeps, very chill. Maybe it's someone who came in for the Fourth. I mean, we are a tourist destination, you know. But I wouldn't worry about that. This is a sweet spot, man."

I had about as much information as needed, so I thanked him for his time and stepped away.

On the walk back to the car, I muttered to myself about Tiffany, her wine cellar story, and her rehearsed mannerisms. Too much didn't add up. She'd lied to me, and I wished I'd dug deeper. I thought about calling her back but decided it would probably be counterproductive, which also meant there was nothing else for me to do.

The damn sports coat felt like a vise on my chest, so I took it off and tossed it in the back seat. I leaned into the CR-V, started the engine, let the A/C work its magic for a few minutes, and then got in and headed back to Miami. I could use the thinking time, and we had other cases.

I was forty-five minutes out when Michaels called. I picked up the call on the car's Bluetooth. "Malone."

"This is Detective Sergeant Brian Michaels, Mr. Malone."

"What is it, Sergeant?"

"I'm afraid it's not good news, sir. A body washed ashore not far from Overseas Resort this morning."

CHAPTER 10

barked at the Bluetooth. "Who?"

I slammed the inside of the door with my fist, taking out some of my frustration on the car—frustration at what Michaels had just said and at the opposing traffic that kept me from turning the car around. *I need to get back!*

"We do not have positive identification—"

"Who, Michaels?"

"You understand any potential identification comes from photographs. We cannot fully rely on that."

"Been there and done that, Sergeant. Spare me the cover-your-ass bullshit and spit it out."

"We think it's Christine Raymond."

"Fuck!"

"The ME is only now taking the body back, but he thinks the victim was in the water for a couple of days."

The horn from the car I cut off swallowed my answer as I threw the CR-V around in a U-turn, heading back to Key Largo. I'd have flipped them off if I had time to waste. Instead, I focused on just two things: what Michaels had to say and the road in front of me. That, and silently urging traffic to move faster.

Michaels had shared that last piece of information to make me feel better, so I'd know Christine had likely died before I took the case, that there was nothing I could have done. I didn't have it in me to thank him. She was still dead, and I was still pissed. And I had a more pressing, a more frightful question to ask.

"Just one body?"

"Yes, sir." He had the good sense not to add "for now," at least not out loud. I didn't know MCSO's exact protocols, but I had a fair idea. They'd probably already called the Coast Guard to search the area in case this was worse than it looked. It was the kind of call that said *look hard, look everywhere, but please don't find anything.*

"When will the ME do his thing?" I asked.

"It should be today. We'll also be driving the Raymonds down to identify the body."

To identify their daughter's corpse, I translated. "Driving the Raymonds down to where?"

"To the medical examiner's office in the Marathon Substation."

"Understood. I'm on my way to you. And Sergeant? Thanks for keeping me in the loop."

"Yes, sir. You're welcome. And speaking of that . . ."

"Yes?"

"Given the new circumstances, we expect to execute a warrant on the house where we met last night. We will execute at 1600 hours. Captain Tornero invites you to observe and requests you arrive early."

"I'll be there at 1530 hours. And thanks for having my back." I wasn't naive—Tornero didn't know my name from some divine intervention and had not invited me to observe out of a random act of kindness.

"Captain Tornero may be grouchy sometimes, but he is fair and a good officer," Michaels said in his most official voice.

"Thanks for having his back too," I said. "I don't know if he's the kind of officer who tells you he notices those things, but he notices. Take it from me."

"Thank you, sir," Michaels said, still sounding like some Robocop, his tone as much a part of his armor as his uniform.

I hung up without another word. I had another call to make, the worst kind. I hadn't had to make a death notification since I'd left the MPs, and I'd never made one alone. I had a bad feeling this was going to be my turn, and it sucked. The timing sucked too. I might not make it back to Overseas until after MCSO picked up the Raymonds to take them to Marathon Key. This was not something I could do over the phone. I resorted to calling General Overby first.

He answered on the first ring. "You a mind reader, Malone? I was just about to call you."

One day, we may call each other John and Coop. That day would have to wait until after we took care of business, when this case was over.

"What do you see?" I asked.

"A hell of a lot of official personnel and vehicles out by one of the docks not far from here."

"It's not good news, General. Christine's body washed ashore. Officers will be over shortly to escort the Raymonds to identify her. They did not find anyone else at this time."

Unlike Michaels, I did not leave the worst unsaid. I gave the general all the information he needed, officer to officer. He needed one more piece of information from me.

"I'm on my way," I said, "but I may not get there before MCSO arrives."

A few seconds elapsed as Overby digested my words. "Jesus, Malone, I'm no stranger to death, but when it comes to families, I usually wrote condolence letters, at least at first. What do you suggest I tell the Raymonds?"

Other people might have tried to get out of this situation, to find a way to delay the Raymond's departure. I never thought the general would be one of those people, and he did not disappoint. He wanted practical advice, nothing more and nothing less. He had way more time in the army than I did, but I had more experience with these kinds of situations. He knew that and respected it.

"Tell them . . . tell them the body of a young black woman was found near that pier. Tell them we don't know for sure it's Christine but that it does not look good and that the police will arrive soon to talk to them. All we can do for now is prepare them to deal with MCSO, prepare them for what they'll likely have to do in the next ninety minutes. MCSO may allow you or Bill to go with them, but the Raymonds may not want you along. Everyone deals with something like this differently."

"Understood." Overby took a deep breath over the phone. "You said to tell them we're not sure. I understand why. But between you and me, how close to sure are we?"

"It's the same in their world as in ours, General. It's not official until all the right stamps are on all the right papers. There's always the tiniest chance of a mistake. But yeah, it's her."

"Thank you, Malone."

He hung up. He did not need to tell me to hurry, so he didn't. I cursed traffic all the way to the Overseas.

I parked haphazardly a car's length away from my clients—or some of them. The Overbys were here, as was Bill Berger. Jennifer was nowhere to be seen. The Raymonds' absence told me I was too late.

Jill Overby was in front of me before I could walk around the car. She was in no mood for hellos. She ripped her sunglasses from her face and launched. "I heard what you told Dad and what he told Cassie and Reggie. Now give me the no-bullshit version."

I did as she asked. "It's Christine. The cops identified her from the photographs in the missing-person reports." I had several inches on her, but it felt like she was the one looking down at me as I continued talking. "It means practically nothing new for Chloe and Ann. I'm still not bullshitting you. We already knew they'd been taken. Christine could have been killed by accident. It may even be why the other two were taken. Or it happened afterward. Or it happened if she tried to escape and bring help. Christine's death is a punch in the gut, a bad one, but as far as I'm concerned, there are still two living women to find."

"And what are you doing about it?"

The general put a hand on his daughter's shoulder. "We only hired the man yesterday."

"That's alright," I said. "I'd be asking the same question." I leaned against the car, just to take half a step back. I understood Jill. I told her father the truth. I'd be the same way in her shoes.

"I have a lead," I said, "one that got MCSO interested even before they found a body. I might tell you more if I was working solo, but I don't want to jeopardize their cooperation. They can be useful to me. I can tell you I'm meeting with them this afternoon to dig into it. It's just one lead—nothing more, but nothing less, either. I've got a scent, and I'm not letting go."

Jill nodded, keeping her gaze down. She hooked her thumbs in her shorts, the way some people do to keep themselves from fidgeting.

"It's one more lead than we had yesterday," General Overby said.

"Uh, what kind of a lead?" Bill Berger asked, stepping into view.

"Again, I'd rather not say at this time. Our chances are better if I stay on MCSO's good side." I wondered why he cared. He had not been as hostile as his wife but had never seemed eager for me to investigate, either.

Jill nodded again slowly, eyes downcast. I'd seen her guilt flare up the day before over what had happened. It had to be flooding her now, mixed with pure terror that her child could be next, a body ending up in a swamp, half eaten by wildlife. There was nothing I could do about that now. All I could do for her was find her Chloe.

The hurt of knowing I was too late for the Raymonds, that I could not do for them what I could do for Jill and the Bergers, was wrecking my brain. I needed to focus on Chloe and Ann. I had work to do. I turned to those girls' parents.

"I can't promise you I'll find your daughters," I said. "No one can. But I promise you this. If they can be found, I'll find them."

Jill looked back up at me. "Good," she said. She put her sunglasses back on and walked away.

I glanced at my watch. I had some time before meeting MCSO to execute the search warrant. I zeroed in on Bill.

"Walk with me, Bill, will you?" I asked.

"Sure."

"Where's Jennifer?" The Edge was the only Ford by the cabin Jennifer had rented for Ann and her. I guessed the Explorer was Jennifer's, and it was gone.

Bill shook his head. He tried to shrug, but he was tense. "I wish I could tell you," he said. "Jennifer does not talk to me. She does not talk to Ann either, except to fight with her. It's like I don't have a wife or daughter anymore. Jennifer yells at Ann, and Ann yells back at her. Then Jennifer goes to work or church, and I might as well not exist. My life has been a nightmare the last couple of years."

"If Jennifer and Ann are at such odds, why the cabin? Why the curfew?"

"That's Jennifer digging in. And truth be told, she never liked the other parents. She never felt like she fit in." He took his oversized glasses off, rubbed his eyes with the palms of his hands, and put them back on. "Reggie retired from an IT career with a good amount of cash, Cassie runs a downtown branch for a business bank, and Jill runs a whole airline in town. They've got incredible careers. Jennifer has a nine-to-five job for an insurance company, and I have a small CPA practice working from home. No one else thought anything of it, but Jennifer did, and she cut people off. She cut everyone off, even me."

"Not to be nonchalant about it, but if it's that bad, why stay?"

Bill ran a hand in front of his mouth. "I don't know. Everyone says family's the most important thing, that you must fight for it, so I'm fighting. I do everything I can. Maybe I should give up. It's been years. But things change. It got bad after Ann met Chloe and Christine. I mean, I'm not saying it's their fault or anything. It's just . . . it's what happened. Maybe this is a blessing in disguise."

"It's no blessing for Christine," I said.

Bill took off his glasses again and slowly polished them with his shirt. "No, no, of course. This is terrible. But maybe it will get Jennifer and Ann to speak again, and my nightmare will end."

I took a long look at Bill Berger while he focused on his glasses. I had yet to see a genuine emotion cross his face. I'd thought it came from the stress of Ann's kidnapping. Now, I wasn't so sure. He didn't show any empathy for the other parents who were going through the same ordeal or worse. I started wondering if he felt any emotion at all, or what kind of things happened in that house and what that had done to him.

I redirected the conversation to my original topic. "Do you have any idea at all where Jennifer might be now? Any at all? She may want to cut me off too, but I need to speak with her."

He shrugged and pulled out his phone, answering me in a low, sad monotone. "There's this church she likes—big surprise. It's down the highway, maybe fifteen minutes away or something. She spends a lot of time there. She sent me a picture of the facade, as if it mattered or I would care. I swear church is all she cares about. She's gone from religious to obsessive. It's not healthy."

He looked up at me. "I'm sorry. I'm babbling. I don't often get to talk about this. Anyway, you should see the church from the road. Let me send the picture to you."

He sent me the photo without another word. I did not have one for him either. I mumbled some thanks and went on my way.

Either traffic was worse than usual, or Bill underestimated how far away the church was. I found it on my left twenty-five minutes later. It was a brick building with a steep roof, a broad door, and a large cross rising from the top of the roof line. I parked near the entrance where an awning stretched out from the door, creating space for congregants to linger outside and chit-chat after service, sheltered from the unrelenting sun.

I walked inside. A single woman sat in the pews. She had faded, graying hair. Her shoulders were slumped. It could have been Jennifer. She did not turn around to see who came in so I couldn't be sure. As I approached her pew though, I could tell it was her and went to sit down.

She barely moved her head to see who I was.

"I don't want to see you," she said. "Especially here. This is my safe place."

"I thought you might want to know that Christine's dead," I said. I felt no incentive to deliver the news gently. As it was, Jennifer offered only a shiver, the way someone might react walking out on a cold day. "And Ann?"

"I'm still looking for her."

"I will pray for Christine's soul."

"That won't help me find Ann, or who has her, or who killed Christine."

"Vengeance is the Lord's," Jennifer said, "and the police will find Ann. You'll only get in the way."

"The police and I are on the same side. I'd think you would want all the odds in your favor."

Jennifer looked down, picking at her fingernails. "Do you believe in God?" she asked.

"That's private."

She snorted, a response that did not exactly endear her to me.

"When you've seen the things I saw when I was in the military, different people react differently," I told her. "Some throw themselves on the grace of God to survive it. Others conclude there can be no God in a world like this. And there's everything in between. But one thing we all have in common is we keep it to ourselves. Whatever we each come to believe, we're still one team. The part deep inside matters only to each of us individually. It was that way for me then, and it's that way now. Hopefully, you can respect that."

"Well, I believe in God, Mr. Malone, and I'm not afraid to shout it from the rooftops. I believe in Him and His Church. I do not believe in the likes of you, and I don't want to talk to you. Now, please leave."

I was not ready to concede defeat, to give up on Jennifer opening up. She may have nothing pertinent to tell me, but I wouldn't know either way until we had a productive conversation. Looking at the heat creeping up in red blotches on her neck, though, I could tell such a conversation would not happen today. I kept my mouth shut this one time, gave her a curt nod goodbye, and left. I had a house to search.

CHAPTER 11

I drove back the way I had come and made it to the house with the padlocked door. Its long driveway was already crowded with law enforcement vehicles, their lights flashing. Uniformed deputies milled about. I couldn't tell if it was organized chaos or just chaos.

I saw Michaels right away. He was talking to the same mustachioed officer he'd met in the parking lot I'd trailed him to after we met for lunch. There was a third person in their party, a tall woman in a pant suit. I killed the engine and walked toward them.

The dark-haired officer Michaels was talking to pointed toward me. Michaels nodded. The three of them strode toward me and met me halfway. Michaels made the introductions. The other officer, as I'd guessed, was Captain Tornero. He was a short man. Both Michaels and I had nearly a head on him.

The woman's name was Tanya Kesso. Up close, she looked about fifty, with too much makeup and stiffness in her face from too much Botox. Neither made her look twenty years younger like she wished. Michaels mentioned a title that sounded made up. She was a paper pusher by any other name. They had a role to play too.

"The warrant is in hand," she said once introductions were made. "Ms. Skidmore—she's the realtor—agreed to open the house for us. Captain Tornero said it was okay to wait for her as he secured the perimeter."

I nodded my thanks. After all, this was for my benefit. The others already knew all that.

As I pondered whether to let them know I'd already met Skidmore, together with the details of my little deception this morning, Tornero turned to me. He faced me, his eyes lasered on mine, his features frozen, and his hands on his hips.

"Mr. Malone, when I'm right, I'm right, and when I'm wrong, I'm wrong. I was wrong about those three women. That puts you ahead of us in this case. So, on paper, it's advantageous for us to work with you. I'm prepared to do that. That said, I have not had time to do my due diligence. Your website bio, while impressive, does not cut it."

"What do you want to know?"

"Who's the last cop you worked with? Not your favorite guy on the force, the last one to be on the same case as you."

"Jorge Rodriguez, MDPD Homicide. We worked a double last month."

Tornero arched his eyebrows. "You had a double homicide last month? You a trouble magnet, Mr. Malone?"

I took some water from the deputy who was walking up and down with a case of bottles, paying his dues, making sure everyone stayed hydrated. I twisted the cap open, took a swig, and looked back at Tornero. "Professional hazard," I said.

"Give me Rodriguez's number," the captain said.

I pulled up the detective's v-card on my phone and turned the screen toward Tornero. He tapped the number in his cell and walked a few steps away.

He needn't have bothered. The bits I overheard were in Spanish, and I would have picked up precious little even if the call was right next to me. I kept promising myself to learn the language, working in Miami and all, but I never found time to make it happen.

"He said you're a major pain in the ass, but you know your stuff," Tornero said when he returned.

"I'll own that."

"Good enough for me. Stay behind us for protocol's sake and chain of evidence, but you're welcome to stick around."

My thanks—I hadn't decided whether they were about to be sarcastic or sincere—were interrupted by the arrival of a familiar Mercedes SUV. It pulled up the driveway, stopped suddenly, seemed suspended in time, then backed out and parked on the street. Tiffany Skidmore emerged with a scowl, eyebrows low over her eyes, and slammed her car door.

"Oh, dear," Tanya Kesso said. "I don't think she realized there'd be quite such a police presence when I talked to her about opening the house for us."

"You always need to overcommunicate with civilians, Tanya," Tornero said. "It's easy to forget in the moment, but you invite drama if you don't. Go talk to her. Let's not have trouble here."

"Yes, sir. Sorry."

Kesso might have been right, and Tornero wasn't wrong about handling civilians, but I wondered if something more contributed to Skidmore's angry face.

Either way, Kesso hurried to Skidmore, looking at ease power-walking in heels. She pulled a piece of paper from her purse. I looked on from a distance. Skidmore launched into a tirade I could not hear. She swept the driveway's expanse as she talked. Kesso presented the warrant and put her hands together, pleading. Skidmore harangued her again, gesticulating toward the driveway some more. A hair may even have fallen out of place.

Kesso squared her shoulders and said a few more words. She pointed to the house. Skidmore gave a short nod, and both women strode to the front door. Tornero, Michaels, and I fell in step behind them.

Skidmore retrieved the key from the lockbox and opened the door. "This way," she said.

She had one high-heeled shoe in the entryway when Tornero touched her shoulder. "I'm sorry," the captain said, "but you need to wait outside."

"Absolutely not!" Skidmore yelled at Tornero, cheeks flushed.

"I'm afraid so," Tornero said. His voice was both firm and friendly in just the right proportions. He'd worked that out over decades on the job.

"This is unacceptable," Skidmore said.

"I am sorry you feel that way," Tornero said, walking past her.

I followed suit. That's when Skidmore first noticed me. She pointed at me, arm and index finger outstretched, her voice nearly a screech. "What's he—"

She never got to finish. A deputy put one hand on her arm and pointed to the end of the driveway with his other. "You need to step away and let us do our job, ma'am. Now."

Skidmore huffed away, eyes shooting daggers at me over her shoulders, as an officer escorted her back toward the end of the driveway.

"What was that about?" Tornero asked, looking at me.

"I'm a royal pain in the ass," I said, putting my bottle of water down on the porch and following them into the house.

Tornero did not press for details, not just yet. He had more pressing matters. Deputies were spilling into the house. One of them, carrying bolt cutters, exchanged a few words with Michaels, then went straight to the padlocked door. Tornero and Michaels followed closely behind. I gave them the space they'd requested for protocol, chain of evidence, and all that jazz—because they were working with me, and I wanted to keep it that way. That did not mean I liked it.

As it was, less than ten seconds went by before Tornero called out, "Get in here, Malone."

I took the stairs down and walked into the once-locked room. As I'd expected, steps led down to some kind of storage room. As I'd also expected, there was not a wine bottle in sight. I made my way down carefully, paying attention to where I put my feet. The place smelled vaguely of grease or oil.

That, and . . . piss.

I stepped around a receipt laying on the third step down as I made my way.

Tornero pointed to the receipt and a fast-food wrapper in a corner. "Someone was here. Can't say for certain it was the three missing women, or anyone else held against their will, but with that padlock, it doesn't pass the smell test."

"You mean it stinks to high heaven," I said.

The three of us scanned for clues, craning this way and that, trying not to move our feet to better preserve the scene. There wasn't much to see. The room looked bare, though it was large enough that we could miss something. The crime scene folks would take a closer look. The drywall was in bad shape. It looked patchy, a thin layer of paint peeling in places. The Pulltons probably never used this room, not as a wine cellar and not as anything else.

My eyes kept being drawn to a spot in the wall, like there was something there I should be seeing. Some of the pockmarks in the drywall formed an unlikely straight line. "Hand me your flashlight, Sergeant," I said.

Michaels pulled it out of his belt and did as I asked. I shone a light on the area that interested me. The pockmarks were tiny, but they definitely formed a line, and they were definitely not random.

"SOS," I read out. The small, improvised dots and dashes had probably been made with a fingernail or maybe a piece of jewelry. *Dot dot dot, dash dash dash, dot dot dot.* The one Morse message everyone knew: SOS. Save our souls. I'd heard that SOS meant nothing at all, that it was just a signal that's easy to transmit and recognize, but if that was true, I liked the popular legend better.

Three more combinations of dots and dashes trailed behind them, just as tiny as the SOS. Two of them were identical to each other. I was reaching for my phone to pull up a Morse alphabet when Michaels said, "CCA."

"You know Morse code?" Tornero and I asked in unison.

"Yes, sir. I had a very geeky childhood. It's C, C, and A."

"Chloe, Christine, and Ann," I said, stating out loud what everyone was thinking. Tornero and I looked at each other, and I verbalized another thought we shared. "Now we know. They were here."

"Alright," Tornero said. "Everybody out. Get the techs in here."

The three of us retraced our steps, walking with care to disturb the scene as little as possible. At the top of the stairs, we were met by the disapproving glares of technicians waiting to do their jobs.

Tornero winked at the lead man. "Don't worry, Andres. We left the place nice and clean for you."

"Sure, Cap," the man said.

We filed out and congregated on the mansion-sized porch. Tornero started us off. "We'll see what the body and the scene tell us. So far, all we know is one or more persons broke into an empty house that half the island probably knew was for sale and that one or more persons, possibly the same people, kept others there—likely the three women who disappeared—against their will. We're no closer to knowing who did either or who killed Ms. Raymond."

"I'm willing to bet the realtor knows something about it," I said.

That triggered Tornero's memory. His head snapped in my direction. "She acted like she'd seen you before."

"That's because she has," I said. "I met her this morning, pretending to be an interested buyer. She lied to me about what was behind that door—an elaborate lie at that. I doubt she made it up on the fly."

I finished giving Tornero and Michaels the details of the encounter. The captain looked straight at me, his jaw clenching tighter and tighter as I told the story. "That's cause for concern," he said when I finished. "Still, be careful with her. She has friends in the right places."

"Big fish in a small pond?" I asked. "No offense." After all, the small pond was his turf.

"None taken. In her mind, she's probably a shark in a koi pond—untouchable."

"Please take Captain Tornero seriously," Michaels said. "Ms. Skidmore can cause trouble."

I scratched the side of my nose to hide part of my grin. "It's like you know me already."

And he knew me pretty well, too, predicting I would strike on my own. I didn't care how much trouble Tiffany Skidmore could cause. She knew something, and I wanted to know what. The only thing that mattered was information leading me to Chloe and Ann.

Tornero looked down at a spot on the ground between our feet. He didn't take long. When he spoke, his eyes were lasered on me.

"Okay. Malone, it looks like Rodriguez was right about you. You're a pain, but you can play ball. Play ball with me. I'd rather have you with a foot in the door than on the outside causing trouble on your own."

He paused for a second. When he started again, he split his attention between Michaels and me, pointing a finger at each of us. "This is what we'll do. I'll authorize OT for the ME and the techs and get a prelim from them by tomorrow morning. Fuckers get to work late for once. We three will reconvene at 11:00 a.m. after they brief me. We'll go through everything we have and come up with a plan of action. Until then, you two, don't go cowboy on me. I want your word."

Michaels agreed right away. He didn't have a choice. I took longer. I looked at the house, so close over Tornero's shoulders. I pictured the three girls whose photos were still in my car's glove box stuck in that room. I wanted action. But as much as I hated to admit it, there was precious little I could do right now, and none of it was worth getting on MCSO's bad side. The house was off-limits and Skidmore probably still too hot under the collar to handle.

I turned my attention back to Tornero. I forced my jaw to unclench and extended my hand. "You have my word."

He shook on it, and I got back in the CR-V. I pulled out my phone before driving off and texted Courtney. "Before you leave tomorrow, I need everything you can find on Tiffany Skidmore, realtor in Key Largo," I typed. "Not her listings. I want personal stuff. Criminal history. Shit like that. But put a hard stop on your time. I don't want you falling asleep on the road."

A bubble from her came nearly instantaneously. "Thanks, Coop. With all the adrenaline in my blood right now, this is great."

"Don't forget the hard stop," I texted back.

"I promise," came her text. I could just about hear her sigh.

I could not think of another thing to do on the island. I could update the office from the car. All that was left was the drive back to Miami, and maybe, just maybe, shed the events of the last two days for just one night.

CHAPTER 12

The drive back felt like an out-of-body experience. I had let CJ know there were developments, sending quick voice texts from the car on my way to Overseas, and then again back from the church after talking to Jennifer. With time ahead of me, I dictated a longer voice memo giving her and Courtney a reasonably coherent narrative of the day's events. They had enough to do without me interrupting them— they'd put the report in the file when they found it.

I listened to my memo again before clicking send. It sounded like someone else was talking in the car, someone saying logical and sensible words, someone who wasn't a ball of pissed-off energy because one of the women he had been hired to find was already dead.

I sent Amy a voice text too, asking her to meet me at Barrels instead of riding together, and a bit later than planned. By the time I remembered to give her the address, she'd already answered it would be no problem. I knew it wouldn't be. I hoped *I* wasn't going to be the problem. I needed to go home for a deep breath. I needed to shower and scrub death off. I needed to change clothes. I had not been anywhere near Christine's body, yet death clung to me.

I pushed the accelerator on every empty stretch of highway I encountered, speed limits be damned. I didn't know if I had an angel or a demon over my shoulders, but I could sure feel the Grim Reaper hovering over me, proud of his latest coup, a young woman snuffed before she had truly lived.

I got home and did all the things. I focused my mind on Amy. She was life. She was what I needed, *who* I needed, more than anything. I left the CR-V in the driveway for Courtney and took the ol' Indian Chief. The bike and I took to the side streets tonight, seeking as much solitude as Miami could offer.

I got to Barrels just as Amy was walking to the door. Something must have caught her eye—or her ear. It could have been the bike's engine. It could also have been women's intuition. She stopped in her tracks, looked at me and smiled—*that* smile—a smile brighter than her platinum blonde hair, a million-dollar, make-your-knees-weak smile. I loved her for it, and I hated her for it. It just wasn't fair.

Amy walked to me. More accurately, she sashayed to me. She twirled around once she reached me. She wore high heels and a backless dress that barely covered the goods.

"I felt like overdressing a little tonight," she said.

"Is that overdressing or underdressing?" I asked. It was barely dressing at all and had exactly the effect she intended.

"You can call it either one," she said, wrapping her arms around my neck. "Are you complaining?"

"Not one bit. I look like a slob next to you, though."

She shook her head, then whispered in my ear. "Hell no. You know what a good leather jacket and biker boots on you do to me." The kiss that followed might have been meant to remind me.

We walked in, and I asked for a table to the side, against the wall, to get a better view of the room. We hadn't sat down for a minute when Todd came to say hi. I'd told Barrels' owner he could stop by. He did not have to pretend not to know me—just avoid talking shop unless I did. I introduced him to Amy. She stood up to give him a hug, and he put the first round on the house.

A waitress dropped off two waters, a single-page food menu, and a wine-and-beer list thicker than a phonebook.

"My kind of place," Amy beamed at the waitress. And yet, she did not pick up either one. She leaned my way, her elbow resting on her armrest. She gave me a look that came close to a glare.

"My bad days are not like your bad days," she said. "They're just office politics."

I looked back at her so she knew she had my attention. She was going somewhere. I did not interrupt.

"All the same," she went on, "I've had a couple of rotten days. That puts me in a mood. And no, not only 'that' mood, though that too. It puts me in a . . . blunt mood."

"Blunter than normal?" I asked. Amy had never been one to beat around the bush.

She cocked her head and spoke very slowly, dragging one syllable into two. "Yes."

"Duly noted. Shoot."

She spoke in a soft voice, a kind voice—a loving voice, even—but her words left no room for imagination. "What the fuck is wrong with you tonight? Get it out now."

So much for leaving the pall hanging over my head behind. Amy never needed sugar-coating, so I didn't try. "One of the three missing girls I've been looking for turned up dead."

"Then what are you doing here?" She sat up straight, and a flash of anger passed over her face. "I'm not some kind of fragile little woman who's going to get all emotional over a canceled date."

"Give me some credit," I said. I was firm. Direct. She deserved no less. But I felt no anger, and there was none in my voice. "You know me better than that. Fact is, there's nothing I can do about this case tonight. I can do no good to anyone in it. Not a damn thing. And I'd rather spend time with you than all the alternatives put together, so long as you don't mind me like this, mood and all."

Amy had leaned toward me again halfway through my speech. She put a hand on my leg and her eyes on my soul.

"I don't mind you in any mood, Cooper Malone."

I put my hand on hers and looked at her. She was beautiful inside and out, with a huge, generous spirit. And she was here with me. I still didn't know what I did to get that lucky. I'd wondered that more than once in the past few weeks and would probably never know the answer. I didn't even understand why not knowing didn't bother me. Not knowing anything else would drive me to the edge of insanity. But that's how it was. That's what Amy did to me, and I'd decided, just this once, to accept it.

"Is it . . . was it the general's granddaughter?" Amy asked.

"No." I didn't need to tell her more. Christine's death was the worst kind of punch in the gut. Chloe's would have been all but unbearable. Somehow, Amy knew. She seemed to have picked up an awful lot about me in an awfully short time. Maybe that's what people mean when they say things "click." Maybe it's some soulmate bullshit. All I knew was it felt good not to have to explain.

And sure enough, Amy voiced my inner thoughts out loud. "Still . . . she was just a kid, right? Not even twenty?"

"Not even. Her parents seem like good people too. Death is death, and it shouldn't matter if the parents are nice or assholes, but it hurts a bit more when it happens to the nice ones. From the moment I met everyone, those two were more concerned about everybody else, even with their own child missing."

"What about the other two girls?"

"I'm still looking for them."

Amy squeezed my hand. "If they can be found, you'll find them."

I chuckled despite the gloom. "That's pretty much word for word what I told their parents."

"Good," she said and picked up the wine list. "We need drinks more than ever."

"What kind of wine do you recommend for an old whiskey drinker like me?" I asked, grateful for the change in topic.

"I thought you'd be all over the beer list."

"I might try a change of pace tonight."

"Really?"

"Yeah."

Amy sat back, square in her seat, the bible-sized wine list open on her lap. If I'd known sharing her love of wine with me would make her as happy as she looked at that moment, I'd have asked her long ago.

"We need a big red," she said, half to herself and half to me. "Really big and really red, something that will dye your teeth purple." She flipped pages as she spoke, thoughts pouring out into words. "I'm thinking a Spanish Rioja or a Portuguese Touriga."

She looked up long enough to make sure I was paying attention. "They're really the same thing," she said. "The name changes when the river crosses the border into Spain. Which is kind of weird, and also kind of cool. Most varietal names carry across. Not all but most."

She returned to the list and kept talking while turning pages. I kept on looking at her and listening. "Here we go," she said. "Perfect. They have a nice, honest Callabriga."

"What's that?" I asked.

"A big red from Portugal. It will work. It's a good, strong wine, middle of the road for that region, so you'll have a good idea of the style."

"Then that's what I'll have."

We ordered our wine. Amy picked a white that got her all excited—a kind I'd never heard of—and a bunch of appetizers. She looked up expectantly when my wine came. It was dark red as if someone had mixed in black ink. It tasted strong and dry, filling my mouth with a burst of flavor that lingered on my palate after I swallowed it. Amy had chosen well. I could get used to that.

"What would a connoisseur say about it?" I asked, handing her my glass.

She swirled the wine and dipped her nose in the glass. Then she did it again. Then she swirled it one more time and took a sip, rolling the wine over her tongue. "Bold," she said. "Dry. Robust. Earthy."

"Shit. You wine people have a weirder vocabulary than the army."

"Pfft. Not even close!"

We laid back to a light, leisurely dinner. We talked about a little bit of everything. I dragged office-politics stories out of her. Nobody may have died as a result of her shit days, but they may have been more maddening than mine.

I liked our talks. I liked listening to her. That night, I was a little distracted by the way she looked in that sliver of a dress. I figured she did not mind me staring, or she would have worn something else.

In spite of all that, I managed to keep an eye on the room. And true to form, Amy did not miss a beat.

"See anything interesting for your vandalism case, Mr. PI?" she asked. "It's bullshit someone would trash a place like this, by the way."

"It is bullshit, and maybe."

"Really? I *am* in your world now. What is it?"

"Three guys over your left shoulder. All three of them are drinking light beer. This is not the kind of place a group will come to if everyone is happy with beer you can buy at a gas station. It makes sense that Todd sells it. Not everyone in a group will be all over the microbrews. But if everyone goes for this, why come here? The vibe is great, but it's still weird."

She thought about that for a moment. She picked up her glass, swirled the wine, closed her eyes, and took a sip. Then she said, "You notice all those little things, don't you?"

"Little things can break big cases," I said. "Fuck, I just sounded like a cheesy TV slogan from the fifties, didn't I? You're probably cringing inside."

"I am," she said, shaking her shoulders like a Nor'easter had just blown through. "Don't ever do that again."

I caught Todd's eye, and he stopped by our table to ask if everything was alright.

"It is," I said. "Great, actually. What about the three boneheads drinking donkey-piss beer to my left. How are they doing?"

Todd had a little grin. "Busy as we are, not quite as great. They're semi-competitors. They own a dive bar three blocks away. We don't tend to attract the same crowd, but they still like to see how we do things, what we serve, stuff like that."

"They're nervous enough about the competition to try and take it down?"

"You mean by . . . no! They're harmless."

"Are you sure?"

Todd looked at me for a second, mouth hanging open. He brought his hands together, fingers intertwined, and rested his chin on them. "I guess I'm not sure of anything anymore."

"When the waitress comes back—"

"Becca," Amy said, shooting me a look. "She has a name."

"You're right. When Becca gives us our check, slide a piece of paper in there with their names and the name of their bar on it. We'll run the names down. You're probably right, and it's harmless, but we'll check it out all the same."

"Okay, thanks," Todd said as he turned away.

Amy was doing some kind of happy dance, rolling her shoulders, that smile of hers bright as a Florida sunshine.

"What's that for?" I asked.

"Being here together. Noticing the little things."

"That's how it works."

Her smile morphed into something more mischievous. She ran her hand along the seam of her dress, tracing her cleavage. "What other little things have you noticed?"

"That you told the truth about shitty days putting you in *that* mood. Your nipples look damn gorgeous under that dress. That you're naked everywhere under it. I noticed that when we kissed hello. That you're enjoying the small talk and that second glass of wine, but that's mostly because you love the release that follows prolonged anticipation. And because you like teasing me and leaving me mildly uncomfortable with a semi under my jeans, the one you keep checking is still there. Don't worry. It is and will not be going away while sitting next to you."

"Check, please." Amy looked straight at me, mouth open just a little. She was not kidding. I signaled Becca, paid the check, slipped the list from Todd in my pocket, and headed out.

"Take me back to your place," Amy said. "I Ubered down."

I looked at the bike and then at her dress. "We may have to Uber back up," I said, scratching my cheek.

Amy turned around to face me. With agonizing slowness, she raised her dress over her hips, daring me to stare at her nudity—daring anyone in the parking lot. Then she straddled the Indian. "Ride fast, honey, before I leave too big a spot on your bitch seat."

My excitement would make riding a challenge at any speed. I managed to take my seat, start the bike, and peel away from Barrels. I stuck to narrow roads and side streets. I didn't want a cop with no sense of humor to take exception to my riding with a half-naked woman behind me.

I rode down them fast, pushed by the urgency within me. A dark alley caught my eye. I wasn't sure I could control my actions if I took us down that road, so I rode on. I wasn't sure Amy could control her actions either. She sat glued to me on the bike. The warmth of her body radiated through my riding jacket. She reached around and scratched my chest under the jacket.

"Faster, babe," she shouted in my ear over the din of the wind, urging me on. "You know that wet spot I was talking about? You're going to need a good cleaner for your seat." She didn't make us crash, but as she bunched my shirt in her hands to cries of "I need you, and I need you now," I opened the throttle another notch.

I dismounted the Indian Chief the moment we made it inside the garage. Amy didn't move. I stood behind her. My hands on her hips, I pulled her off the bike. She spread her legs in her giant heels and leaned over the seat. I opened my jeans and took her right there, just like that. Hard. We didn't say a word. There was no foreplay. We didn't need it. There was just her and me, needing each other and needing to forget the world outside us.

When we were done, she straightened up and leaned back into me. Her hair tickled my nose. Our bodies breathed in unison.

"I saw you glance at that alley on the way here," Amy said, sounding out of breath. "Why didn't you go in?"

"I thought it might be a bit much."

"A bit much?" She turned around to face me. There was something new in her eyes, maybe anger, maybe disbelief. She brought her hand to the side of my face so hard she damn near slapped me. Her fingernails dug into the skin behind my ear.

"Do you want to keep me?" she asked.

I was too stunned to answer—at least not quickly enough—so she asked again, enunciating every word. "Do. You. Want. To. Keep. Me?"

"Yeah," I managed to say.

"Then you better start learning to feed my wild side. Too much? Too much is what I want. Too much is what I need. Too much. Out of control. I need that from you."

"I hear you, and I'm not intimidated by your wild side. It's just that with the mood I'm in—"

"Your mood? Your big, scary, dark mood?" Her nails dug deep enough to hurt. The pain felt good. The pain felt real. "Take a good look at my dark side, Cooper Malone. I dress to kill, and I don't give a fuck. I want things *ladies* aren't supposed to want. I do things *ladies* aren't supposed to do. I am not polite company. I act out. Sometimes, I act out with sex. I am showing you *my* dark side, you son of a bitch. All of it. So don't you dare hide yours from me. Don't you fucking dare!"

I pushed her backward. Then I picked her up around the waist and carried her past the bike. I reached around to open the door and slammed her against the wall in the house, harder than I'd ever done with anyone.

I yanked the part of her dress that still covered her chest so violently it ripped. Amy leaned her head against the wall, eyes half closed, while somehow still looking at me. She whispered one word, one word that meant everything. "Yes."

The rest of the night, I showed her my dark side. I showed her how I needed her to make me feel alive, maybe even sane, amidst the death and chaos that surrounded me. I showed her what it took to do that, even when I felt no one could want me that way. And she showed me what wild meant to her, who she was behind closed doors when she was free to be herself, what she needed from me.

There were times I thought I might break her. There were times I thought she might break me. By the time we made love once more, bathed in dawn's light, I knew we could never break each other.

CHAPTER 13

The boots and jacket went back on, the coffee went into a ther-
mos, and I started up the Indian for the ride to Key Largo. The
CR-V was gone, and Courtney's Betty sat on the driveway, all rust and
duct tape. I also had a text and an email Courtney had sent late last
night when I'd had other things on my mind. The text just said *play
me* and had a voice memo attached. I couldn't read or listen to either
on the bike. It wasn't rigged for business. I decided they could wait. I
wanted to get going.

As I sped away, Amy, still sleeping in my bed, was the only indication this was the weekend. The days of the week wouldn't matter to
Chloe and Ann. They didn't matter to those looking for them.

I got to Key Largo with plenty of time before my meeting with
Michaels and Tornero. I had something else I needed to do first.
I dreaded it, but that was no excuse, and I eased the Chief into the
Overseas parking lot.

Jill Overby and her father sat at a picnic table, each with a mug in
front of them. I could see the Raymonds seated on the retaining wall
that surrounded the lot, their back to the world, hand in hand, shoulders stooped, looking out at the ocean.

The general saw me coming and turned to the Raymonds. Cassie
nodded and swung her legs over the wall with some difficulty. I met
her next to the table.

"I'm so sorry for your loss," I said. I tried to muster genuine sincerity in my voice to make up for how stupid those words sounded. What else could I say?

Cassie nodded. She spoke in barely a whisper, her gaze lost somewhere. It was as if all life had been drained out of her.

"Thank you," she said. She took a breath. It sounded like an effort. Tears started streaming down her face. "The doctor said it probably happened on the fifth. One day, she's taking selfies from the beach, and the next day she's gone. How does that happen?"

"There's no answer to that, ma'am. There's just not."

Jill stood next to her friend. Cassie took her hand, looked at her, and then asked me about Chloe and Ann.

"Are the Bergers around?" I asked.

When shrugs and headshakes were my only response, I turned to the elder Overby. "Will you update them as you see fit when they arrive, General? I don't want to delay."

"Of course."

"Let's sit down," I said.

The Overbys reclaimed their seats at the table. Cassie walked past the table to the retaining wall and began speaking to her Reggie, but he shook his head, and she joined us at the table.

She took a seat next to me. "Our children are our world. Both Reggie's and mine. But Christine and him?" Her eyes glistened. "His heart was just torn from his chest."

Tears stung everyone's eyes, this tough guy included.

"He's not ready to hear about all this, and I understand that," Cassie said. "But I need to know."

I nodded, wiped my eyes, and angled my body to address everyone at the table. "As I told you yesterday, MCSO is working with me on this. They'd rather I say nothing. That's policy. I want to keep them on my side—not that I can't investigate without them, but it's easier with them and, more importantly, often quicker. By the same token, you have a right to know what's going on, so I'll tell you what I can. Just keep even this much to yourselves."

Everyone nodded, three pairs of eyes riveted on me. I went on. "We have clues about what happened, but we do not know anything with certainty. It's more than a guess, but keep in mind there could be surprises later."

I gave everyone a second to take all that in before diving in. "It appears that Chloe, Christine, and Ann were taken the night of the Fourth and brought to a house not far from here. The kidnapper or kidnappers likely broke in by smashing a glass door. We found evidence of the girls' presence in that house. We do not know what happened there, but something caused Christine's death, and Chloe and Ann were moved to another location."

I did not tell them that Chloe and Ann might have been killed along with Christine, and we had not found their bodies yet. I refused to work off that theory, and I refused to talk about it. This was the *I'll Fucking Find Them* ship, and I was taking them aboard with me.

Jill shot me an angry look. She leaned in, her hands balled into fists on the table. "So, we have no clue where they are now? Or who took them? We know nothing more than before?"

"I'm telling you everything I can. I have a person of interest who's about to hear from me. There's no doubt in my mind this person is involved or at least knows something. I don't know how or what yet, but I will. I'm working the case."

That must have been enough, at least for now. Jill relaxed her hands and sat back. She closed her eyes for a moment and took a deep breath. "Alright. Alright. Just please, please find them."

"I'll keep you posted when I can," I said.

"Thank you, Malone," General Overby said, speaking for all of them. There was not enough energy left around this table for more talk.

"Let me ask one more thing while everyone's here," Cassie said as I pushed away from the table. "Will you find who killed my Christine? Will you take that case?"

Jill frowned, her eyes narrowing down to slits across the table.

"They are technically two different cases," I said. "I could find Chloe and Ann and still not know who took them or who killed Christine. Or I could know and not be able to prove it. And yes, Cassie, I am taking that case too."

Tears flowed down her cheeks again. "I just wanted to make sure it was okay since it's two cases like you said."

"No question," General Overby said.

Jill leaned across the table and took Cassie's hands in her own. "If he doesn't find out, I will."

I got up, saying something stupid like, "It's settled." I swallowed hard, unclenched my fist, and walked away before things became more emotional. I wished to hell that CJ was here, but she was already carrying two people's workloads—three today.

Reggie Raymond called after me before I could make my escape. I turned back twenty feet short of the bike.

He put a hand up before I could offer my condolences. "I just need to ask you one question," he said. His voice was hoarse, his eyes puffy and red. He was the oldest of the parents. He looked ancient now.

"Go ahead," I said.

"It may be an unfair question, but it weighs on me and I thought, maybe . . ."

"Don't worry about that. The worst that can happen is I can't answer it."

Reggie closed his eyes. "What do I tell my son? He's sixteen. He doesn't know yet. How do I tell him?"

The question deflated me. My bones felt like they were turning into liquid, like they'd be unable to hold me up much longer.

"I have mercifully little experience telling people about things like this," I began. I had trouble pushing the words through. I cleared my throat, apologized, and went on after another breath. "From the few times I have, and from what my time in the army taught me, everyone reacts differently. Some need handholding. Others need to rip the band-aid off. I don't have children, and I don't know your son, but I'd start in stages."

I puffed my cheeks. How do you tell a teenager, a boy really, that his sister was killed, that she washed up on a beach, full of bullet holes? I kept talking, grasping for the right words. "Tell him something bad happened. Then that it's about his sister. Lead into what happened, but if he gets impatient, that's your clue to tell him straight up. It won't be as easy as I make it sound, but that's the best I can give you."

"Yes. It makes sense. Thank you for that." Reggie's rasping voice reduced to a whisper, like a stream drying out. "I don't know how I'm going to make it through this."

I shook my head. "We live in a world where children are supposed to bury their parents, not the other way around. I'll find out who did this. Maybe it will help, maybe not. That's all I have to offer."

"You're a good man, Mr. Malone," he said. "An honest man." He nodded, more to himself than to me, bobbing his head a few times. Then he turned around and went back to look at the ocean.

CHAPTER 14

I thought that meeting with the parents would have been the worst part of my day. Instead, I went from the frying pan into the fire. It didn't look like it at first. Jumping through hoops to get past the lobby at MCSO's Key Largo station was merely irritating. Sitting with a visitor's badge around my neck while I waited for Tornero and Michaels, who were late, was at most annoying.

Then Captain Tornero entered the room, and the temperature soared. He had his hat in his hand. It flapped against his leg as he stormed in. His shoes pounded the floor. He strode to the conference table, dragged a chair, and sat across from me. Michaels sat down next to him, still as a statue, hands folded in front of him.

"I just had a very unpleasant call with the sheriff," Tornero said without preamble. "It took a good hour to convince him not to turn this case over to SIU."

I stirred in my seat. Working with MCSO was necessary, maybe even useful. But I didn't need hotshot assholes from the Special Investigations Unit, sheriffs, or whatever office politics were happening here getting in the mix.

"Does SIU normally handle this kind of case?" I asked, my jaw feeling tight.

"No. But our friend Ms. Skidmore made a lot of very angry calls to a lot of very powerful people in the Keys."

"She didn't waste any time."

"No, she didn't. I'm still not sure I convinced the sheriff, but it's our case for now. However, we are under strict orders not to bother Ms. Skidmore or interfere with her business without good reasons, and it seems that lying to Malone here is not good reason enough."

I was starting to feel as hot under the collar as Tornero, who got up and started pacing the room, burning some energy. Before I could vocalize just what I thought of the sheriff, Tornero told Michaels to fill me in on what they had. I kept my constructive comments to myself and turned my attention to the detective sergeant.

"Yes, sir," Michaels said. He pulled out his notebook. He went back and forth between looking at his notes and looking at me as he talked. "The ME's preliminary report came in. Ms. Raymond died as a result of multiple gunshot wounds from a heavy caliber weapon, a forty-five."

"And I don't like that," Tornero said without breaking his stride, pointing a finger at me. "Pamela Howard was killed by a nine-millimeter bullet. You know what this means as well as I do. We likely—*likely*—have two different shooters. Go on, Michaels."

Michaels did as ordered. "Time of death, well, it's more difficult to determine when the body has been submerged. The ME had to make some assumptions, not least of which is that she was put into the water near the shore. If that assumption proves correct, we have a good idea of water temperature, and we know how water impacts decomposition. The examiner can work backward from the decomp fluids in the body."

Michaels kept reading from his notes. "Our doctor—he is quite experienced with at-sea deaths—also examined bloating, skin slippage, and the extent of damage from aquatic life. If we accept for now that Ms. Raymond's body was put in the water close to the time she was shot, the time of death falls somewhere during the evening of July fifth. The ME cannot be more specific until specialists can examine aquatic insects.

"Let's see . . . stomach contents were fully digested. Ms. Raymond had not eaten since that morning or the day before. She sustained some scrapes and minor injuries, but nothing to indicate a violent interaction. There were no defensive wounds or biological material under her fingernails, though the water may have washed some evidence away. There was no sign of sexual assault, to the extent the ME could determine after several days in the water."

"Where was she hit?" I asked. "From how far?"

Michaels flipped through his notebook. "There's no way to tell about gunshot residue—the water would have washed that away. From the bullet pattern and force of penetration, we're estimating she was shot at close range. She was shot four times, three times in the chest and once in the shoulder. We recovered three bullets. They're out to ballistics."

"Do we have to *assume* her body was submerged close to shore? Can't we figure it out?" I put a hand up. I was getting amped. "I'm not challenging you, Sarge. My MP days were in Kansas, and there haven't been that many corpses around me in my PI practice. I know squat about floaters."

"Yes, sir," Michaels said, his answer to nearly everything. "The Coast Guard and our ocean people are working on the tides and currents of the past two days. The marine entomologists will help too. Different bugs live in different parts, I'm told. It probably wasn't far from where she was found, but all we have so far are best guesses."

He was right, and I hated it. It wasn't just about where the body was dumped. It was true of the entire case. All we had were goddamn guesses.

"Anything else?" I asked.

"Tissue samples and her personal effects have been sent to the lab. There's a rush on it, but we don't have anything back yet."

"What about the scene?"

"Regarding the house in general," Sergeant Michaels reported, "there was heavy traffic and a lot of cleaning since the house is for sale. The lab has some stuff—we put that at a lower priority than Ms. Raymond's effects. As to the room where the three victims were likely kept, we swabbed every surface. There's evidence of urine in the far corner—the lab will confirm. Closer inspection of the wall revealed no other hidden message, or really anything else. The lab will study the swabs—"

"They won't find anything," Tornero said. "We may get something useful from the victim's body or her personal effects, but I doubt this will be a forensic-driven case. We're going to have to earn this collar." He turned the chair he'd recently vacated backward and straddled it, arms resting on the back. "The question is, what do we do now?"

The answer seemed obvious to me: "We talk to Skidmore."

"We are under instruction not to do that," Michaels said, like a good Boy Scout.

"You are," I said. "I'm a civilian. That shit does not apply to me."

"Skidmore won't see it that way," Tornero said. "The moment you talk to her, we lose the case to SIU, and you lose MCSO's help."

Before I could object to how Tornero balanced his priorities, Michaels piped up. "Maybe we could . . ." He stopped for a moment, as if hesitant to step in between Tornero and me. We both stared at him, waiting, so he continued. "We could do a wide and very public canvassing," he said. "And as part of this canvassing, we'd happen to go by all the properties listed by Ms. Skidmore's office."

"I admire your sense of compromise," I said, "but we're not going to find anything looking through windows."

"The house from yesterday was broken into," Michaels said. "You never know. We could find something, even without going into Ms. Skidmore's listed properties. Or the publicity may shake something loose."

"I have a better chance of getting something out of Skidmore," I said.

"At great cost," Tornero said.

"Would Chloe and Ann see it as a great cost?"

Tornero shook his head. He was actually smiling. "You're sure you're not Latino, amigo? I love the passion and the hot blood, but you're assuming you'll find them if you can just talk to Skidmore.

That's a big assumption."

He wasn't wrong. "I'm not denying that," I said, "but I'm pretty sure I'll find them faster by talking to her than not. And I'll try not to let my Irish temper get in the way of your Latino heat."

Tornero raised his hands to the skies. "Damn it, I'm not blind, Malone. Skidmore is in it somehow. And finding the girls quickly is all that matters. It matters to me just as much, in case you had any doubt. But I can't pretend the world around me does not exist, and I want to preserve my chances of finding them—and finding Pam Howard's killer, too, by the way.

"Give me a day, at least. We'll implement Michaels' plan and see if the lab has anything for us. If we've made no progress by the start of business tomorrow—the lab should have some prelims by then—I turn you loose and let the chips fall where they may."

I wasn't his to turn loose. I had gone private so I wouldn't have a Tornero or a sheriff or an SIU to answer to. And I did not like his idea one bit. I had a lead. I had to pursue it. I was right and I knew I was right. MCSO's cooperation was valuable to me, but speed was more valuable.

I heard CJ's voice in my head pleading with me to let the system work. She liked the system. And I had information on Skidmore from Courtney still sitting in my inbox that I'd want to look at before I talked to her anyway. After that, I could not make promises, and I would not make any.

I looked Tornero straight in the eye as I stood up to leave. "I may be a pain in the ass, but I'll never bullshit you. Search fast. I'll hold off as long as I can stand it, and I don't know how long that will be."

"You give pain in the ass a new meaning," Tornero called after me. "Don't you forget it!"

I left the sheriff's office, throwing my visitors' badge on the desk on the way out, without anyone trying to put cuffs on me. From there, I went to the Secret Passage for a bite to eat and a place to review what Courtney had sent me.

I picked a table in a corner of the patio, heat be damned. The place was nearly empty in the midday sun. Summer was bleaching the wooden tables another shade lighter. The restaurant friers belched smells of sugar and fat into the air. A couple of pups had found shade under their owners' tables. They were the smart ones.

I settled at my spot and ordered lunch, watching the dogs stretch and beg for food. I envied their simple lives. My meal came. No one was sitting at the tables next to me, so I played Courtney's recording while munching, keeping the volume low and the phone to my ear. It did say *play me* in her text. Sometimes, I do as instructed.

"Hi Coop," Courtney's voice greeted me. "I just sent you a PDF file about Tiffany Skidmore. There's quite a bit in there, and I'm sure a lot of it will be boring and irrelevant. I erred on the side of over-inclusion. So, I am sending you this summary in my own live voice. Smart, huh?

"Anyhow, Tiffany Skidmore—a story of the rich getting richer. She's from a prominent family in the Keys. That allowed her to hobnob with powerful people who own and sometimes sell expensive houses. Her pre-ordained success in real estate—though, in all fairness, she does appear to work her butt off—put her in contact with even more people, and she became even more successful, a virtuous circle spinning full speed ahead. She's super connected.

"She married young and divorced quickly. Never remarried. I have no clue whether she's an asexual monk or a very discreet slut. That would take more time to find out, it's probably irrelevant to the case, and I promised you I'd put a hard stop to it at a decent hour."

I tapped pause and checked the time when Courtney had sent her text. I shook my head. What qualifies as a decent hour must change with age.

I pressed play, and Courtney's voice resumed. "She has one kid, Zach, from her marriage. That's probably why she kept her married name after the divorce. He's twenty-two and lives at home. I did not have time for a deep dive on him, but I don't think he ever had a serious job, and he did not go to college either, so I'm not quite sure what he spends his time doing. He has one of the most hateful social media pages I've seen in a long time. It's not bigotry, nothing that simple. He mocks and hates e-ve-ry-one.

"He's in an online group with two of his friends. No time to look up those fine citizens either, sadly. The group's called Skull and Coins. I don't know why or what that means. The group's private. I'll have to put getting into it on my later list, and you know how much I hate later.

"And voilà. Hopefully, you'll enjoy all that light reading I sent you. I'm off to bed. Oh, and say hi to Amy for me! Wink, wink, nod, nod, and ta-ta for now."

I rolled my eyes and opened the PDF file in my email. Courtney was not kidding about over-including. It looked even longer on a phone-sized screen. Maybe that was for the best. I had some good grouper left on my plate and words on my phone. Courtney had just made Captain Tornero's day.

I put the phone down for a minute and tried to find the peace a dog feels napping under a table. Courtney had done a good job of cyber-sleuthing. She'd be in Gainesville now. There was nothing cyber about that, no more typing and staring at a screen. And she was flying solo. I wondered how she was doing right that moment.

CHAPTER 15

I don't know why Coop always complains about traffic—not in this car. If I'd driven from Miami to Gainesville with Betty, trusty ol' girl that she is, I'd be a little tired and sore, maybe even cranky, not to mention an hour or two later. Not so with the CR-V! I'm feeling relaxed and ready to roll. The worst this car did to me was get me pulled over for driving a wee bit over the speed limit. I got out of a ticket with my usual charm, so I don't even have to tell CJ. Maybe I will anyway—if she lubricates me with enough vodka on our next girls' night.

By all rights, I should be tired after that longish night yesterday. I followed Coop's instruction about stopping at a reasonable hour, but there was a lot online about that Skidmore person. I hope he's enjoying his reading material.

I swear the weather here feels twenty degrees warmer than in Miami. Where's my ocean? Okay, maybe I exaggerate a smidge, and regardless, my walk from the car to Broward Hall feels like a breeze. All the online stuff is fun. It's like a puzzle. But I'm loving this assignment! I'm walking the street, doing real PI work.

I'm not impressed by the UF campus. Granted, I'm a Miami girl—by adoption, but a Miami girl all the same. I went to the U. That's the University of Miami for the uninitiated. Go Canes! Now, that's an urban campus, sleek and elegant. This Gator thing is in the middle of town, but it's not urban. And it doesn't have the big green spaces I associate with *far-out campuses, either. All I can see between the car and the dorm are clusters of buildings. But it's early, and I reserve judgment.*

I am impressed with me, though, if I do say so myself. I parked the too-new SUV a couple of blocks away. Score one for good thinking. And while there aren't that many students around in July, the ladies I see still wear the shorts-and-tank-top uniform I remember from my college days. I dressed the part. Score two for Courtney.

I planned my route last night and decided to start with Ann Berger's place. That's where I'm headed now. She's the only one who lives in the dorms, and dorms are always open. Plus, I have a secret weapon.

Ann doesn't just live in the dorms. She lives in a beastly, massive, boring dorm. All I can see is a mega brick rectangle that blocks the horizon, and I know from the map on my phone that it's just one side of a giant H-shaped building. I'm starting to wonder if I'll ever find Ann's room in there. I may not even find the front door—if there is one. It looks like there may be several entrances. No matter. I put some pep in my step and aim for the middle of the building. When I find a door, I walk in like I belong there.

And . . . I walk forever and a day. Or maybe it's a few minutes, but it feels like forever and a day. Maybe Coop's legendary "patience" is rubbing off on me, but I find that absolutely normal when every corridor looks the same and the room numbering system—if there is a system—is clearly designed to confuse.

I eventually find Ann's floor. It just took walking a 5k to get there. There's a group of girls chatting two doors down from her room. I wave at them with a friendly "Hi."

They give me the side eye, so I slow down and go talk to them.

"Hi, I'm Courtney," I say. "I start here in the fall. Transferring."

"Oh, cool," an African American student with curly hair answers. "Where from?"

"Miami Dade College."

"You'll be staying in Broward?" another girl asks. She tries to sound friendly, but she looks grumpy. She is wearing workout shorts and a loose

tank with no bra. She was not expecting to see anyone today but her floor sisters.

"Yeah, I think so."

"Lots of freshmen and second years here," the grumpy one says.

I shrug. "It's cheap, though. Cheaper than some of the other halls, anyway."

"And it's really close to classes," the third girl says. She's African American and ready to go out in a super-cute top and skinny jeans.

"And I'm friends with one of the girls here," I say, "Ann."

"Ann's super cool," the first girl says.

"Even if she takes forever in the showers," says the grumpy brunette, and we all chuckle.

"Don't be mean," the first girl says. "I don't think I've ever heard Ann say no. She's sweet."

"That's Ann," I say. I feel like I'm doing a pretty good job selling that I know her. It's time for phase two. "Hey, she said I could check out her room before I sign up for sure for Broward. Is it okay? I mean, it's your floor and all."

"I don't think she's home," the brunette says. She hasn't quite looked me in the eye this whole time.

"Oh, I know," I say, brandishing the key on an alligator keychain that Coop gave me yesterday morning. He'd gotten them from Ann's dad. No other parent had keys to their college-age kids' places on them. From what Coop's been saying, the Bergers would be the ones.

"Oh, then, for sure, no worries," the third girl, the dressed-up one, says. She's ready to get going, and I take my cue from her. I say my thanks and wave at them again on my way to Ann's room. I open the door. The group scatters behind me as I walk in, and I close the door behind me.

It's not much of a room. It's a single, of course. Having Jennifer Berger's daughter rub elbows with the wrong kind wouldn't do. I'm standing in a white rectangle with a plastic-looking desk on one side, a tiny closet next to it, and a bed on the other. There's an oversized pillow on the bed with a big "A" for Ann, and she hung a throw blanket with an image of an ocean wave on the wall.

My day immediately takes a turn for the better. There's a laptop on the desk. There are nicknacks too: a framed menu, a fidget spinner, and some kind of paperweight. But I only have eyes for the laptop. I wriggle my fingers in anticipation. I can already feel the keys under my fingertips.

It's weird it's here. I thought Ann had gone home for the summer. But it's an awesome break for me. I waste no time lifting the lid, powering up the machine, and sitting at Ann's desk.

I interrupt the bootup routine and access the admin screen. I sigh. Poor girl, so naïve. The Windows defaults are all intact. This is going to take no time at all. In a flash, I become Ann Berger, or so the computer thinks.

I don't need to get past her email, which opens from the auto-start menu, unprotected, to find scandal. First, Ann has boyfriends. Plural. You go, girl. It looks like she's pretty good at the cloak-and-dagger life too.

Second, mother and daughter are really, really not getting along. As I scroll, I find out that the nasty back and forth started as soon as Ann moved into the dorm. Jennifer did not want Ann at UF.

I scan through the emails. This isn't the right place for you . . . I'll pay for a private college . . . You belong in a Christian school . . .

Ann dishes it out as good as she gets. Her nicest answer is I like it here. *Then it escalates.* Stop it! . . . I'm staying, period . . . I'm not going to a prison run by nuns . . .

I scroll and scan, scroll and scan. Mother does not like what she sees on daughter's social media. Daughter says it's none of mother's business. Mother wants to pull daughter out of UF. Daughter . . . oh, my! Daughter says she'd rather earn tuition money on her back than leave campus. That starts a screaming fight that goes on for a month.

Make that two.

I get to last May. Ann's emails to everyone except her mom are happy-go-lucky. Well—except that she's not emailing her dad at all, good or bad, not even to get him on her side. That's weird, especially since the emails with Mom only get angrier. You'd think Ann is enjoying fighting, the way she needles her mom. These two need therapy.

I hum, and my nose wrinkles—it does that when I'm in the zone. Ann writes that she's not coming home. She found a summer job in Gainesville and is staying in town. She'll come to the Fourth of July in the Keys, but that's it, and that's for Christine and Chloe. Mom says they'll talk then. That's the last email between them.

I sit back in Ann's uncomfortable chair and mull over what I just read. This explains why the laptop is still in her room and why she was in Key Largo. I feel myself slumping. I'm excited to have found something. I don't see what it has to do with the case, though. I take a thumb drive from my purse anyway—I never leave home without a couple of those. I plug it in and copy the email file.

I grumble to myself while the file transfers, doing my best to imitate Coop. "You do it because it could matter. Everything matters. You build the file. You never fucking know."

I open Word and the plain-text app Ann has on her machine. The first one has nothing but schoolwork showing in the "recents" menu, and the other has nothing at all. A quick look at the File Explorer shows nothing that doesn't sound like college classes, either. Her internet history is what I'd expect from a college girl. Mine looked pretty much the same once upon a time—a lot that fits research for papers, a bunch of nighttime hangouts, and a healthy dose of sex. I shut down the computer and look in the desk's only drawer, and in the closet, even under the bed and under the mattress on the bed. My hopes for a journal or diary of some kind are dashed. It's time to move on.

I go back to the CR-V and drive to Christine's apartment. I don't think this will be more than a pit stop. Sure enough, I take the elevator to her floor to find yellow crime scene tape in front of her door. Monroe County must have asked the local cops to do a search the moment the Raymonds identified the body.

"Wrong floor," I singsong to myself even though no one's here. I go back down and leave the building. My work here is done.

It's only a couple of blocks to the house that Chloe rents with some roommates. It's funny how life goes. As close as those three girls are, they each went their own way. That's part of college though—finding your own way outside of old relationships, even those that stay strong.

I park, take a deep breath, and head to the door. I called CJ from the car this morning. I love Betty, but I can't lie. I rather like having Bluetooth in the car. Anyway, I asked the boss whether I should mention Chloe is missing if one of her roommates was home. CJ was kind. She did not laugh at my overthinking. She just told me I was doing it. Chloe's parents filed a missing-person report, and there had to be a reason for me to show up. Of course, I tell them.

As it happens, someone is home. The door opens and reveals a tiny brunette who looks like she's closer to fifteen than nineteen. "Yes?" she asks in a muted voice. She has yet to fully open the door.

"Hi! My name's Courtney. I'm a friend of Chloe. Sort of." I wince on the inside. I sound like a dork.

"What do you mean, sort of?"

"Do you know she's missing?"

"Missing how?"

"She was at a Fourth of July party, and no one has seen her since, not a word from her."

"Oh my God!" Her tanned skin turns pale. Clearly, she did not know.

"I work with a private investigation agency in Miami. That's where Chloe went missing. Well, Key Largo. Her parents hired us to find her." I hand her the generic company business card, the one with the "info@" email on it. She takes it and looks down at it with a blank look on her face.

"Is it okay if we talk inside?" I ask.

"Sure." She sounds hesitant. She's been speaking so softly that I have a hard time hearing her. In the end, she steps away from the half-open door, and I follow her in. The house is small for however many of them live there. A tiny living room with mismatched furniture opens up five feet from the front door. We both pick somewhere to sit down.

"You're one of Chloe's roommates?" I ask.

"I will be, I guess. Officially, I start in the fall. I moved in early to take a couple of summer classes, get my feet wet, you know."

"Yeah, sure."

"I met Chloe and Maddie and Emma too, when I answered their ad for a roommate a couple of months ago. They said a fourth girl was leaving at the end of the semester. Then Chloe and I crossed paths for about a week or two after I moved in, but she spent more time back home than here. So, I've met her, and we've talked a little and all, but I don't know her that well."

"Did you know she would be in Key Largo?"

She shakes her head. "I thought she lived in Orlando."

"She does. She was on vacation with her mom."

"I had no idea," she says in her squeaky little voice.

I try not to slump in my seat. This chick probably has less of a clue about where Chloe is than I do.

"You two did not talk about summer plans or anything?" I ask.

"Not really. We just talked about school and family a little bit, and about the town, places to go, good places to eat for cheap, that kind of stuff. I can tell you she's NROTC, but not where she was going to spend her summer."

"Have you heard from her since she left campus?"

The future roommate shakes her head, barely a movement of her chin left and right. I can't figure out if she knows nothing or is playing dumb on purpose. I force myself not to sigh. CJ wouldn't sigh. Coop definitely wouldn't sigh, but God only knows what Coop would do.

"Have you met your other roommates—Maddie and Emma?" I ask. "I mean, after you moved in?"

"Just for, like, a week. After that, everyone went away for the summer, so I have the place to myself until fall classes start."

"Was there any bad blood? Did you see any fights?"

I think she's shaking her head again. Her movements are so slight it's hard to tell. I'm frustrated. I'm nervous. I think about asking to see

Chloe's room, but even if she left a computer behind, I can't exactly hack it with her roommate over my shoulder.

Am I missing something? Am I asking my questions wrong? Am I doing this right at all? I feel like CJ would think of more questions to ask, but I can't come up with anything.

I stand up and point to the business card that's still in the roommate's hands. "I wrote down my cell on the back. Call me if you hear anything, anything at all, okay?"

She flips the card over. "Yeah. Sure. Absolutely."

"Thanks. Oh, and I never got your name."

"Sophia. Sophia Zava."

"Thanks, Sophia." I give her a quick wave goodbye and make my way to the shelter of the CR-V. I realize my hands are shaking. This was barely field work—okay, so it actually was—but still. My hands are shaking, for Pete's sake!

I take a moment to compose myself, then I check the time on my phone. It's not even three. I have a drive ahead of me, but something's bugging me. I pout as I consider my options. The tension behind my eyes has a name—Zach Skidmore and his Skull and Coins secret bullshit group. I put the shady group in the "later" pile last night, but I don't like it. It's weighing on me.

I don't hesitate for long. "Fuck it," I say out loud. "I'm sure this car has great headlights." Not that Betty doesn't have good headlights, mind you. Well, one good headlight anyway.

A few minutes later, I pull up in front of a cybercafe—plenty of those in a college town. Before I go in, I dictate a full report on my work so far in a voice memo so we can put it in the file later. I don't have the guts to call CJ directly. I'm terrified she may think I messed up. She's on my mind as I make my report, though. I can hear her business voice in my head—clear, concise, thorough, professional. I try and say everything the way she would.

Once I finish recording and settle at a computer, the fun begins. Zach's account is pretty tight, but he has two other losers in the group with him. It only takes one of them to be less than careful one time. That's where I focus my efforts. I randomly create anonymous email addresses and play around with some social engineering to invite myself to the group. Those guys are not quite as clever as they think, and leetspeak is so yesterday. Have they never heard of random password generators or two-factor authentication? It takes a few tries, but I am in. All I have to do now is send a request to join the group from the fake profile I just created. Then I go back to the hacked account and accept my request. Voila. The best part is that the real Skull-and-Coins moron—not Zach Skidmore, but one of his posse—has no idea it happened. Ha! I love this rush!

I look at the posts, and I don't like what I see. Those bored kids are turning themselves into less bored criminals. And it's not small stuff, either. Skull and Coins is named for bashing the first and stealing the second. They brag about attacking people at gas stations late at night and other charming activities. They get off on violence.

They mostly do their thing on the mainland, I notice, not in the Keys. They're at least smart enough not to shit where they eat. The violence is random, widespread, and increasing. It's scary. I mean, really scary. They beat up homeless people and get off on it, going on and on about how much fun it is and the look of pain and fear on their victims' faces. Any more of this, and I'm going to throw up.

If they can't find an easy victim— because, of course, they never go after anyone who might fight back—they throw bricks or whatever else they can find through windows. We aren't talking about stealing hubcaps here. The more damage, the funnier they think it is. There's even . . . there's even . . . oh, shit! I catch a reflection of myself in the monitor, my eyes wide and my jaw hanging loose.

Out comes the thumb drive. My hands are shaking again as I put it in the computer. My whole body is shaking. It's all adrenaline, and I need to get a hold of myself. The download seems impossibly slow. I urge it along from the edge of my seat with a silent "come on, come on!"

The moment it's done, I resign from Skull and Coins and sign out of the account I used to accept my request. It all seems to take too long, but if I'm lucky, they'll never know I was there.

I nearly fall over my chair as I rush back outside. I slam the CR-V's door behind me and don't bother starting the engine before dialing Coop. No wonder he never says hello. Who has time for hello at a time like this? I don't even let him answer the phone. Words spill out of my mouth the moment the connection opens on my screen.

"Coop, I've got something! You won't believe this."

CHAPTER 16

Courtney was excitable—the privilege of youth. She was also smart. If she said she had something, then she had something.

"Talk to me," I said, sitting back to listen.

She took me through the whole story. I already knew the part about Zach and his Skull and Coins club. Part of it was new to me—what the name meant and just how bad it was. I let her go on for a bit, extraneous comments and all. She deserved to be heard. But my patience had well-known limits.

"Get to the point," I said.

"Okay, okay, sorry. All the criminal stuff is violent and horrible and disgusting and all that. I still can't get over the fact they're proud of it, you know? But it's also drive-by stuff, like robbing a lonely guy at a gas station, beating somebody up if they can because they're that gross, or throwing a rock through a window."

"Courtney . . ."

"Yes, yes, I'm getting there. Three weeks ago, there's a whole bunch of posts where they're bragging about how they went 'next level'—their words. They broke into a business and trashed it. They one up each other with every post, how each one did worse things than the other guy, so they end up going into detail about it. Coop, they're talking about Barrels."

"What?"

"I'm sure of it."

"Son of a bitch!"

I started thinking about what to do with information we were probably not supposed to have when Courtney kept going.

"That's not all," she said. "There were more posts about it over the last week. They think it would be oh-so-funny to do it all again now that it's all fixed up—make the owner's life a total nightmare and ruin him."

"Don't fucking bury the lede with me! When?"

"I'm not. You needed to know how I got there."

I closed my eyes. I breathed in Florida's summer heat and let the sun burn my face. This wasn't college. You didn't show your work for partial credit. I made a mental note to include making a police-style report in Courtney's training. She did not know how yet, that was all. That was on me.

"When?" I asked again, a little gentler.

"Tonight. After close."

"You're still in Gainesville?"

"Yes."

"Get back to the office ASAP. Don't worry about speed limits. I'll pay the fines. Just don't make it bad enough to be detained. And you better start pounding those energy drinks you like. This is going to be a long night."

"Okay . . . I'll see you there."

Courtney sounded hesitant. She was probably trying to figure out how it would be a long night for her. I wasn't sure either, but I intended for her to reap the fruit of her labor.

"Be safe," I told her. "And Courtney?"

"Yes?"

"Good job, kid. Really good job."

I hung up and took a moment to process my own thoughts, come up with the first few sketches of a plan. There was no reason to rush back to Miami, so I ordered another Coke, a slice of key lime pie, and made the Secret Passage my temporary headquarters. I polished off the pie before I knew what I wanted to do. Leaning back, I unlocked my phone and started putting my plan into action. I had three calls to make to get started.

"Detective Sergeant Michaels," my first victim answered with his usual professionalism.

"This is Malone. You can tell your captain that Skidmore is safe for today. I have an emergency on the mainland." That emergency could also be a break in the Overby case, but I did not tell him that. He'd want to know the details, and I did not want to tell him. Better let discretion be the better part of valor.

"Captain Tornero will be glad to hear that," Michaels said.

"Did beating the bushes and pushing the labs yield anything yet?"

"Nothing. Captain Tornero is getting red in the face, but we received no new report from our officers, the crime scene technicians, or members of the public. That's quite disappointing."

It was also no surprise. If someone knew something and didn't speak up before, they wouldn't come out now out of shame or fear of getting in trouble for not saying anything earlier. Any call Michaels was likely to get was from the wrong kind of nut job. But there was no point in twisting the knife, so I thanked him, asked him to keep me posted, and hung up without sharing my wisdom.

My next call was to Todd, Barrels' owner. I would need his approval to make my skeleton of a plan work. I explained why I needed his help and that this was the only way to kill two birds with one stone.

"I see," he said when I finished, "and I want to help, but money's tight after what happened, and my insurance company may not play along with your plan."

"Do you have an agent or an 800 number?"

"An agent and a good one." He sighed over the phone.

"Todd, this may also be the only way to get the perps dead to rights for the vandalism."

"Boy. I need to think about that. Is your other case as dire as you said?"

"It is. No bullshit."

"No, you've never seemed the bullshitter kind. All right, let me call my guy and see what he says. I'll call you back."

"You can share with him that one of the perpetrators' family is loaded. They can afford restitution, and families often pony up as part of plea deal negotiations."

"I'll tell him."

Half an hour later, Todd was on board, and I made my last call to CJ. I gave her the law-enforcement-style summary of everything Courtney said, and we agreed to meet at the office before Courtney made it back. I needed to talk to her alone.

Then the Indian Chief and I were back on the road.

I had time to stop by home. I showered, got some extra caffeine in me, and dressed in tactical black. For an old army guy, I'm not particularly fond of guns, but I owned two, and in situations like the ones I was expecting, I carried both.

The .45 automatic I normally kept in the CR-V was in my gun safe at home. I'd pulled it out before Courtney borrowed the car. Now, I retrieved and cleaned it before heading out to meet with CJ. It didn't need cleaning. It was habit, and it helped settle me. It helped keep me in the moment. It kept my brain from traveling without permission, back in time to other places and other guns and blood spilled, back when I was working from safe houses, not home and office. Those times would always be with me, but I didn't have space for them now.

I would use the stub-nose 38-caliber I keep at the office as a back-up piece. I had a custom-made holster for it that fit comfortably in the small of my back. Ankle holsters never did it for me. It's too far to reach in a pinch.

I slammed the front door a little too hard on my way out. I had a plan in mind. It was the only plan I could think of, but that didn't mean I loved it. Fuck, I couldn't remember a case when I carried both guns. That was enough to keep me on my toes as I made my way down Miami's streets.

To no one's surprise, CJ was already at the office when I got there, seated at the conference table with a legal pad in front of her. Bullet points covered half the page, most of them crossed out. The wheels were turning. I sat down across from her.

"Working both cases at a time will be tricky," she said. CJ never wasted time when it came to business.

"I want to ambush them," I said, "let them break in, get in trouble, then jump them with guns drawn, putting us in a position of strength and them at their weakest. It will give us the best chance to convince them to talk."

"Guns drawn? Are you serious?" She sounded horrified. CJ was neither timid nor naive. All the same, she came from the corporate world. She may know how to shoot as well as I do, but guns outside the firing range were not part of her natural habitat. I hated to disappoint her and drag her to the dark side, but I had no choice in the matter.

"I am serious. It's not only the shock value, though I'd do it for that reason alone. Zach Skidmore is likely to be armed."

"Even so, that's pushing the envelope."

"If that's pushing it, then pushing it is what we need to do. We can't be caught with our fingers up our butts and Zach firing at us."

CJ hesitated a moment longer. "Alright. This is your arena. I trust you. I'll think of some of my friendlier contacts at MDPD to coordinate the arrest. I have someone in mind, actually."

I'd already dragged CJ out of her comfort zone. Now, I had to drag her even further. I shook my head. "I don't want the police at the takedown. I want to be there alone. I will be the one—the only one—interrogating Zach and his posse."

"Then what?" CJ spat the words, her eyes shooting daggers. "You get what you need and let them go? Maybe rough them up a little first?"

"Don't be ridiculous, as tempting as it may be." I knew she did not mean it, so I did not take offense. CJ may not raise her voice when she was mad, but she was not above sarcasm, and I'd made her a little angry pushing like that.

"I have no problem if a friendly MDPD officer happens to show up on the scene to take them into custody once I'm done with them," I continued. "But until then, they're mine. I don't have time for paper-work and fucking Miranda."

CJ stared at me. As usual, I could not read her at all. She could be mad, or she could be sad, or she could be just about anything else.

"Why can't you ever work within the system?" she asked. She might have been asking a teenager why they never come home before curfew. "How can you even be sure six or twelve hours will make a difference?"

I frowned at her. Sure, that was our most frequent fight at the of-fice. She liked institutions, liked working inside the system. I didn't. But that was the weakest argument she'd ever made. She barely attempted to change my mind.

"I don't know about the system," I said. "Maybe I'm just too high-strung for bureaucracy. But the timeline? Every hour counts if you're kept against your will. You know that. I know that you know that. I know you want the girls free the second we can spring them."

"I do," she said softly. "I don't want to lose my soul in the process, either."

"And I don't want that any more than I want to prolong Chloe's and Ann's ordeal. And I don't want to fight with you over this. Talk, yes, but not fight. I can't pull it off without you anyway. I can't corner all three of them by myself."

"I know," CJ said in something approaching a whisper. "I have your back, you know that. I had to try. I had to push back at you to see if I could spur you to come up with a different idea. Because I could not come up with one." She held up her legal pad with all the crossed-out bullet points on the page. "Any other case, I could, but not a kidnap-ping. I really hate your side of the business sometimes."

I wasn't sure where she was going with that, so I looked back at her, waiting to hear where she was leading.

CJ went on, still staring blindly at her notepad, her voice firm. "I already pulled my gun out of the safe and have my tactical gear in my office closet. And I called my friend Philippa to be on alert. She's MDPD, and we're pretty close. We shoot together sometimes because she hates the department's range. Anyway, I'll call her back with the details. She's the friendly officer I had in mind, and I'm pretty sure she'll agree to show up when I call her in. You better be right, Coop. This insanity had better lead us to these two women."

"It's the best shot we have."

"I know," she said again. She needed to keep convincing herself of it. She hated this situation, and I hated bringing her into it. But we both hated leaving Chloe and Ann alone with their captors even more.

"One more thing," I said. I nearly loathed myself for springing another surprise on her. I did anyway. "We need a third gun in there."

CJ put her hands in front of her mouth. "If you say we do, then we do. That's your turf. I'm not sure how we do that, though. Philippa can pretend she doesn't know something is happening until I call her, but she can't disregard her badge. Maybe we can call some of the PIs we've worked with in the past."

"We've never worked with any of them in a tactical environment. We don't know them in that setting. It's doable, but it's risky, too risky."

I'd improvised riskier before. I'd improvised riskier moves just last month, going undercover on a SWAT raid with a team I'd met a half hour earlier. I was grateful CJ did not remind me of it. She kept her face toward me and said, "I take it you have a better idea," through a tight jaw.

"I want to take Courtney with us."

CJ gripped the table. Her face contorted and turned red, a look and a color that the stoic Grandma Vinh, who had provided a quarter of CJ's DNA and half her upbringing, might not recognize. "Absolutely not!"

"We agreed to take her into the field."

"We agreed to train her." CJ did not blink. Her stare could have easily turned me to stone, but she did not raise her voice. She never did. She shut you down with a few firm words.

"She can't train behind a computer," I said.

"She can't train in front of bullets either. That's not training. It's foolhardy. I cannot believe you are seriously arguing for that."

"Hear me out," I said. It would be a hard sell. CJ disliked needing guns. Putting one in the hands of her young protégée was beyond the pale. But she wouldn't hold Courtney back, either, so I pressed on.

"We have the advantage here," I said. "The odds of shots being fired are as low as they can get with guns drawn. And Courtney's not just a good shot. Her gun safety is top-notch. You told me that."

"At the range! This is different." If CJ gripped the table any tighter, she might break it. The muscles in her arms had gone rigid, and her knuckles were turning white.

I leaned in and put my hands flat on the table. I was not trying to confront her, just talk. For the first time in history, I might have been calmer than my partner.

"That's the point," I said. "It is different. If Courtney goes through with her plans to become a full-fledged investigator, she'll have to come out of the range and know what it's like to draw in real life. This is early, I agree. But it's as controlled an environment as possible while still being tactical. I'd rather she knew how she reacts to that now than later with bullets in the air."

CJ sat back, hands now flat on the table, and delivered her verdict. "It is too early."

"You're protective of her. So am I. My instincts may be more sink-and-swim, and yours more methodical, but we want the same thing. And there's something else at play here."

"And what's that?"

"She helped break the case. She deserves to see it through and not from behind a desk."

"And not from behind a gun." That was as close as I'd heard CJ come to snapping at me.

I sat back against my chair in exasperation, causing the wheels to roll back. That's when I noticed Courtney's shape filling the doorway. She had made better time than I thought she would.

"I could hear your two sniping the moment I opened the front door," she said. "If 'she' is me, maybe I could have a say?"

I cocked my head and extended a hand to CJ.

"You have a say," CJ said, emphasizing the *a* in her declaration. "You do not get the *final* say." She adopted her business voice and summarized our plan and the role I wanted Courtney to play. She presented both sides, and to her credit, she did not slant it. I had not expected her to.

Courtney wrung her hands and thought for a long moment. "I trust you both, and I definitely don't want the final say. I don't know enough." She looked at me, then turned to face CJ. "This is a lot. I want to get in the field, but I did not expect to need my gun. I never really thought about it. It's foreign to me away from the range. But I'd only be backing you two up, right? And I'll take all my cues from you, and I'll be super safe. I guess what I'm saying is, I'd like to do everything I can for this case . . . if that's okay with you, CJ."

CJ stood up and squared up to Courtney. "Fine. Coop is right that you earned it if nothing else. But you do as I say when I say it, at all times, no exceptions. Understood?"

"I understand. I will." Courtney knew fewer words were best with CJ in a situation like this.

"Good," CJ said. "Now go home. Eat something to back up those infernal energy drinks I know you guzzled to get here this quickly. Something light with protein and complex carbs for some no-crash energy. Clean your gun. It probably does not need it, but it will keep your hands busy and on your weapon. And one last thing. You know your gun safety as well as anyone, but this is different. Stay focused. If I see your gun pointed the wrong way or your finger leave the trigger guard and it's not because you have to fire your weapon in your own defense or ours, I'll shoot you myself."

"Got it," Courtney said, looking a little pale, her eyes not leaving CJ's. Her jaw moved in a chewing motion. Her mouth was probably dry. Good. She was taking this as seriously as she needed to.

CJ nodded and looked at me. "Anything else?"

"We'll reconvene forty-five minutes before closing in the back of Barrels. We'll review the plan then. Courtney, keep the CR-V until this is over."

Courtney nodded and left without a word. She would follow CJ's instructions to the letter. Then I stood up and took a long look at my partner. Her jaw was set, eyes fixed on the spot where Courtney had been a moment earlier.

"If she gets hurt, you'll be the one I shoot," she said.

I nodded, knowing she might actually mean it, and headed to my office to work up the details. I had a lot to do and not much time to do it.

CHAPTER 17

We gathered at Barrels at the appointed hour. It didn't take long to brief the team and make a couple of superficial changes. Not that many people were involved, and we only had to worry about three targets. Not only that, but we pretty much knew where they would be, so we could plan our positions to cover them. We could plan. It wouldn't survive contact with the enemy because plans never do, but it was a good framework.

I made sure Courtney was good to go and gave her a last chance to pull out if she did not want to be included in something involving guns just yet. Wild horses couldn't have dragged her away.

Todd insisted on staying. It was his place, and I had no problem with that. I even had a role for him to play. It was nothing crazy—he'd have three buttons to push at specific times. That, not moving, and not making a sound. That was his job. I went through the plan with him several times and was confident he could handle it.

All that left me crouching behind the bar in total darkness fifteen minutes after closing. An hour earlier, Barrels would have been filled with glasses clinking and conversations bouncing off the walls. The silence now was as oppressive as the darkness. Barely a sliver of moonlight looked for its reflection in the wine bottles behind me.

My ears strained for a noise, any noise, something to tell me what we were expecting would happen tonight was happening. I'd put a lot of faith into this plan. I needed it to work. I needed it, somehow, to lead me to two kidnapped women. That meant the vandals had to show up.

We lived in a screwed-up world.

I ignored the protests from my leg muscles. I was banking on impetuous youth showing up soon. My quads were backing up my bet. Thankfully, I guessed right. It only took a few more minutes before glass breaking announced a crime in progress. I pictured Todd wincing in the back room. Frosted glass wasn't cheap. I knew something about it. Having my name on the frosted glass of our suite's door still felt badass—I wasn't above those feelings—but I'd nearly given up on the idea when I'd first seen the price.

More sounds of glass crunching followed. I pictured those boys using whatever they'd broken the glass with to remove sharp edges hanging around the door's frame. They wouldn't want to risk a nick to their pretty faces. They were taking too long and making too much noise, but their amateur act was no solace. Amateurs were unpredictable.

I kept track of them by sound, staying low behind the bar. There were footsteps, heavy breathing, and low voices as they walked into Barrels. They did not seem concerned about making noise. They spoke among themselves, barely bothering to whisper, their banter a mix of bravado and snickering. They could have been college kids sneaking out of their dorms. I shook my head. This was no prank, and those kids had a sordid history.

Todd's phone briefly lit up, right on cue, as he pressed the first figurative button and sent the number one in a text to CJ and Courtney. To CJ, waiting out of sight behind the building, it was the signal to move toward the front door. For Courtney, behind the main room in the beer garden, it was a signal to remember to breathe. Her heart would be beating out of her chest.

The plan called for a twenty-second wait, which we'd figured would be enough time for them to do some damage and get in trouble but minimize the repairs for Todd and his insurer. I knew from experience that those twenty seconds would feel like twenty minutes. Sounds of vandalism reached my ears already. Chairs were toppled, cushions slashed, wood broken. The snickering increased. I envied CJ. Walking around the building was not exciting, but it was more action than waiting, hidden behind the bar.

My hand closed around my gun. I pulled it out of its holster, felt its weight. The magazine was full, and there was a round in the chamber. My thumb caressed the safety. My lips pulled away from my teeth. Twenty seconds or not, I'd had enough.

I flipped the safety off, looked at Todd, and nodded. His phone flashed again, sending out a text with the number two. That meant *NOW*, and I sprang into action.

I rose from behind the bar to find three shadows hunched over furniture, more shapes than people. They stood right where I expected them to be, toward the front of the room, having yet to work their way back. They all crowded the same area. There was no efficiency, no division of labor. There was neither purpose nor organization. This was crime for crime's sake. The sight pushed the words out of my mouth in an angry growl.

"Drop whatever you're holding and get on your knees, hands behind your head. It's over, assholes."

Damn, that felt good.

That was the signal for Todd to push the third button by flipping the switch that would turn on half of Barrels' lights, the ones where we'd installed red light bulbs earlier. The red glow wouldn't blind me after spending so much time in the dark, but it would give me a good look at those three idiots.

At least, that was what Todd was supposed to do. He flipped the switch all right. He flipped the wrong switch, and blinding light instantly bathed the room.

It would take a few seconds to recover my vision. That was a few seconds too many. I started shouting, "On your knees! On your knees!" to make the scene more chaotic for the vandals than for us.

All I could see through squinted eyelids were brown shadows, the color of the spots you see after looking straight into the sun. I blinked rapidly as if that would help. I listened for clues to their reaction, trying to match the sounds to what little I saw. There was a strangled "Oh, God!" and a thump, and one shadowy shape got smaller. One of them listened.

At the same time, I caught movement to my right, toward the door, along with hurried footsteps. I yelled, "CJ! Coming your way!" A door opened to my left. That would be Courtney, and I moved it to the back of my brain.

The third asshole did not look like he was moving. Shit! He was not dropping or running. That left two options. He froze, or he was drawing.

I dodged to my left, lowering myself until I could barely see above the bar. I was nearly too late. A gun fired, its deafening thunderclap followed by a bouncing echo in the enclosed space. My ears rang even as glass broke behind me. The smell of wine mixed with cordite as broken display bottles oozed their contents onto the floor.

I kept moving. Two more deafening shots boomed, and more glass broke. The shots were erratic. The kid was barely aiming. But he was still shooting. I rounded the bar, straightening up, gun in front of me.

The world slowed down the way it does in moments like this. My vision had sufficiently recovered to take a snapshot of the situation. It took a fraction of a second for the scene beyond my gunsight to imprint on my brain.

The leftmost target was the one on the ground, head down, licking hardwood. His hair was slicked back like a wise guy from the thirties, but piss and fear wafted from his direction. He kept mumbling something into the floor, something that sounded like "I surrender, I surrender."

On the other side of the room, the one with enough brains to run was now walking backward in lockstep with CJ, her gun, unflinching, an arm's length away from his eyeballs. He had come to ransack the place dressed in slacks and a golf shirt like this was a country club event. He backed up, one step at a time, as CJ pushed forward. He could have been a robot programmed to imitate her in reverse. CJ had total control.

The shooter stood in the middle. It was Zach Skidmore. He held a nine-millimeter pistol one-handed. The gun was jumping in his hand from the third shot's recoil. His mouth hung open, and panic filled his eyes.

To the far left, barely visible from the corner of my eyes, Courtney stood in the doorway, staying out of the light as much as possible while still covering the trio with her weapon. She'd made the soundest move of the night. Her stance and grip were range perfect.

And she was shaking, just enough to put a slight tremor in her barrel. I'd have been disappointed if she weren't the first time she pointed a gun at a human being. And in any event, she was not shaking badly enough to miss.

My reaction was immediate. I shouted my next words at the top of my lungs. "Hold fire! Hold fire!"

That caught even Zach's attention. He stopped shooting long enough for me to talk.

"Do you want to die out here, kid?" I asked in the temporary lull.

Zach looked left and right with jerky movements of his head. He was still blinking from the sudden light. I kept my gun pointed at him, center mass. In my peripheral vision, Courtney also held her gun steady on him. Zach's gun, on the other hand, was pointed harmlessly at the bottles behind the bar. I thought the picture should be clear, even for a dumb fuck like him. Then again, thinking too much can get you killed.

I lowered my gun to a point on the floor in front of Zach and squeezed off a shot. He jumped back three feet. Then I raised my gun again until the barrel lined up with the spot right between his eyes.

"I never ask the same question twice," I said.

Zach's face turned red, and he flung his gun. The piece slid on the floor until it came to rest against a table's leg.

"Fuck you!" he said. Spit flew out of his mouth. Some landed on his T-shirt and blended into his sweat. I left him his two words of bluster. His gun was on the floor. That's all that mattered.

"On your knees," I said.

With evident reluctance, Zach complied, his knees crunching like an old man's as he crouched. Tiffany Skidmore's son looked like any other punk. He'd shaved the sides of his head. He had deep-set eyes, hollow cheeks, and a tiny scar to the left side of a pointed chin.

"You too," CJ told the delinquent in front of her gun. He smoothed his golf shirt and kneeled slowly as if to challenge CJ to make him move faster. He tried to look tough, but his eyes never left CJ's automatic. His crew cut and clean-shaven face made him look young on the floor, with three armed people towering around him.

CJ glanced at Courtney, who'd stepped into the main room. Courtney nodded. She had all three covered. She wasn't shaking anymore, except for that slight tremor from too much adrenaline that takes a while to overcome.

I moved in front of the bar. I picked a spot where either Courtney or I could cover all three without putting CJ at risk as she moved about. Once CJ was happy with our positions, she put her gun away.

CJ put on crime scene gloves. Ever prepared, she pulled out an evidence marker from a pocket and placed it where Zach's gun had landed. Then she photographed the weapon, picked it up, ejected the round in the chamber, removed the magazine, and placed the lot in a Ziplock bag.

Once done, she zip-tied each of the Skull and Coins members' wrists behind their backs and frisked them for any other weapon. She had to pull the one who'd dropped back up to his knees by the back of his shirt. The front of his pants was soaked, and there were traces of vomit around the corners of his mouth.

CJ worked methodically, neither slowly nor quickly. This was not her favorite part of our job, but it was a job, and CJ did it right, by the book. We had a plan that went awry, but it was resurrected, and she was executing it. End of story.

The next step called for her to take my place. She stood next to me and pulled her gun back out of its holster. Our eyes met. There was no jubilation in her expression or mine. There was no Hollywoodian banter, no joke, no witty line, no victory dance. There was only relief. We wouldn't be shot at again, not tonight.

I glanced at Courtney. She was a little paler than usual but holding her own. Her eyes were alert, dancing back and forth between the three people she was covering. She pointed her gun down, aiming in front of the sorry lot. She kept a dynamic stance, finger on the trigger guard, ready to switch her aim in an instant if she needed to.

I had a vague idea of what was going through her mind. I'd been there. It's different for everyone, but a lot goes on in moments like these. Not that you could tell. On the outside, she was cool as a cucumber. There were things I wanted to tell her, things she needed to hear, how she should be proud of herself. These things would have to wait.

I started pacing in front of the three menaces to society, my gun still in my hand. I needed answers from them. I needed them now. And I did not a hundred percent care how I would get them.

Before I started talking, though, the smartass who tried to get away found his voice. He shot one word at me.

"Lawyer."

CHAPTER 18

One corner of my mouth inched up in a leer at the wise guy as I made my way to where he kneeled, hands tied behind his back. I walked slowly, tapping the barrel of my gun against my thigh in cadence with my steps. His smug expression dissipated one muscle at a time.

"I'm not a cop," I said once I stood in front of him, keeping my voice low.

"It doesn't matter," he said, not sounding all that confident. "We have rights."

"I'm not a cop," I said again. "I don't work for the cops. I am not operating, as they say, under the color of law." I paused for dramatic effect. "You have no rights with me." And to make my point clearer, I jammed the barrel of my gun against his temple.

"What do you want?" The whimpered question came from the sidekick with slick hair and wet pants.

"Shut up, Matty," Zach said.

I lifted my gun and went around to stand behind wet pants. I leaned over his ear, so close I could smell the product he'd used to slick his hair back.

"Is that your name? Matty?"

When he didn't answer, I straightened up, resting my gun on his shoulder. He yelped. I looked at Courtney. "Is that his name?" I asked.

Courtney nodded, unsure of her role at first. I nodded back at her, standing as I did behind the trio, willing it to her. *Come on, kid, you got this. Play the game with me.*

"Yeah," Courtney said in a clear voice. "Matthew. Matthew Stewart."

"Matthew," I said. "That's a good name, a kind name—God's gift. Matty, on the other hand, reminds me of a petulant toddler. You let your buddy talk to you like that?"

"It doesn't matter," Matthew said.

I pushed down on his shoulder with my gun. He would be feeling the cold metal against his flesh. He whimpered louder.

"What I'd like to know, Matthew," I said, "is whether the bullet that killed a woman doing nothing more than watching fireworks came from the nine-millimeter your buddy here shot at me with."

"Shut up," Zach said again. He sounded pretty mad. Some might even think he was worried. I was starting to get irritated myself, not taking well to being interrupted by some punks.

"What's your buddy's name?" I asked Matthew, pretending not to know.

"Zach," Matthew said.

"Zachy, then," I said, adopting a nasal singsong. Zach was the toddler now, and this was my lullaby. "Did the bullet come from Zachy's gun?"

"I don't know. I don't know anything about that."

"That doesn't sound very convincing," I said.

"I don't know," Matthew whimpered again. "I really don't. I don't know anything about guns or someone being killed. I hate guns." He spoke faster and faster as if saying more words would give him a better chance of convincing me.

"There. You heard him," the golf-shirted smartass said, the one who wanted a lawyer. "Now, let us go!"

"Fat chance," I said. I paced around the trio of misfits, windmilling my gun around, trying to appear less and less in control of myself. It's all about appearances with people like that. And I felt control slip by anyway. It wasn't all an act.

I turned to Courtney, angling my gun toward Mr. Let-us-go. "What's that one's name?"

"Robert Cornell," she said.

"How the fuck . . .?" the esteemed Mr. Cornell started.

"Bobby, then," I said. Then I turned back to the polo-shirted smart mouth. "Shut the fuck up, Bobby."

"My name is Robert."

"Right. You need to learn to shut the fuck up, Bobby, before I accidentally put a bullet in you."

Cornell opened his mouth, then thought better of it when he found himself staring at the business end of my .45.

I started pacing again, faster, using movement to ratchet up the tension. I turned my head to Courtney without breaking my stride. "Remind me, what does this sorry lot call themselves?"

"Skull and Coins," Courtney said. She was in the zone now, playing her role, acting off my lead.

"Yes, that's right. We know all about that, don't we?"

"Yes, we do."

"Bullshit!" Zach said. He turned to Matthew, twisting at the hips, looking mildly ridiculous as he tried to stare down his friend from his tied-up position on the floor. "They're bluffing. They don't know anything. It's a private group."

Courtney actually laughed out loud in the middle of all the tension. "You did a shit job of keeping it that way," she said.

Atta girl.

I stopped moving and turned to CJ. She stood in front of the bar, impassive and inscrutable, not a hair out of place even as she held her weapon at the ready. A certain authority emanated from her calm. She was the good cop to my bad cop, the one who did not fly off the handle or jam guns in people's faces—the one who could be trusted. I needed her now. I turned to her.

"Since that little group of theirs just broke in here and fired a gun," I started, "well, would you like to explain to Matthew what that means, or should I?"

CJ hesitated for a fraction of a second, evaluating the best strategy, and took it herself. "Matthew," she said, "you broke into this establishment with your friend Zach. Then Zach shot at my partner. This makes you guilty of attempted murder, among a few other things, same as Zach. It does not matter that you never fired a gun or didn't even carry one tonight. You're going away for a long time."

Matthew blinked rapidly, looking back and forth at CJ and me, trying to comprehend the words coming at him.

CJ had more for him. "I have also reviewed the Skull and Coins file. The prosecutor will be able to tag on priors involving violence. Many of them."

I took over from there. CJ was more trustworthy. I was more threatening. I felt more threatening. It was time for these boys to be scared.

"They'll only need two, though," I said. "Two violent priors and this little stunt of yours tonight make three strikes. Three strikes, and you're in—in for life. You will never get out. You will die in prison. And I feel an anonymous tip going to the cops about it."

I had no idea whether this was true or not. It could be, and it sounded good. All that mattered was that Matthew believed it. He was already fighting back tears.

Robert Cornell shouted before I could keep going. "He's lying. Don't say a word, Matty."

I whipped around and fired a shot three inches over his head and into the wall. *Sorry, Todd.* The gunfire reverberated in the room. I might get in trouble for that one. I had no legal ground to discharge my weapon. No one was shooting at me or even threatening to. But I couldn't afford to let Cornell interrupt me, let him break the flow of my interrogation. And I was getting seriously pissed off.

"I told you to learn to shut up," I said, shouting the words at him once the echo of the gunshot died off. "Learn quicker."

"He's not lying," CJ said, putting the weight of her authority behind me and getting us back on track.

I turned back to Matthew. "Of course, there's always the possibility that I forget what I saw. And maybe, just maybe, I could oversleep when it's time to testify at your trial. Maybe I put a good word in with the prosecutor. I know a few of them. It all depends on my mood. And my mood can only improve if you tell me what I need to know."

I let that sink in for a moment. He looked defeated enough, but you could never be sure. This was the moment of truth. I asked my next question in a slow cadence.

"Was it Zach's gun? Did he kill that woman?"

"I don't know," he said, tasting tears. "Maybe. I told him to stop bringing his gun around all the time. I told him, I swear. I told him 'no guns' like a thousand times."

Zach and Robert glared at him, but I'd shown my willingness to shoot, so they kept their mouths shut.

I had Matthew talking. I leaned in closer and whispered the question I had been building to all this time, the one that truly mattered.

"And what did you do with the women who saw it happen?"

I was guessing here, but it was a logical chain of events, especially after seeing how trigger-happy Zach was. Chloe and her friends might have witnessed Zach firing. Whatever happened next, those three numbskulls ended up kidnapping them at gunpoint and stashing them in a house listed for sale by Zach's mom, a house he would have known about. I was on a limb, but it felt like a sturdy one.

Matthew did not contradict me. The surprise came when his face brightened up. The corners of his mouth bent up. "Oh, they're safe," he said, sounding relieved to have a good answer for me. "Zach says they're safe."

"What about the one who died?" I growled.

"Nobody died," Zach stammered.

That was interesting. He sounded like he meant it. But it wasn't interesting enough to stop what would happen next. It wasn't interesting enough to stop me. I was seeing red. I pushed the barrel of my gun into Zach's mouth.

"Where are they?" I demanded.

Next to me, Matthew recoiled. He started sobbing. He repeated, "They're safe, they're safe, they're safe, they're safe," over and over again. He was distracting, and I needed to hear what Zach had to say, gun in his mouth or not.

CJ appeared next to me, walking at an unhurried pace. She may have hated this side of the business, but she knew how to work it when needed, and she'd already agreed it was. She planted herself in front of Matthew, put the sole of her boot on his chest, and pushed him onto his back.

"Shut up," she said.

Matthew strangled the next "they're safe" before the words left his throat. He nodded vigorously. He squirmed, trying to stretch as much as his hands tied behind his back allowed.

CJ turned her gaze to Zach. "And you, if I convince my partner to take his gun out of your face, you will answer his question, correct?"

Zach nodded over the barrel.

CJ put a hand on my shoulder. "Let's see what the boy has to say, shall we?"

In response, I pulled my gun out. I even turned it sideways so the sight wouldn't break Zach's teeth.

"They're at my mom's," Zach said, sounding hoarse and deflated. "Until we figure shit out, that's all. And nobody . . ."

I'd already turned around and stopped listening. I walked away with CJ next to me.

"Call Philippa," I whispered.

CJ holstered her weapon and pulled out her phone. I did the same and texted Todd it was safe to come out. He was pale when he walked out from behind the bar. He rested his hands on it and looked around the room with a blank stare.

"That's them?" he asked.

"They're your vandals," I said. "And a few other things."

Todd kept staring at them. There were no words available to him for something like this.

"Philippa will not be able to use what we got," CJ said next to me. There was no reproach in her voice. She knew from the start this would be off-book, something Malone style, get what we need and worry about the rest later. Even so, she was not entirely right.

"Not the interrogation, no," I said. "But she'll have the gun Zach used to shoot at me. That's legit. Ballistics will tie him to the Pamela Howard murder. That will open a new window to the kidnapping without having to eat from the fruit of my poisonous tree."

"And I think Matthew will end up cooperating even from a police interrogation room after having his rights read," CJ said, thinking a step ahead of me.

"I hope you're right."

A few minutes later, Barrels was bathed in red and blue lights. Phillipa and half a dozen uniforms had taken control of the scene. She had not been far and had brought some friends. She had all three vandals in the back of police cars, crime scene techs moving in, and more on the way. She directed traffic when she wasn't talking to CJ.

I let the cops do their thing and went to find Courtney standing by the door. "You did a hell of a job, kid," I said. "I'm proud of you."

"What?" Her eyes widened, and she looked up at me, shaking her head. "No, I didn't. I was shaking like a leaf. I—"

"If you didn't shake," I interrupted, "I'd be firing you right now."

"Huh?"

"If you pointed a gun at a fellow human being for the first time and did not shake, you'd be a psychopath, and I'd be firing you. Fact is, the shakes felt worse to you than they were. You kept your stance and your grip the way you were supposed to. You stayed tactically relevant and ready to act when shots started flying. You were always in position, always at the right spot, even when the lights came on and surprised everyone. Then you backed me up on cue during the interrogation. So don't you fucking be down on yourself. You did a better job than most seasoned investigators would have."

Courtney was a hugger, and my little speech made me her victim. "Thanks, Coop," she said when she released me.

"It's the truth—nothing to thank me for. Now hang around for MDPD, okay? They'll take a preliminary statement from you. Tell the truth when they do. I don't think they'll harass me for going too far, but if they do, they do. I knew what I was doing. Don't start spouting half-truths for me. You don't go there, understood?"

Courtney nodded, a tad too reluctantly for my liking. "Let me hear you say it."

"I understand."

"Good. When you're done with MDPD, go home and get some rest. You've earned it."

"Where are you going?" she asked before I could turn around.

"To find Tiffany Skidmore," I said over my shoulder. "Alone."

A voice rang out behind me. "Like hell you are!" CJ said. Except that she did not *say* that. She yelled it. CJ never yelled. I'd never heard her yell in all the fights we'd had over our short-ish time together as a couple and in our years as business partners. Not once. I stopped in my tracks and faced her.

"We're a team." She spread her arms, gesturing to the scene around us, and continued, her voice once again calm. "We did all of this together. Courtney and I got in a gunfight with you. Alone? Alone, Cooper? Fuck you! Fuck you if you think that's going to fly."

That made the pit in my gut, the one built up from of all the tension and rage, even heavier. It felt real, physical. It hurt. It was getting in the way of words coming out. But I also knew CJ was right, so I forced air out of my lungs and told her so.

I took a breath and gathered my thoughts. "You and Courtney, park a block from her house," I said. We had the address from Courtney's profile. "Be there by 0600. I still want to interrogate her alone, one-on-one, but I'll keep a phone line open. Back me up as appropriate. I can be hot-headed, but I do trust your judgment. Both of yours."

"That's a plan," CJ said. That was typical CJ. In tough situations, fewer words meant the most.

I started out again when another thought occurred to me. I turned to face CJ one more time. "CJ?" I called out.

"Yes?"

"Why aren't you telling me to call the police, to report what we know and let them go in? That's what you'd do. That's the world according to CJ."

CJ smiled. It dawned on me that it was the first time she had done so since I'd found her with a notepad in front of her in the conference room. "We're a team, remember?" she said. "I'd like to still be your partner tomorrow. I know you need to see this through."

"Thanks," I said. There was nothing to add. I straddled the old Chief and sped into the night. I let it surround me, barely seeing the road ahead. If I allowed the night to fill my eyes, the engine's roar to fill my ears, I would stay here. I wouldn't flash back. I tricked my mind into ignoring the smell of cordite on me. I stayed in the present, riding, just me and the road. Hello, darkness, my old friend.

CHAPTER 19

It only took me an hour to reach Key Largo from South Miami in the dead of night. I found an all-night diner, somewhere to fuel my body and give the adrenaline time to recede. Greasy spoons did not serve the healthiest food on earth. People went there to soak up the remnants of boozy nights, not prepare for battle, but I could always count on a serving of steak and eggs to do the trick.

Even before I'd talked to CJ and Courtney, before I straddled the bike back at Barrels, I'd decided to wait a few hours to act. It did not help the angst I felt for every minute I was not getting Chloe and Ann out of whatever hole Skidmore kept them in. But if I banged at the door at zero dark thirty, Skidmore would call the cops and try to talk them out of searching her place. She'd make me the bad guy. If I broke in, her alarm would do the same thing, except it would be worse. So, I waited.

Until I didn't.

I rode the Indian to Skidmore's house at dawn. It was big, a monstrosity by the Keys' standards. It sat at the end of a secluded street, backing up on three sides to a man-made canal that reached toward the Gulf of Mexico. The fourth side had so much foliage it looked like Skidmore had planted her own private rainforest.

The house was raised on stilts to avoid damage from floods and storm surges. That created a carport as an extra benefit. I parked the bike next to Skidmore's SUV like it belonged there and found a spot among the trees where I could watch the house. It was just past six. I checked in with CJ.

"In position?" my text asked.

"Standing by. We parked farther than planned, before the entrance to the neighborhood, but we're ready." I grunted in approval. If she'd parked any closer, she'd have attracted attention.

My fingers mashed the screen one more time. "I'll open the phone line when I go in after I see movement in the house. Hang tight." I waited for the read receipt and put the phone back in my pocket.

An hour passed before I saw what I was looking for—a figure walking by a window, one way then the other. I probably wouldn't see more than that. If I lived here, I'd take my coffee on the other side, overlooking the waves.

I gave it another ten minutes to let Skidmore settle in. The heat was unbearable already, even in the shade of her trees. Sweat was dripping down my stubbled face, making it itch. I ignored it by focusing on the target, keeping my eyes locked on the house. A shower and a shave would wait. They'd waited longer than this before.

When the time came to act, I dialed CJ's phone and put mine back in my pocket, keeping the line open. Then I walked to the front door and rang the doorbell, just like that. And just like that, the door opened, and Tiffany Skidmore appeared, barefoot, wearing dress shorts and a fitted top. The moment she saw me, a rictus formed on her lips, and her neck muscles strained against her skin.

"How dare you?" she asked through a clenched jaw. "Get off my property! I'm calling the police."

She slammed the door in my face—or tried to. It hit my boot's steel toe. I put my hand flat on the wood by my face and shoved the door back open. Skidmore tumbled backward, bewildered. I saw myself in.

The house was pretty, I gave her that, with an open feel, light-colored walls, a tile floor, wicker furniture at one end, and redwood shelves at the other. Skidmore looked in her element here—or she would have, were she not awkwardly walking back, a look of fear in her eyes.

She punched a finger in my direction, stammering. "I know who you are, you know. Oh, I know, Mr. Malone. I know all about you. I'll have your license for this. You won't get away with it."

"Where are they?" I asked. I kept walking, and she kept backing up. "Chloe and Ann? Or do you even know their names? Do you care?"

"I don't know who you're talking about. I don't even know what you're talking about."

I took a glass plate from a table near the entrance, the kind of decorative piece someone like Tiffany liked to own, colorful touches, everything in its place. I threw it on the tile floor hard enough to shatter. Skidmore screamed. Maybe it was the surprise. Maybe it was the violence of my actions. I didn't care.

"I can trash this house from one end to the other and find them, or you can tell me where they are," I said.

I made my point clear by taking a lion figurine from the nearest shelf and giving it the same treatment I'd given the plate. It turned into hundreds of shards on the hard floor.

Skidmore threw her hands in her hair. "You're out of your mind." Her voice faltered as if she couldn't decide whether to scream or whisper. "I swear I don't know what you're talking about."

"If I am out of my mind, imagine how Chloe's and Ann's parents feel. And you know exactly what this is about."

"I don't." Skidmore had backed herself into the kitchen and against the refrigerator. She stood there, staring at my face. She held her hands at her side, flat against the stainless steel. She had nowhere to go. "I don't know," she said again as I picked a glass from the counter. "You don't need to break anything else. I don't know anything."

I dropped the glass on the tile with predictable results. Skidmore flinched. I put my face two inches in front of hers. "Your bullshit's not helping. Where are they? Where are the women your son and his gang of cowards kidnapped?"

"You're mad."

"I'm about to be. You see, Zach said the girls were safe. Zach said they were here." I pulled my gun out of its holster. "Now, you're telling me they're not here? You're telling me they're not safe?"

Skidmore's eyes widened with each word. "Zach!" she screamed. "Zach!"

"Zach's not here. I've got him all tied up in a bow. I've got his gun, too, the one he killed Pamela Howard with. The only question is, what am I going to do with him?"

"Leave my son alone!"

"Where are Chloe and Ann?" I put my gun on the counter, where she could see it, where she couldn't help staring at it. "Where are they?"

"My son . . ."

"Your son is a fucked-up piece of shit, and there's only one thing you can do to help him because I sure as hell don't give a damn what happens to him. Tell me where you're keeping Chloe and Ann."

I gave Skidmore two more seconds with my gun in front of her and my breath in her nostrils. Then I reached for my weapon, and she spilled her next words, her head hanging in front of her. "They're in the shed. They're fine. They're—"

"What shed?"

"The green shed in the front yard. It's quite big, and they're—"

I punched the fridge next to her body. Skidmore shrank, knees buckling, eyes down, looking at her feet. I punched the fridge again. It was that or punch her. The frustration and rage had to go somewhere. *A shed. The front yard. I could have freed them hours ago. Without breaking in, with no alarm, no risk.* I wanted to throw up.

"On the ground, on your belly, hands behind your head," I said. I pushed some broken glass away with my boot, and she had enough sense—or enough fear—not to mistake my instructions for suggestions or worry about a few shards. She collapsed on the floor, sliding against the fridge door. I pushed her face down and zip-tied her wrists behind her back. Then I pulled another zip tie for her ankles. When that was done, I took a rag hanging from the dishwasher and shoved it deep enough into her mouth that she would not be able to scream or spit it out, not anytime soon.

I took my gun from the counter and started running. "Get in here!" I yelled over the open phone line as I rushed out of the house.

"We're on our way," CJ's disembodied voice said out of my pocket, the sound of a revving engine in the background.

Years of training had me moving the way I always did with a gun. It was an ingrained habit. I held the weapon in a shooting grip, pointed at the ground. I moved in wide, even steps, going from tree to tree. It did not take long.

In daylight, and knowing what I was looking for, I found the shed in seconds. It was painted green to match the vegetation. It may have been big for a garden shed, but it was still a prison cell. A lock through a latch nailed into the wood door kept the makeshift jail closed tight. And I wasn't going to waste any more time, not one more second, not to look for something as useless as a key or bolt cutters.

"Chloe! Ann! Can you hear me?"

I overheard a whispered conversation through the door. I'd probably scared the shit out of them. *Nice job, Malone, you dumb fuck!* I kept my voice as low as I could and still be heard. "My name is Cooper Malone. I'm a private investigator. Your parents hired me to find you. Can you hear me?"

"Yes!" an excited voice answered. "Yes, we're here. We can hear you."

"I'm going to shoot the lock. Stand back as far back as you can. Tell me when you're ready."

"We're ready."

I still had my gun in my hand. I squeezed three shots, point blank, just above the latch. The wood splintered, and I yanked the whole thing, latch and lock, off the door. It swung open. Chloe and Ann were standing against the far wall, hand in hand, straight-backed and clear-eyed, looking back at me.

They were alive.

They still wore the same shorts and bikini tops they'd worn on the Fourth of July. The shed where they now stood was empty but for two cots and a bucket. It was a jail cell alright, a jail cell of the worst kind.

I holstered my weapon and took a step back. "It's okay," I said, "you can come out now."

They took a few hesitant steps, still holding hands. "Is it over?" Ann asked. "Is it really over?"

"It's over."

Chloe let go of Ann's hand. She walked to me. Then, all of a sudden, she collapsed against my chest, laughing and crying at the same time. She shook with the intensity of a thousand emotions. Ann ran to us, hugging Chloe, who was hugging me. If words were needed, I had no clue what they were.

"Chloe!" Ann said. There was a tone of alarm in her voice. She stepped back, pulling her friend with her by the shoulders. Her eyes were glued on two women running toward us with guns in their hands.

"It's okay," I said, "they're with me." CJ was closest, so I pointed to her first, even as she smiled and put her gun away. "That's CJ. She's not as scary as she looks right now."

I pointed to Courtney next. She'd already holstered, and she was shaking her blonde mop loose from a scrunchy. With that giant smile on her face, she looked downright innocent. "And that's Courtney. She's probably scarier than she looks." That was enough to draw a chuckle from Chloe and Ann, and their shoulders relaxed.

Chloe looked up at me. She wiped a tear off her cheek. "Are our parents here?"

"Not yet. We can call them now. Your grandfather's here too."

Chloe laughed. It was still a nervous, strained laugh, but at least it was a laugh. "I bet. He probably stole some secret army time machine to get here before Mom even called."

I pulled my phone out of my pocket. CJ had already closed my open line to her. I had my fingers poised to dial, but Chloe was on auto-talk. Words erupted from her faster than thought.

"It's Christine, isn't it?" she asked. "She led you here, right? I knew she'd find us. No one stops Christine." She turned to Ann. "We said it over and over, right? Christine would come through. She always does."

My hand fell to my side, and my heart sank right along with it. I put my fingertips on Chloe's arms to get her attention. "I'm sorry, hon. Christine didn't make it."

"What do you mean? Of course, she did. She escaped. We saw it." While Chloe talked, Ann just looked at me with eyes begging me to tell her it wasn't true.

"I'm sorry. She's gone," I said as softly as I could. "She was killed."

"No!" Ann cried. She collapsed first, knees hitting the ground hard, with a cry of anguish sounding like she had splintered in half. Chloe rushed to her. Both girls' tears mixed as they held each other right there, on the ground, in front of the garden shed that had been their prison.

I stood there with my mouth half open and my phone in my hand, not sure what to do.

CJ put a hand on my shoulder. "Give them a moment," she said.

And so I did, and CJ was right. It took a few minutes, but Chloe looked up and asked if we could call their parents now. The world started spinning again. I dialed General Overby. His number was high on my list of recent calls.

"Morning, Malone," he answered, wide awake with the sun already up.

I didn't bother with hello. "General, I have Chloe and Ann with me," I said. "They're free, and they're safe. Medics will want to take a look, but they appear healthy. I can text you the address."

The general did not answer. His distant voice echoed a moment later as he still carried the phone but was not talking into it. "Jill, come quick. Chloe's safe. They're both safe. They're with Malone. They're safe."

The next voice was Jill's. "Chloe?"

"Let me put her on," I said.

I handed Chloe the phone and stepped away from her to give mother and daughter some privacy. CJ smiled at me. I guess that was the emotionally intelligent thing to do. I wish I could take credit with her, but I had ulterior motives. I had work to do.

"CJ, I need you in the house. Make sure Skidmore is still secure. Also, find some Ziplocks or paper bags to preserve evidence on the girls' clothes. You know the drill."

"I do," she said, already on her way. She also knew I couldn't help spelling it out anyway.

I turned to Courtney next. "Get the office contacts list on your phone and hand it to me. I presume you have another?"

Courtney nodded even as she handed me her phone, tapping as she did. I'd have been shocked if our office cyber-maven did not carry a second phone as surely as I carried two guns. "Text your backup number to your phone, then go up front and secure the property."

"Okay but . . . I'm sorry. How do I do that? I've never secured an area."

"No, I'm sorry." I'd gotten so used to Courtney doing what I needed when I needed it done that it was easy to forget she'd only started training as an investigator. "Go up front. Make sure your gun is visible. No one enters but the parents and MCSO. If anyone gives you any trouble, call me. When MCSO gets here, consider yourself relieved and go in the house to help CJ."

"Okay, got it."

I turned around. Chloe was still on the phone, and Ann was glued to her. I dialed Jill's number from Courtney's phone.

"Overby," her father's voice answered.

"It's Malone. I'm calling from my associate's phone. I will text you the address from this number, and you can come over. Only you and the parents for now. And bring a change of clothes for Chloe and Ann."

I was all business, and the general answered in kind. "Wilco. We will be on our way in five."

We hung up, and I pulled another number from the office's contacts list.

"Detective Sergeant Michaels," the voice answered, brisk and professional in the early morning.

"This is Malone. I have multiple updates. I need you to listen carefully."

"Go ahead," he said.

"Chloe Overby and Ann Berger are free and safe. They were being held prisoners on Tiffany Skidmore's property. I have the girls with me, Skidmore in custody, and the property secured."

"We're on our way."

"I'm not done. Tiffany's son, Zach Skidmore, is in custody in Miami-Dade County on charges of burglary and attempted murder."

"Whose attempted murder?" Michaels was collecting what relevant information I had not included.

"Mine. I'm pretty sure that when ballistics comes back, it will be a match to the bullet that killed Pamela Howard. I could always be wrong, but I doubt it. Dade should give you first dibs at him."

"Understood."

"And if you received a report of gunshots at this location, it's just me shooting off a lock. You may disregard. I guess I won't be known for my subtlety around your office either."

"I'm not aware of any report but will forward the information. Anything else?"

"Just one thing. Give it some time before you bring in the cavalry. Let the families have a little time together without an army of badges surrounding them and tugging at them every which way. I will secure the evidence, document the chain of custody, and keep the scene secure. You have my word."

Michaels did not hesitate. "I can't help it if you took another twenty minutes to call me."

"You're a good man, Sergeant. Thanks."

I looked around, feeling suddenly aimless. Ann had the phone now. Soon, both girls' families would arrive. Everyone would cry, hug, laugh, talk too loudly—all those things people do when overcome with emotion. CJ and Courtney would be there. They'd make everyone comfortable and still preserve evidence while the girls changed.

I would be of no use in the house. Big cases filled me with energy and purpose, and this one was not over. I needed to find Christine's killer. But part of it was. Life could go on for Chloe, Ann, and their families, a life where I had no role to play. It was the way it was meant to be, but that didn't ease the emptiness inside.

I put my hand on Chloe's shoulder and whispered to her to stay put for a couple more minutes. She nodded, and I went to find Courtney. She had pulled her hair back in a ponytail, wore her gun on her hip, and did her best to look official. She didn't do too bad a job of it. A couple of neighbors were whispering on a driveway, but the neighborhood had not woken up to chaos yet. That would come when their front windows started reflecting police lights.

"Ann and Chloe are still by the shed," I told Courtney once I caught up with her. "Go to them and get them in the house. I'll relieve you here. Once inside, CJ will know what to do. The two of you are responsible for keeping everyone happy while preserving evidence."

"Understood."

And just like that, Courtney was gone. When the families came, I directed them to the house. They rushed in, just as they should, then they were gone too. I stayed at my post. I wasn't too worried about neighbors barging in. I looked a tad scarier than Courtney on her worst day. My thoughts were miles away, though, even by the time the first lights and sirens intruded into the neighborhood. I had told the girls it was all over.

It was for them.

CHAPTER 20

The afternoon sun burned high in the sky, beating on my unprotected forehead. John, Jill, and Chloe Overby, reunited, sat around the same picnic table where I'd sat the day before—the same wooden table, the same long benches on either side, the same two RVs parked next to it, the same beach across the low retaining wall behind it. The Raymonds were there too, hanging on to every scrap of conversation, living out the friendship their daughter no longer could.

The Bergers—well, the Bergers were nowhere to be seen, and both Fords were gone from the resort parking lot.

I watched from across the lot. I had no right to interfere, to throw a rock into the waters of their reunion. And yet, I had to. I needed answers, even now. I had a trail to follow, and it was getting cold.

I sensed a presence next to me moments before a familiar body leaned into my arm, a hand resting on my chest.

"Hello, Mr. PI." Amy's sweet voice rang in my ear.

I leaned in for a kiss, and dark clouds lifted as if by magic. "Hi yourself," I said. I didn't know what she was doing in Key Largo, and I didn't care. At least not yet. I knew myself well enough to know questions would force their way out eventually. They always did. It wasn't only a professional hazard, it was my nature, good or bad.

"You took off work?" I asked. That came quicker than I'd anticipated.

"It's Sunday, silly." Amy gave my arm a playful squeeze and rested her head on my shoulder.

I had no concept of time, not in the sense of days of the week. It was day six from the abduction, day three from the time I had been hired. Case days mattered, days of the week did not.

Amy answered my next question before I had to ask. "CJ called me after you told her and Courtney they could go home. She put it delicately. You probably ordered them home."

"She thought I needed sassing?"

"She'd approve, I'm sure. But she mostly thought you'd need company. She's a good friend."

"Yeah, she is. But how . . .?" This time, I answered my own question. "Your phone number was in the Morrison file."

Amy and I had clicked so well, felt so close, that it was hard to remember how short a time we'd been together, or that I'd met her on a case, that the first time I saw her, it was because she was a witness in a murder investigation.

"CJ put it to good use," Amy said. "I'm glad she called."

"I am too."

Amy turned her head toward the ocean and the people around the picnic table. "You need to talk to them, don't you?"

"Yeah, I do."

"Go do your thing, then. I'll be here when you're done. Go!"

She let go of me, and I felt instantly empty. I took one more deep breath and walked. I focused on the act of putting one foot in front of the other toward faces I knew would change the moment I got to them.

Chloe saw me first and ran to me, wrapping herself on me in a big bear hug. "I'm so happy to see you," she said. "I never got to thank you properly."

"I'm pretty sure that's well and done now," I said as she let go, only to pull me by the arm toward the picnic table. Everyone beamed. Even I couldn't help it.

Jill met us halfway, squinting in the sun, her big sunglasses still resting on the table. She took both my hands in hers and looked straight at me. "Thank you. Thank you for finding Chloe."

"You're welcome." I squeezed her hands. Then we let go and headed toward the RVs and the table between. "The Bergers aren't here?" I asked.

Jill grimaced. "They're on their way back to Orlando. Jennifer picked a fight with Ann in the police station parking lot. I couldn't believe it, after everything that happened. Ann desperately wanted to stay with Chloe. She and her mom shouted at each other something awful. Poor Bill tried to calm things down and got shut down fast. He looked ready to collapse—sat down on a bench and stooped, his big glasses nearly falling off his nose, desperation pouring out of him. And Jennifer just shouted louder. Ann yelled back at first but eventually relented and got in the car."

Chloe glanced at her phone. "I haven't heard from her yet."

"They're probably still on the road," I said. Ann wasn't driving. She could text if she wanted to. Chloe knew that as well as I did. Maybe things were a little too tense in that car. It was something for her to hang on to.

"Yeah," Chloe said. She did not sound any more convinced than I was.

We sat down, and I shook hands with Reggie and Cassie Raymond, exchanging soft hellos.

Then, I returned my attention to Chloe. "I know you've just spent hours with the cops," I said, "but I was hoping to ask you a few questions myself."

"Of course. Anything. But only if you tell me how you found us. I still can't figure it out. Not without . . ." Chloe glanced at the Raymonds with a sad smile. "Well, without Christine. You had nothing to work from."

"Sure. No problem. Let's start at the beginning, though, okay? Tell me what happened on the Fourth."

Chloe's face fell. She looked up, her gaze fixed on the horizon, somewhere far away. For a moment, there was only the sound of waves crashing ashore. When Chloe started talking, her voice was clear, yet barely more than a whisper.

"The three of us were hitting the beach, watching the fireworks. That's why we love it here, and this year was even crazier than usual. It's hard to imagine so many people on a beach like that, just gathering around with fireworks, not some big commercial display by a city or a sports team. Or Disney. I mean, we do live in Orlando."

She gave me a glance and a quick smile to let us all know she still had her sense of humor and she'd be okay. Eventually. Her body was tense. Her eyes danced all over the place, even when her head didn't move. She showed signs of hypervigilance, the kind that soldiers coming back from war experience. Some crime victims have it too.

Chloe leaned back again, eyes turned to the sky, and she continued. "It seems so long ago now. At the same time, I remember it like it was yesterday. I remember all the explosions. Everyone tried to fire something bigger than the person next to them, something louder, something brighter. The smell of the fireworks was stronger than the ocean air. It was surreal.

"Lots of people were drinking. Most drank beer. Some people brought stronger stuff. Us too, I guess. We mixed screwdrivers in red solo cups before going down."

"Giant solo cups," Jill said, ever the mom.

"Yeah," Chloe said. "I can still taste it when I think about that night. It felt like such a happy time. Everyone was laughing and enjoying themselves. There were some obnoxious types too. But there always are, and they were harmless. At least they seemed harmless. Then, this one guy started acting up more and more, just being loud and pissy. He was uneven on his feet, stupid drunk, tripping all over himself."

I pulled up a picture of Zach Skidmore on my phone. "Him?" I asked.

"Yes." Chloe shuddered as if a cold chill had just come over her. "I identified him in a photo array at the police station too."

"I don't know what the cops told you," I said, "but he's in a Miami jail, booked on first-degree felony charges. More charges will be brought here, in the Keys. He's not going anywhere for a long time."

"Good, and thanks. The cops were very nice—polite, solicitous, and everything, but they were the ones asking questions. That young officer . . ." She paused, searching for a name.

"Michaels?" I asked.

"That's right. He told us we had nothing to worry about anymore, but that's it. It's good to know he's going to prison."

"He is, and he'll stay there. What happened with him on the Fourth?"

Chloe pressed her fingers against her temples. "I can still hear it. That guy you showed me on your phone started yelling, 'Shit, we're out of fireworks.' One of his friends said something like, 'Yeah, man, we're done. This thing is pretty much over anyway.' Then that first guy said, 'Fuck that, I'm not done,' and he pulled a gun. Unstable as he was, his first round went straight up. That idiot did not realize that what goes up must come down. Then he nearly fell and shot that damn gun again, and it was pointed straight at the crowd."

Chloe took a deep breath, her eyes once more somewhere over the ocean. "I'm a midshipman, Mr. Malone, UF-NROTC. I have a pretty strong sense of right and wrong. But Christine . . ." She looked at the Raymonds, a hand over her heart and a smile on her face. "Christine did not need anyone to reinforce hers. She had more integrity and courage than anyone I know. Anyone. She shoved that guy and told him he was crazy, that she was going to go make sure he hadn't hit anyone, and he was going with her."

Chloe stopped and looked at me. "Did he? Hurt anyone? From what the officers were asking, I started to think maybe he did."

"He killed someone. A woman here on vacation. Her name was Pamela."

"Oh God, this is horrible." Chloe bowed her head in her hands, shoulders slumped. I'd added an extra weight to her day. I consoled myself that there was no point telling her anything other than the truth. It was small comfort.

I could hear CJ's voice in my head telling me to give Chloe a moment, the same advice she'd given me next to Skidmore's shed this morning. She'd been right then and was right now. After a while, Chloe lifted her head and continued her story.

"Anyway, Christine and that guy kept fighting, pushing each other and arguing on the beach. Ann and I looked at each other, unsure of what to do. Christine was right, but the guy had a gun. We didn't wonder long, though. Christine was our friend, and we backed her up. People started walking away." Chloe turned to me. "People are cowards, Mr. Malone. Goddamn cowards."

"You better start calling me Coop so we can stay friends, and unfortunately, that's something I know all too well."

Chloe resumed her story. "We were becoming a bit isolated because of all the people leaving, and I don't mind saying I was getting nervous. There's safety in numbers, and we were losing it. Even with that, I never imagined . . . well, that what actually happened would happen." She seemed to falter for a moment, on the verge of breaking down.

"Take your time," I said.

"I'm okay. As okay as I can be. It's just . . . the guy with the gun just grabbed Christine by the hair, like it was no big deal, and he jammed his gun in her ribs."

Cassie Raymond's hand flew to her mouth, but other than that, she didn't move, and neither did Reggie.

Chloe didn't notice and kept talking. "Christine yelped as the gun hit her, and the guy said he'd kill her if the three of us didn't shut up and go with him. He told his friends to grab Ann and me."

"They went along with it?" I asked.

"Yeah. They did not look super happy about it, but they did. Have they been arrested too?"

"They have. They won't see the outside of a jail cell for a long while either."

"Good, because they sure helped. Maybe three-on-one, we'd have tried something, even with Christine having a gun poking her side. The way it was, we had no choice. We were stuck. That guy looked crazy enough to shoot Christine, and the other two had their hands on Ann and me. So, we went where they walked us."

"You did the smart thing," I said.

"I hope so. They dragged us to a house a couple of lots away, broke the sliding back door, and locked us in some kind of basement."

"That was our first break," I said, holding up to my end of the bargain. "I had an associate fly a drone along the shore, and we found the broken glass. I got into the house that same night. Eventually, MCSO got a warrant and searched it."

"You broke into private property, Malone?" General Overby asked with a shit-eating grin.

"You sponsored me to MIC," I shot back, using Army Intelligence's official acronym, the Military Intelligence Corps. "I do what needs to be done."

"I may have to consider UAVs in the service," Chloe added, using the military's designation for drones, "now that one helped save my life."

"You were gone by the time we went in," I said, picking up the thread, "but you'd left us a clue. Which one of you knows Morse code?"

"You found our message!" Chloe said. "You found our message. Ann did that. She used the post from my earring. It was all we could think of without leaving something so obvious the bad guys would see it. It was just to say we were there and needed help. And we weren't there for long.

"That guy, the gang leader, brought us some fast food the next morning. Then he came back, but much later. When we heard the lock jiggle, Christine acted on instinct. She ran up the stairs, reached the door just as it started to open, and barreled right over him. Ann and

I ran up after her. Maybe I could have caught up to Christine with my conditioning from NROTC, maybe not, because she acted so quickly. But that wasn't even a thought at the time. No way Ann and I weren't going to stick together. One could escape and bring help, but we could not leave just one of us locked up.

"By the time we reached the top of the stairs, he'd locked us in again. We couldn't get out. It didn't matter, though. We were giddy. Christine had escaped—or we thought she had—and she'd get help. It would be over soon." Chloe looked at the Raymonds again. "I'm sorry. We should have been quicker. We should have run out with her."

Reggie Raymond found a smile. "Don't do that, honey. Don't blame yourself. You did nothing wrong. You were with my Christine through thick and thin to the end. I'll love you and Ann forever for that."

"We both will," Cassie said, clasping her husband's hand.

Chloe continued through pinched lips. "A little later, the gang leader came back with that woman, the one who kept us in the shed. They both had guns. They shoved us into the hatch of an SUV, tied us up, blindfolded us, and moved us to where you found us. Was that woman his mom? She kinda sounded like it."

I wondered if Skidmore's piece was a forty-five, even as I answered Chloe. "That's his mom, alright. And she's in jail too. She's a realtor, and the first house they held you in was one of her listings."

General Overby nodded. "So now you had a name. You were like a dog with a bone."

"I wasn't working alone. My team uncovered a lot of the information we used, and we were able to connect the dots later."

"I don't doubt that. We met your people at the house. They are two formidable women."

The general hadn't lost his touch. He was a good judge of character.

I turned back to Chloe. "She kept you in that shed for a long time. What did she want?"

"For us to forget, I guess. It was horrible in there, no two ways about it. We were fed twice a day, mostly fast food. I never liked that stuff, but now, the sight of a grease-stained bag of fries makes me want to hurl. We got to use a bathroom when that woman took us, one at a time, at gunpoint. Most of the time, we had to use the bucket. We asked for a change of clothes but didn't even get that."

I felt the weight of every hour when I did not find them. I felt the Florida heat beating on their skulls all day, every day, with only each other and the smell of their piss in a bucket for company.

Jill brought me back to the present. "Did you try to scream or shout for help?" she asked. It was difficult for her. She did not want to sound like she was criticizing her daughter, but she needed to know.

"At first, on and off. But we never heard a car or voices, so it was pretty obvious it was pointless, and we saved our energy. Ann and I agreed that if we saw someone on a bathroom trip to the house, we'd scream and run to them and bring help, but we never saw anyone."

"You said she wanted you to forget," I said, bringing us back on track.

"She spent a lot of time on the other side of the door, trying to tell us that if we could convince her we'd say nothing about the shooting and our kidnapping, she'd let us go."

I sat back. That made little sense. The girls wouldn't change their minds, and Skidmore would never be able to tell if they were lying. "Did you try to convince her?" I asked.

"Hell, no! We told her no way. We knew—we thought—Christine had escaped, so we knew help would come." She turned to me, the corners of her mouth inching up. "And it did, after all."

"As your grandfather said, we had a name. Still, we needed a few more pieces of information to put a picture together. We clued in on her son first—a filthy excuse for a human being. He led us to his mom and your makeshift prison."

"Thank you," Chloe said. "I can't tell you . . ."

"Will you tell me more about how Christine escaped before I go?" I asked as her voice faded. "Obviously, you heard no gunshot."

"We probably wouldn't have from our cave. But Christine had the jump on him, and he took the time to lock the door again. I don't understand what could have happened. Christine's a good runner. She's fast. There is no way."

"I tend to agree with you," I said, mostly to myself. I got up from the table, my mind swirling with thoughts, already thinking ahead. Everyone got up with me like I was the fucking king of England.

General Overby extended his hand. "Thank you, Coop."

We shook. "Thank you, John. I wouldn't be here without you."

"I'll never be able to repay you for what you've done. You did an admirable job."

"That's bullshit. I have not yet begun to repay you. And the job's not done. Not yet."

Caught up in Chloe's return, General Overby gave me a questioning look. Then he caught sight of the Raymonds at the end of the table, tears coursing down both their faces, too drained to move or speak.

"Of course," he said.

His granddaughter was more direct. "Damn right, it's not."

I finished their thoughts. "I have a killer to catch."

CHAPTER 21

I nodded to the Raymonds as I walked away. They managed to nod back, their eyes vacant. I was so far inside my head that I nearly bumped into Amy. She was half sunshine smile and half lasers in the eyes.

"I know that look," she said. "We're not going to argue over big dark moods again, are we?"

"It may take me a hot minute to get used to not hiding it, but no argument."

"Good, because I got us a room on the island tonight. I figured it might come in handy."

"Can you cancel it?"

Amy shrugged. "Cancel it, use it, not show, whatever. Why?"

"Let's go back to your place, then. When you're done purging my mood and I'm done satiating yours, I'd rather we greet the new day from that magical deck of yours."

Her million-dollar smile added a zero to the tally. "I knew there was a reason I liked you. Done—if I get to glue my body to yours on the bike. I'll come back for the Jeep later."

I took her by the hand, headed to the Chief, and we got going. I rode faster than we needed to. That did not mean we made good time.

That afternoon, I did not keep going when we passed a dark alley. I didn't want to wait, and I was beginning to know Amy well enough to know that waiting was not her first choice either.

That night, she was the light to my darkness again. Whatever it took. And I embraced her wild side because it was not just a side of her. It was a part of who she was, inseparable from the rest of her. I wanted to take all of her in so we could have a future together.

The next morning, before dawn, it turned out it was Amy who needed to talk as we lay next to each other.

"Why aren't you?" she asked out of the blue.

"Why am I not what?"

"Back at your place after we went to Barrels, you said you weren't intimidated by my wild side. Why not?"

"Why should I be?" I asked, raising myself on one elbow to better look at her.

"It gives me a colorful past. That can put some guys off."

"Well, I'm not 'some guy.' And anyway, I haven't exactly lived a choir boy's life either. I'd be a jerk if I were put off because you got into the same kind of trouble I did."

"It's different, though."

"Because you're a woman?"

"Yes. I even had someone ask me once if I'd been abused, if that's why I was like that."

"Were you?"

"Abused? No. It's a pathology. I read up on it since, even in people otherwise perfectly well-adjusted. But no. It's just . . . that someone should assume I had been pissed me off."

"I get that," I said. "Now, it's out of the way. You weren't abused. You have a wild side. It could be said I have one too. Sometimes, it helps lift each other out of our dark moods, especially mine. So, we're good, right?"

Amy reached over and caressed my cheek. "We are, but it's still not the same, Mr. PI, and you know it. Party girls can get pretty much anything they want with a smile and some cleavage. You guys have to work at it."

I pressed my forehead against hers. "Maybe so. It still makes no difference to me. I'm still not intimidated, no matter how colorful your past."

Her hand moved from my cheek to the back of my head, nails digging in. "You're sure about that?"

"I'm sure"

She kissed me, her tongue invading my mouth. "Prove it."

So, I did.

After the sun rose, we showered, dressed, and drank coffee in silence on her deck. We didn't need any more words. We sat back, enjoying nature, the scent of our brew, and the physical connection of her leg over mine and her head on my shoulder. I dropped her off at work after that. It all felt so normal.

Then I headed to the office to hunt a killer.

Forty minutes later, CJ sat across from my desk, ready to start a different kind of conversation. She sat straight against the back of her chair, legs crossed, eyes glued on me. Courtney sat in the chair next to her, head down on her tablet, bringing up the file. I hadn't even powered up my computer and needed another coffee. It would have to wait.

CJ started off like Hussain Bolt on the hundred-meter dash. "Explain this to me. Why are we sure Zach did not kill Christine? She escaped on the fifth of July, and she was killed on the fifth of July. Zach was at the scene. Zach is trigger-happy."

"All true, but other aspects of the case trump all that."

"Hit me."

I started extending my fingers, one by one, ticking off my thoughts. "One. Christine was shot with a forty-five, and Zach's pet automatic is a nine-millimeter. He could have had two guns, but that's not likely. Two. He's a lousy shot, which plays into another point I'll make in a moment. Three. He sounded genuinely surprised anyone had died when we caught him at Barrels. The whole gang did. And four, there's something Chloe told me yesterday. I haven't had a chance to write it up in the file yet."

Courtney turned to CJ with a devilish smile on her face. "So, you did get a hold of Amy."

"She did," I said before CJ could answer. "And thank you."

"She sounds like a good person," CJ said. "And good for you."

"She's all that. Now—"

"I know," CJ said, hand raised, palm out. "Back to the case."

I did just that. "Chloe said Christine got the jump on Zach when he brought food. She ran right over him, took him by surprise, and kept running while Zach locked the door. On top of all that, she's a fast runner. In theory, I could buy Zach squeezing out a shot. He can't control his weapon, but he could have gotten lucky.

"Except that it doesn't fit the evidence. Christine was shot from the front at close range. Zach would have had to catch up with her, get face-to-face, and shoot her in cold blood, sober, while looking at her in the eye. Put it all together, and I don't buy it."

CJ looked up at the ceiling, processing what I'd just said. When she finally spoke again, she did so in a clear, measured voice.

"I'm not sure you're right. He could have had a second gun, as you said, and Christine could have stopped when she heard the gunshot rather than risk being hit."

"Then why shoot her? Why not bring her back to that basement? If that's what happened, and Zach caught her, Christine didn't escape very far. He's got her. In that scenario, he wouldn't shoot."

"Maybe he's so mad about her trying to escape that he shoots her in a fit of rage," CJ said. She raised her hands and leaned in toward me. "What's the alternative? Christine escapes, then she somehow runs into somebody with a forty-five who shoots her dead? That's even less credible. And remember, as we just learned, she's a fast runner. She only had to cross three backyards to get back to the resort, including the one for the house where she was held. There's no way some rando with a gun happens to stop her and kill her in that short amount of time."

"I don't think it was random," I said. "She was shot multiple times, and the rounds scattered despite the short range. Whoever killed her may have fired more bullets that went wild."

I turned to Courtney, switching to mentor mode for a second. "What do multiple shots at close range sound like to you?"

"It sounds personal," Courtney said.

"Someone she knows," CJ said softly. She had not processed that part yet. This was my world, and I had spent time mulling it over. I'd connected a few more dots.

"Or someone who knew her," I said, "people who had a personal stake in stopping her. Tiffany Skidmore has already shown she'll protect her son at all costs. And the other two Skull and Coins idiots were facing a long prison time over the kidnapping alone. They weren't stupid enough not to realize they were in deep. Any one of those three could have gone to the house with Zach that night to help him out. Maybe they were outside when Christine came out and fired on instinct when they saw her run."

"That could make sense," CJ said. She kept talking, playing the scene out in her mind. "Christine runs the way she came, out the back. She runs right into Tiffany or one of her kidnappers. She's unable to stop. She's all momentum. Or she decides not to. She doesn't have far to go. She can run right through them like she just did to Zach. In a way, she's right. She takes whoever is out there by surprise. But it plays against her. They're armed. They raise the gun—pure reflex—and empty it in Christine's direction." CJ paused. "It could have happened that way, and it's more likely than Zach killing her. I agree."

"That's the theory," I said, "and you'll be the first to remind me it's only a theory, and you'd be right."

"So, what's our next move?" Courtney asked.

I looked at them both, glaring across the desk. I didn't fucking know. I gave them a non-answer, which was all I had. "Both of Zach's sidekicks are in jail cells, all Mirandized and shit. Not much we can do with them. Same goes for Tiffany."

I drummed my fingers on the desk. It didn't help. "Let me write up the closed-file report for Chloe's and Ann's cases. Maybe that will spur a thought. Truth is, I don't have a next move right now. You two keep digging as well. You get an idea, shout it out. Don't wait for a case conference."

"Will think, won't wait," CJ said, getting up. She seemed to think sassing me was the best way to help. Since I didn't have a better idea, I could not dispel her illusion.

"Got it," Courtney said as both women left my office. I powered up the computer, forced some space to open between my teeth, and got to work.

I couldn't tell how much time passed. I was half typing reports and half lost inside my head. I kept picturing Chloe and Ann, giddy with joy when I freed them, their hearts broken when I told them Christine was dead. I wanted to feel good, elated that I'd found the girls. But I couldn't. I'd only found two. The unresolved death was mine to solve. Every question, every doubt was a storm cloud, thundering at my head with an ache no pain pill could take away.

I had the word processor up on one screen and Christine's autopsy report, courtesy of Sergeant Michaels, up on the other. I kept trying to figure it out, looking for some detail of the events around her death that would shed light on it.

Where was Christine when she was shot? Who could have gotten that close to her that quickly to spray bullets at point-blank range? Who? Who fucking killed her? Nothing in the report confirmed or dispelled my theory, and even that theory, the one where people close to Zach helped him and killed Christine, left three suspects to sort through. I kept trying to talk myself in or out of possible scenarios without proof any of them were true. Wishful thinking was no way to work a case.

My phone rang, jerking me out of my thoughts. The display lit with a South Florida number I did not recognize.

"Malone," I said, taking the call.

"Hi, Malone. This is Captain Tornero."

That was a surprise. The captain and I had gotten along well enough, but we'd kept each other at arm's length. With both Skidmores in custody, I hadn't expected to hear from him.

"Morning, Captain. Anything I can do for you?"

"As a matter of fact, there is. You and your team might be able to help us speed things up a little, if nothing else."

"Go on." Tornero was speaking my language, and he knew it. I was always interested in things speeding up.

"That young associate of yours . . ."

"Courtney?"

"Yes, that's right. How good is she?"

"She's green, she barely started training, but she's got good instincts." I cut in with my own question before Tornero could say more. "Why are you asking? I thought you were pretty good at getting things done within the system."

Tornero took a deep breath on the other end of the line. "As you can imagine, Ms. Skidmore's arrest generated a political shitstorm, even with all the evidence of her part in kidnapping three women."

"That will die down. The rich and powerful will drop her ass on the side of the road soon enough."

"All the same, this is a case where I'd rather have more than I need—from her own lips if possible. She lawyered up, of course. She won't talk to us. She sure won't talk to you. But someone her son's age may figure out a way to get something out of her in conversation. We may get lucky."

So that's where Courtney came in. She was the ace in the hole, playing the one hand where the cops still had the advantage, Miranda, lawyers, and all. If anyone lies to them, it's obstruction. But they can lie and deceive all they want. So long as constitutional rights are protected, so long as the letter of the law comes with dotted i's and crossed t's, they can trick a confession out of a suspect to their hearts' content.

There was one problem with his plan—a big one. "We might get lucky if we use someone Skidmore never met. But Courtney was at the house."

"Your partner had already secured Ms. Skidmore in another room when Courtney walked in with Ms. Overby, General Overby, and the Bergers. She had arranged to keep victims and accused apart, as per protocol. And of course, we made sure to keep it that way when we arrived at the scene—much later than appropriate, by the way. In any event, Ms. Skidmore never saw Courtney."

"Okay, but Courtney will still have to get a waiver of counsel if we send her in. That will limit her usefulness." Tornero knew as well as me that once invoked, the right to counsel stuck, and since we'd be listening in, Courtney would be considered an agent of law enforcement.

"It will be an obstacle, for sure, one of several, but I think it's worth a try."

"Is it? With all you have, I'm not sure we're on the right side of the cost-benefit ledger here. I hear you about getting something more out of Skidmore's own mouth, but the odds of getting it are pretty damn low."

It could be a good experience for Courtney, but it seemed a bit of a stretch. I needed more than that before sending a rookie into the lion's den, even if the lion was behind bars.

"There is one more thing," Tornero said. "Two, actually."

"What are they?"

"First, we searched Skidmore's home, and we found a forty-five-caliber pistol. It will be a couple of days for ballistics to come back with a match-no-match to the bullets that killed Ms. Raymond. With the ladies free, we're back in the first-come-first-served felony lane."

"That's what you meant by speeding things up."

"Yes."

"What else? You said there were two things."

"Second, I want a crack at some kind of interrogation before Skidmore goes to court, one where the answer is not parroting the right to remain silent. I want as much as possible out of her, both on the kidnapping and whether she had anything to do with the Raymond murder."

"You still haven't said why you need it and why you need it now. I don't buy that you can't handle political shenanigans." *Spit it out, Cap,* I thought. *I outrank you.* I was still a major in the Army Reserves, after all.

"Part of those shenanigans includes phone calls from powerful people to other powerful people, orchestrated by Skidmore's attorneys. They are trying to deflect the narrative from her kidnapping to your methods. They're trumpeting that 'outstanding citizen' bullshit and how you mistreated her. I know it's a bunch of crock. I know it, and you know it, but she could make bail this afternoon."

"Hasn't she had her first appearance yet?" It had been more than twenty-four hours since her arrest. I'd assumed she was still in jail because bail had been denied.

"Time was extended to allow private counsel to appear," Tornero said.

Somewhere in the back of my mind, I remembered a provision in the law allowing that extension. It was rarely used because it meant an extra night in jail. Skidmore must have really wanted her high-powered lawyers to be there from the start.

More to the point, Tornero had me. I still didn't think we'd be lucky enough to get anything incriminating. But my methods during the arrest were front and center, so I owed him one. And if I was honest with myself, I couldn't care less how low the odds were so long as there was some chance, any chance, to help keep Skidmore in a dungeon. With her first appearance pushed back to this afternoon, we had a chance to do that.

"All right," I said. "I'll talk to Courtney and call you right back."

I hung up before he could say thank you and asked for Courtney and CJ to come into my office. Once they sat down, I told them about Tornero's call. I didn't hide my opinion.

"It won't be easy," I said, "and it will probably be for naught. We're trying to get something out of her on two separate crimes, the kidnapping and the murder, and she's not stupid."

"I understand," Courtney said. "I'd like to try if you think that's okay."

CJ turned to Courtney and put a hand on her arm. "Take your time to decide. This training thing is moving awfully fast for you, but it doesn't have to. It's up to you."

"CJ's right," I said.

"I'm good, really." Courtney put her hand over CJ's. "I'll need to change, though. Something more college and less business. I'm starting to see why the two of you keep a closet in your offices."

CJ and I exchanged a look that amounted to a shrug. We had no reason to object.

"I'll take you to your place," I said. "We'll call Tornero from the car."

And just like that, we were headed to Key Largo. Again.

CHAPTER 22

CJ wasn't particularly happy staying behind, but we didn't need three people there. She didn't say anything. That wasn't her style. She stayed put and did the work on our other cases. But I knew—I knew it was a sacrifice for her. And she knew that I knew, and that when I said "thanks" instead of my usual "bye"—or nothing at all—on our way out, I meant it.

Courtney was back in her college student uniform—shorts and a tank top. She'd pouted at returning the CR-V's keys but soon returned to her cheerful self as we drove down to the Keys. I wasn't. I fucking hated this drive.

Despite the urgency behind Tornero's call, we had to make time for bureaucracy. We filled out a form, said who we were, who we were here to see, the purpose of our visit, all so the piece of paper could be filed or scanned and retrieved later. Then, and only then, did we get our visitors' badges from the desk officer who had been finishing off his poke bowl while we'd scribbled away. He buzzed us into a waiting room, and Detective Sergeant Michaels appeared in his immaculate uniform to show us in.

The four of us, including Captain Tornero, talked through the broad strokes of Courtney's story. Broad strokes were all we had. For one thing, there was no time for more. For another, it was better to give

Courtney some flexibility, let her change her approach depending on how Skidmore reacted. There was no script for this.

Before we got going, I gave Courtney a receiver to place in her ear. Her hair would cover it, and it was tiny to start with.

"I'll try not to talk to you," I told her. "A voice in your ear is distracting if you're not used to it. It's tough not to react, and that gives the game away. I will only speak if necessary."

Courtney put the earpiece in. "I'm ready."

Tornero picked up the phone and dialed a three-digit extension. "This is Tornero. Please inform inmate Skidmore she has a visitor."

He hung up without waiting for more of an answer than "yes, sir," then he turned to Courtney. "Thanks for doing this. Sergeant Michaels will take you back. Mr. Malone and I will be two doors down. We will hear and see everything on CCTV."

"Okay," Courtney said. She got up and followed Michaels. Her sandals flipped and flopped in sync with the officer's spit-and-polish shoes.

Tornero took me down a corridor, then another, until we reached a door marked *AV Room*. He swiped a key card. The lock beeped and whirred, and the door opened.

A female officer in uniform sat at a console that would have been familiar to any sound engineer. She turned around when the door opened, her chair swiveling under her. She had a welcoming smile and a pixie haircut. She looked tiny in her chair, pale and mischievous. This was her lair.

"Good afternoon, sir," she said as Tornero entered.

I glanced at my watch. The afternoon had just started, but afternoon it was. Time flew.

"Afternoon, Mills," Tornero said. "How are things in AV?"

"All systems green," she answered before swiveling back to her switches and screens.

"Good. Give us sound on three and four, will you?"

"You got it."

Tornero pointed to the screens in question for my benefit, not that they were hard to find. It was where the action was going to be. The first monitor showed Skidmore in her cell. She still wore what she had on when she was arrested, even if the dress shorts were wrinkled now, her top stiff with dried sweat, and officers had removed belt, shoelaces, or anything pointed or sharp. She sat, stooped, on the cell's cot, wrists resting on her knees. She had bags under her eyes.

The other screen showed the corridor in front of the holding cells. Most were empty that afternoon. Courtney walked down the concrete floor. She looked nervous. It wasn't a bad thing. A college student would be nervous walking down a row of jail cells. Fact and fiction came together as Courtney stopped in front of Skidmore's cell and turned to face the bars.

For a moment, it seemed like Inmate Tiffany Skidmore would ignore her visitor. Then she lifted her head, fixing a stare. "Who the fuck are you?"

Courtney put a hand on her chest. "I'm Cindy. I'm Zach's girlfriend." She managed to sound a bit put off.

Skidmore gave her the once over, looking her up and down. She shrugged. "He always did like them with big boobs. But he never mentioned you."

Courtney pouted. She twirled the tips of her hair. "I'm sure he would have soon. He was probably waiting for the right moment. He really cares for me."

Tiffany guffawed. I clicked my microphone while she focused on whatever amused her.

"Lawyer, Courtney," I reminded her in a clipped tone.

"No, it's true," Courtney said without missing a beat.

"Sure. Maybe," Skidmore said as she leaned back against the cinder block wall.

"The cops said I could see you, but I had to tell you that you could have your lawyer if you wanted. Oh yeah, and that you didn't have to see me," Courtney said. "I guess this isn't a private place, so people could hear us."

"No shit! Nothing's private here, not even the bathrooms."

My laugh echoed in the AV room. She was serious. She had made Chloe and Ann shit in a bucket, but she was offended by prison bathrooms. I shook my head, but appalling as it was, it didn't matter. The only thing that mattered was putting Skidmore on notice. She could have her lawyer. People could be listening. If she opened her mouth, it was on her.

Skidmore's eyes narrowed. She looked at Courtney through slits. That was the bad news. Maybe she was going to keep her mouth shut. I stepped closer to the monitor bank, trying to decipher her body language. Had she become suspicious? Suspicious enough not to talk? I tried to read her mind through the screen.

She kept staring at Courtney. She sat up on the cot, stretched, massaged the back of her neck, wincing at some twisted muscle.

"What are you doing here, Cindy-I-never-heard-of?" she asked.

I breathed a sigh of relief. It wasn't a straight fuck-off.

"I went to see Zach in prison," Courtney said. "It was, like, all over the internet that he'd been arrested or something. I wanted to see him. I had to wait over an hour, and there were really weird people in the waiting room, but I saw him. When we finished talking, he asked me to come see you and tell you he was okay and stuff. I . . . I don't think he knew you were in jail too. I didn't know until I got here."

I shook my head in disbelief. I was no stranger to undercover work, but I had years on Courtney. I wasn't sure how she managed to fake being such a ditz when she was so damn smart, how she stayed in character and still strung all the right words together to keep Skidmore talking, all with basically no experience doing that kind of thing. And it worked.

"Is it true? Did you see him? He's okay?" Skidmore machine-gunned her questions.

"Yeah. I mean, I saw him. I don't know how okay he is. Like, I wouldn't be okay in jail, you know?"

Skidmore's shoulders relaxed on the screen. "He's going to be okay. He's strong. They can throw him in a hole and keep his mother away. It won't break him. He's a fighter. He'll show them what he's made of."

"And he won't be there long, will he? I mean, he told me what happened. Those bitches were going to ruin his life. He had a right to defend himself. It's, like, self-defense or something." Courtney was following the basic approach we'd devised—pretend you already know everything so Skidmore might feel free to talk about it. Sometimes, it worked. This time, it got a different reaction altogether.

Skidmore's jaw jutted forward. "I don't know what he told you, but he needs to shut up. And you—" Skidmore pointed at Courtney, jabbing a finger in her direction. "You're going to keep your goddamn mouth shut."

Courtney jumped back. "Yes, sure, of course. I won't say a word."

"Now, get out!"

Courtney kept talking over her. "It's just that I need him out of jail. I love him. And some people online are saying he killed one of those girls. He would never do that, but I'm scared."

Nice job, Courtney, I thought for the hundredth time. She'd managed to bring in the murder on her way out.

Skidmore jumped up from the cot. She stood with her nose inches from the holding cell's bars. Her words came out in an angry whisper, but we could still make them out.

"He didn't kill anyone," she said with a snarl. "I didn't kill anyone. We did nothing wrong. They can't put a mother in jail for helping her son. Now get out and shut up!"

I clicked the mic. "Go ahead and beat it. You got all you could. Good work."

We watched Courtney half walk, half run up the row of jail cells. Once she disappeared from the screen, Tornero thanked Officer Mills and reached for the door.

"Let's talk outside," he said.

He led me down a different corridor to a door with a big red *Alarm*

Will Sound sign on the push bar. He pushed it open. No alarm sounded. I squinted in the sunlight, and Tornero kept walking across the
parking lot to a thicket of trees. He leaned against a trunk, pulled a
cigar from his jacket, and lit up.

"My biggest vice," he said, puffing the cigar to life. "I try to keep it
to one a day."

I looked for a spot with the most shade, not that it provided much
relief from the heat. I was sweating already. I turned to Tornero. "I'm
sorry it did not work out. I wish we could have helped."

"We have more than we had before."

"A mother helping her son?" I asked, echoing some of Skidmore's
last words before Courtney left. "That's not much to go on. It's not going to make or break bail."

Tornero blew a mouthful of smoke into the sky. "No, it probably
won't. But it's one more argument for the lawyers to slip in. And we got
something else in all this, though perhaps not quite what we thought. I
don't think this woman killed Ms. Raymond."

I clenched my teeth. I didn't want to admit it, but he was right.

"I agree," I said. "It's hard to read anyone, especially in jail, and especially someone we don't know and barely talked to. But she sounded
pretty riled up. She hurled the words at Mach one, no filter. Her denial
rang true. The ASA will take another crack at her, but whatever else she
did, she didn't do that."

Tornero heard something in my voice, maybe something that
echoed his own feelings. He squinted at me from behind cigar smoke.
"You thought it was her."

"I did. She could have shown up at the house to help her son with
the girls, confronted Christine as she came out, raised her gun, and
shot her. The scenario made sense. You even found a forty-five at her
house. The only problem is, I'm convinced it didn't happen that way."

Tornero chewed on his cigar. "Who does that leave? Zach
Skidmore? His associates? Ms. Overby thought they were reluctant
to help."

"They helped, reluctant or not. They were facing serious time and didn't want Christine to escape and raise the alarm. Zach could have dragged either or both of them over to help at the beach house. Someone could have fired in the heat of the moment if they had a gun."

"Either of Zach's accomplices known to carry a gun?" Tornero said.

"No," I said. It sounded like an admission. "Matt Stewart claims he hates guns, and I'm tempted to believe him. Cornell might. I don't know. Either way, that's all we've got. What's the alternative? Christine runs into someone who kills her between the house and the resort three lots away?" I was keenly aware I was echoing CJ's words. She'd been right then, and it was still a damn good question.

Tornero puffed and grumbled to himself. He picked a piece of tobacco from the tip of his tongue. "It wouldn't be a homeowner shooting her thinking she's an intruder. The other two houses are empty this week. Maybe someone on the resort who saw her and stopped her before she made it?"

I threw my arms up in frustration. "I don't know who. I talked to the resort's owner, and the place emptied pretty quickly after the Fourth. It's not going to be the parents."

"The Bergers didn't seem too friendly to the other two families."

"They're not. But I don't think they're going to kill a twenty-year-old kid over it."

"I've seen weirder things, and I'm sure you have too. I'm not saying it's them, mind you. More likely, Skidmore is not the only person covering for her son or his friends. We just don't know who else is in the game yet."

I leaned back against the tree that was providing me some shade. "Another accomplice? Shit, Cap, I don't know. Anything's possible. That's the problem. 'Anything' won't give us answers."

Tornero pulled at his mustache. He looked down at the ground, and I looked down at the top of his head.

"We'll execute search warrants on behalf of Miami-Dade tomorrow," he said, "at the kids' residences and their families'—the Stewarts and the Cornells. I'll go with the search parties myself and question the parents. I'll let you know if anything comes up, weapons or otherwise."

I was distracted by the sound of footsteps before I could answer Tornero. Courtney and Michaels were approaching our shady spot, crunching twigs underneath their feet.

"What a horrible woman!" Courtney said as they joined us.

"She is that, but you played her as well as anyone could," I said.

"Thanks."

I turned back to Tornero. "Anything else we can do for you, Captain?" I figured we'd speculated our way to nothing long enough for one afternoon.

"No, but my thanks to you both. I appreciate the assist."

"You're welcome," Courtney and I said in unison. Then Tornero and I promised to talk soon, and I led Courtney away, leaving the captain with half a cigar and a Detective Sergeant to work on.

Courtney added her voice to the chorus of disbelief as we walked to the car. "Do you really think she killed Christine?"

"No."

"So . . . what do we do now? Back to the office?"

"Not yet. There's something else I want to check first."

CHAPTER 23

Later that afternoon, Courtney sat on the back bench in the corner of the Courtroom. Her job was to observe body language up close. I would watch Skidmore's first appearance from the car on a Zoom link. Even if Skidmore saw Courtney, she'd think nothing of it. Courtney's presence would fit her story. Mine had the potential to be, shall we say, disruptive.

I tapped my fingers against the gear shifter, Courtney's laptop resting on the steering wheel. I watched as the judge called other cases, my growing impatience apparent from the staccato beating the shifter was taking.

I passed the time trying to read the judge's mood, his temperament. He was a tall African American man with mahogany skin, wild white hair, and a full beard. He liked to ask questions, even on what seemed like simple cases. Lawyers seemed to know they'd better give direct answers. I shrugged my frustration. I couldn't tell if it would help or hurt us.

A text from Courtney interrupted the monotony. Michaels had seen her in the courtroom and texted her to make sure I wasn't planning to show up. I reassured them both that I had no intention of causing a scene. I'd stay in the car with the engine running and the air conditioning on full blast.

It took forever until the judge gaveled the case I'd been waiting for, Florida v. Skidmore, followed by a case number. When he did, Tiffany shuffled to her table, suddenly appearing in the middle window on my screen. She wore the same clothes and vacant look she'd had in jail. The judge started talking before her lawyer, a big guy in a dark suit, had settled in next to her, and launched into the same kind of announcement that had started every other case.

"Ms. Skidmore," he said, "you are appearing today on two charges of kidnapping. This is a felony in the first degree. The lesser-included offense is false imprisonment. The state has reserved the right to amend or to add charges. You have the right to counsel, and I see you have counsel with you. Have you had the opportunity to confer with your attorney?"

Skidmore and her mouthpiece rose. She looked like a deer in headlights. She turned to her lawyer, who smiled and nodded. "Uh, yes," she said, "yes, Your Honor, I have."

"Very well, then. Did he explain that you will not plead guilty or not guilty today? That will come at arraignment after the State files formal charges."

"Yes, I understand."

"You may sit down." The judge looked down to make a note, then back up at the courtroom—and the camera. "Counsels will note their appearance."

"Assistant State Attorney Dennis Orrin for the State," the prosecutor said from his table without standing up. He'd handled first appearances the whole time I'd been watching.

"Matt Scheer for the defense," Skidmore's attorney echoed.

"I'll hear the State on bail," the judge said, turning his attention to the ASA.

Dennis Orrin rose, standing tall behind his table. Tall did not mean imposing. He was a string bean of a man with an awkward stance and the pale skin of someone who spent too many hours indoors behind his desk. He had a receding hairline, hollow cheeks, and a long neck above a plain navy-blue tie. He held a pair of reading glasses in his right hand as he spoke.

"Thank you, Your Honor," he started. "We filed a motion for pre-trial detention and are asking for the defendant to be remanded into state custody without bail."

"What?" Skidmore's shrill voice rang out.

The judge turned to the defense table. "Do you need a minute, Counsel?" He had the tone of a man used to those kinds of interruptions.

On my screen, Skidmore's lawyer whispered in her ear. For a moment, she looked ready to argue with him. He kept talking, and eventually, she nodded.

Too bad, I thought. If she wanted to piss off the judge, I was okay with that.

"My apologies, Your Honor," Skidmore's lawyer said, looking up. "It won't happen again."

The judge nodded and turned his attention back to the other table. "You may proceed, Mr. Orrin."

"Thank you. The charges here are kidnapping. We intend to seek life imprisonment due to the heinous and gruesome nature of the crime. This qualifies as a no-bail offense. The victims in this case were found locked up in the defendant's garden shed. They had been locked in there for several days in dangerous heat, with nothing but two cots and a bucket in which to urinate and defecate."

ASA Orrin spoke in a dry, monotone voice, not one word louder or softer than the next. It took me a moment to realize that it worked. It wasn't Hollywood, but it worked. It gave the impression he was giving the judge all the facts and just the facts, and the judge had no choice but to agree with him. I leaned in and listened more closely.

"There is overwhelming evidence of guilt at this stage," Orrin was saying. "The victims were freed by a private investigator acting at their families' behest. Without his intervention, they might well still be relieving themselves in a bucket in the defendant's shed. We have the investigator's statement to MCSO and the victims' sworn testimonies.

In light of the circumstances surrounding the crime and the weight of the evidence, pretrial detention is appropriate.

"I would add that Ms. Skidmore is a prominent and powerful woman which, paradoxically, counsels against bail in this matter. She has the money and connections to abscond. She is used to operating in a world of ease and influence and now faces the prospect of life behind bars. She presents a definite flight risk."

"What is the predicate for the kidnapping charge?" the judge asked.

I'd looked up a couple of things while Courtney and I waited for today's first-appearance session. The difference between false imprisonment and kidnapping was the motivation behind the crime. It was also the difference between a few years away and the possibility of life in prison. This judge wanted to know why this qualified as a kidnapping charge.

"The victims were taken to facilitate a felony," Orrin answered. "The victims' testimonies leave no doubt that they were kidnapped to shield Ms. Skidmore's son, Zach Skidmore, from the consequence of firing a weapon into a crowd, resulting in the death of a bystander.

"The victims further testified that they were first held at another location—we also have forensic evidence of that—and Ms. Skidmore and her son, acting together, moved them to the shed. Ms. Skidmore was further heard stating that she was helping her son."

"Has Zach Skidmore been charged with the reckless homicide you mention?"

"We are waiting on ballistics, Your Honor. He is being held in Miami-Dade County on a separate attempted murder charge."

That seemed to catch the judge's attention. I liked that. I didn't like what he said next.

"What troubles me is that there seems to be an overwhelming weight of the evidence in your favor on the false imprisonment charge, but less so for the underlying felony necessary to make this kidnapping."

"Ms. Skidmore will spend years in prison no matter what," ASA Orrin responded. "There is no risk of a miscarriage of justice. I submit that the totality of circumstances supports pretrial detention—the weight of the evidence, the nature of the offense, the flight risk."

"Thank you, Mr. Orrin." The judge turned his head the other way. "Mr. Scheer?"

Matt Scheer, for the defense, was everything ASA Orrin was not. He was pure Hollywood. He was built like he played in the NFL and stood up with effortless grace. He smiled like a movie star, and unlike Orrin, he'd found time for a tan. He talked with his hands, making bold movements as if pontificating for a jury even though no jury was present to hear him. It rubbed me the wrong way, but the judge didn't seem to care.

Scheer huffed and puffed through his "Thank you, Your Honor," adding a grandiloquent "May it please the Court," and kept on going. "This is just ridiculous, Judge. Most of their so-called evidence will be thrown out. My client was arrested in the most dubious of circumstances after a private detective, with a history of harassing her, forced his way into her house, destroyed her property, and hog-tied her for the police to find."

I should have done a lot worse, I thought, glaring at the screen.

"Was the private investigator acting under the color of law?" the judge asked.

"I do not know at this time. We are investigating."

"And the victims *were* found in your clients' shed"—the judge glanced at his papers—"with no air, no windows, two cots, and a bucket?"

"This is where they were found at the time of the arrest. That is all I am prepared to say at this time."

"Please go on."

"Thank you, Your Honor. The point I wish to make here is that such questionable evidence should not count toward the weight-of-the-evidence factor that the Court may consider in determining bail. But even if it did, it supports false imprisonment at most. That's a third-degree felony. In over twenty years in this profession, I have never heard of denying bail on a third-degree offense. Never! The statute simply does not support it."

"Will you address the flight risk?" the judge asked.

Scheer seemed to grow in size, occupying more space than the camera could capture as he gesticulated. "There is no flight risk. Ms. Skidmore has lived in Monroe County her entire life. She is not only a prominent member of the community and a friend of the judiciary but an anchor for the people in her community. Needless to say, she has no criminal record whatsoever. She is of impeccable character, to which the most distinguished people in the county will attest."

I choked on my own spit. Friend of the judiciary! I had no doubt she had contributed to the electoral campaign of every judge in South Florida. With a son like Zach, she'd need friends on the bench.

"But she has the means, and maybe now the motivation to flee," the judge said.

"Ms. Skidmore is as much a victim as anyone here, a victim of harassment and a vendetta. She is looking forward to her trial. And I am at a loss to understand my esteemed colleague's arguments about means to escape. He cannot be serious unless he would have the court deny bail to anyone who can afford a plane ticket."

"What is the value of Ms. Skidmore's home?"

Scheer bent down and consulted with his realtor client. "About two and a half million."

"Any mortgage?"

More whispers followed. "No."

"Thank you, Mr. Scheer."

The judge rested his bearded chin on steepled fingers for a moment. He did not take long. "I find that the weight of the evidence, taken together, as well as the callous nature of the offense, could justify remand. I also find that it evinces a disregard for the law that supports a finding of flight risk.

"However, I am not prepared to order pretrial detention at this time. The State's motion is denied. The court finds that pretrial conditions to release will suffice. Ms. Skidmore, I am setting bail at three million dollars, cash or bond. Additionally, you will surrender your passport and wear a GPS-enabled ankle monitor. You will bear the cost of monitoring.

"You may not go within two hundred feet of any airport or marina. Furthermore, you may not go any further north than Key Largo or any further south than Islamorada. If you violate any of these conditions, you will be back in jail until trial. Do you understand these conditions?"

"Yes," Skidmore said, barely loud enough for the judge to hear.

"Your Honor," Scheer said, "my client is a realtor with listings beyond the geographical limits the Court just announced. Maybe we could—"

"I'm sure she can work with other agents or make other appropriate arrangements," the judge interrupted. Scheer nodded. He knew when not to push. I slapped the laptop's lid close and waited for Courtney.

"What did you see?" I asked her before she sat down, let alone buckled up.

"Skidmore's scared. I don't think her lawyer did a good job preparing her for the possibility of life in prison. And she really hates you. I don't know if you could tell on the Zoom link, but she tensed up every time your name came up."

"I make friends everywhere I go."

"It's your sunny personality," Courtney said, looking away. She sounded a little bit like CJ. I wasn't so sure I liked this development.

"If she's scared enough," I said, "maybe she'll take a plea deal and save the lawyers some headaches. But that doesn't help us find Christine's killer."

"Is that what you were looking for?"

"Yeah. Even if she didn't do the deed, I still think she knows more than she said. I waited for a slip of the tongue, a careless word in their argument that might give us a clue, but we got a big, fat nothing. This was a fucking waste of time." I was grasping at straws, and I knew it.

Courtney looked out the window, thought it through for a while.

"If we couldn't get anything out of her in jail, and they didn't say any-thing sideways in court, maybe she doesn't know anything after all."

I liked that Courtney was getting confident enough to contradict me. It made her more valuable to me. I still disagreed with her this time.

"That may be," I said. "But I'm not ready to let her off the hook."

CHAPTER 24

There was no movement for two days after that. Correction. There was plenty of movement—in other cases. They were all worth the effort. They all mattered. But Christine Raymond's death still hung over me like a dark cloud that no wind could blow away.

Then the office door opened a little after noon, and Courtney's voice rang out with her customary good humor. "Hi, Sergeant Michaels."

"Hello, Courtney. And it's Brian, please."

"Sure. Are you here to see Coop?"

"If Mr. Malone is available," Michaels said, his formality reasserting itself.

Courtney saw me rounding the corner into the corridor and pointed at me.

"I'm available," I said.

We walked up to each other, shook hands, and I escorted Michaels past CJ's empty office to the conference room. CJ was out conducting interviews in a corporate fraud case involving gas cards and expense reports and other things that paid our bills but made my eyes glaze over.

"Thank you for seeing me, Mr. Malone," Michaels said once we'd sat down.

"It'd be pretty shitty of me to close my door when you drove all the way here."

"Yes, sir, I suppose so."

Shit, he might even have smiled at that. There was hope for the model officer yet.

"What brings you up here, Sergeant?"

"With Ms. Skidmore's attorneys trying to make something out of your involvement, Captain Tornero thought an unofficial—make that a private—visit from me would be more appropriate."

"Be careful. I might start liking your captain with that kind of thinking. What have you got?"

"In a word, nothing. We uncovered no weapon. None are registered to Matt Stewart or any immediate family member, and we found nothing at his residence or his parents'.

"Mr. Cornell Senior owns several firearms, but only one of the right caliber. It did not appear to have been fired in some time. We seized it to perform tests all the same, but we see that as a precaution."

"I know the game," I said. "When some defense lawyer scumbag asks if you considered any other suspect, you can recite chapter and verse, even if it's all a waste of everyone's time."

"Uh, something like that, yes, sir. Meanwhile, we are putting as many boots on the ground as we can, canvassing for witnesses. We will also conduct a new search of the house from which Ms. Raymond escaped, expanding it to the surrounding grounds. And we are working with MDPD and the Miami-Dade ASA's office to interview Mr. Stewart and Mr. Cornell."

"In other words, good police work. But not something worth the drive to Miami to tell me."

"Not in and of itself, no. Of course, old-fashioned police work may yield a lead, but . . ."

"But since you have none yet, you'd like to know if or when I might happen to find one, what with my unconventional methods and all."

Michaels didn't move a muscle. He said what he had to say over my sarcasm.

"Captain Tornero asked me to give you his word that we will share anything relevant to your client, and yes, we would love to hear from you as appropriate." He pulled a folded piece of paper from his shirt pocket and laid it in front of me. "This is my personal cell phone number."

"I catch your drift, Michaels. That's fine by me."

We said our goodbyes, and Michaels showed himself out, chatting with Courtney a little longer than necessary. I figured she was being polite. I didn't think she went for the clean-cut, starched-uniform type, but you could never tell, nor was I interested in unraveling that mystery.

I lost myself in my own thoughts. I was fine with Tornero's deal. It was my way of working anyway. I just didn't have anything for them—or anyone else, for that matter. That bugged the hell out of me.

It took another day before CJ knocked on my open door. I wasn't sure why she bothered knocking—probably because she was a civilized human being, and I was a Neanderthal. I barged in whenever I had something to say.

"What's up?" I asked.

"Two things. First, thanks for digging into cases without Raymond or Overby on the file jacket, even when these two still weigh on you. I think we're finally getting caught up."

"Sure."

"Second, you owe Philippa big time," she said, referring to her friend at MDPD.

"Okay. What does she drink?"

CJ rolled her eyes.

"That's right," I corrected, "she's a shooting buddy. What does she shoot?"

"I'll figure out a thank you present from you. She got you an interview with Matthew Stewart. He's still in custody, and she says he's been cooperating with the prosecution."

"Good."

"You do realize the victim of a crime does not usually interrogate the suspect and that you are the nominal victim of the attempted murder? Zach shot at you."

"I know. Why do you think I asked you to pull strings?"

"You're expected at 4:00 this afternoon."

"I'll be there. Thanks, CJ."

I got up and went for a walk. Much as I loved Miami, walks downtown weren't exactly pastoral delights. Horns blared, echoing on walls of metal and glass. Exhaust pipes belched in the air. But the simple act of walking, just one foot in front of the other, helped me think. It helped clear my mind.

Stewart was the weak link in the Skull and Coins gang. Philippa had just confirmed that. I prepared myself for the possibility he did not know anything. But then again, he might, so I wanted to approach him just right. Winging it never worked.

At the appointed hour, I drove along a block of high stone walls capped by barbed wire until I reached a small parking lot. The prison was right off the airport. I always thought there was some cruelty to that, inmates in the yard watching planes take off, carrying the rest of us to places they could not go.

Once in the building, I went through layers of security, one armored door after another. I was a vanilla visitor. I knew enough not to wear or carry anything prohibited, but it still took a while. The pat search was thorough enough to make Amy jealous, had she been the jealous type. She'd probably have asked them to frisk me again just for the thrill of it.

I eventually found myself sitting on one of two metal chairs on either side of a bolted table. It looked the same as any other interrogation room, with its gray walls, gray floor, and metal furniture, down to the ring built into the table to loop handcuffs through. Philippa had called in favors for me to be here instead of talking to Stewart through glass.

I didn't have to wait long. Within five minutes, a guard walked in, pushing a handcuffed Matthew Stewart in front of him. In his prison uniform, inmate Stewart looked pale and soft, eyes downcast. He'd seen better days, but at least he wasn't pissing himself.

The guard started looping the cuffs through the ring welded to the table.

I looked up at him. "You can take the restraints off. I do not feel in any danger."

"No can do," the guard said.

"I hear you. I know the rules, and I know he qualifies as high risk based on the offense. But he's been cooperating with the prosecution, and word is he's behaving in here. Unless you see a danger I don't, I'd consider it a favor."

"You're law enforcement?" the guard asked.

"Used to be. I'm a PI, now."

The guard hesitated. He looked from Stewart to me and back. "You're okay if I keep the live feed on?" he asked as he motioned to the ceiling camera in the corner behind me. "The sound will be off."

"I have no problem with that."

"I guess there's no harm in it," the guard said, sounding gruff. "The leg irons stay."

"Okay."

He removed the cuffs. "I'll be right outside the door," he added as he left the room.

"Thanks for the courtesy," I said.

He glanced back at me, nodded, grunted something that sounded like "sure," and closed the door behind him with a heavy metallic clank.

Stewart was sitting across from me, rubbing his wrists. "Thanks for that," he said, holding up his hands.

"No problem."

I took a long look at the prisoner in front of me. Court records showed the duty judge had set bail. It was unusual in murder—or attempted murder—cases, but Stewart had not carried a weapon or fired a shot, and the judge set bail after all. It was a hefty sum but doable for Stewart's family. And yet, there sat Matthew, in jail. I'd decided it would be my first question, something to open up the conversation, maybe even give me some context.

"I thought the judge granted bail," I said.

"My dad wouldn't pay it. He said I had to make things right and shoulder the consequences. He got me a lawyer, a really good one, so they don't run all over me, but no bail."

"Tough dad."

"Not really. I'm sorry for what I did. Some of it, I didn't know. The lawyer for the State showed me where Zack and his mom kept those women. I had no idea. Zach told me they were fine, that they were staying at his home, and that everyone was working things out. I didn't think they were free to go, but I never imagined it was as bad as it was.

"I'm sorry for that—for all of it. I know I'll have to do time, and it's okay. It has to be." He added that last part with a shrug. Prison was never okay for those inside. Prison was rough. It was supposed to be. It was punishment for the crime. That didn't mean I felt sorry for him.

"What about all the Skull and Coins shit?" I asked. "You're sorry for that too?" I was getting off-topic, but I wasn't going to let him play the "I'm sorry" act free of charge.

"Yes, sir, I am."

He looked at me as he spoke. Most inmates looked down when they played the remorse card. They thought it made them look contrite. It's part of the theater. By looking me in the eye, Matthew told me a little about him, enough to probe some more.

"Why did you do it then?" I asked.

"Zach and Robert are into it, and Robert is my friend."

"Don't feed me bullshit. I don't beat up homeless people because a friend is into that."

"I really like Robert."

"Enough to go to prison?" I leaned into his personal space, challenging him.

His lower lip quivered. "I . . . I love him. I'm in love with him, okay? He's straight, so I never expected anything to happen. He says he hates gays, actually, but that's because he thinks it makes him look tough. I just wanted to be next to him, even with all the stuff he and Zach were doing. That's all."

I stared at him for a long time. Puppy love came in all shapes and sizes. Stewart's puppy love was about to cost him years in prison. *Careful, Malone. Before long, you'll go soft on the guy.*

"I need to ask you about the kidnapping," I said.

"My lawyer said that you can't call it kidnapping."

Stewart was right. His father *had* found him a good lawyer. And just maybe he deserved one, maybe the system was working this time, or this little part of it. I thought about that and about how I'd made the prosecutor's job hard enough, and Philippa had pulled favors for me to be here. I owed some courtesy back.

I tapped the table with the flat of my hand, drumming a short beat. My mind felt like a pinball bouncing off a bumper. "Look," I said, "I don't work for the state. The Assistant State Attorney does not know I'm here. So, your lawyer does not have a right to be here. But if you want him to be, I'll understand." That was the last thing I wanted, but offering it was the right thing to do. Damn it all to hell.

Stewart shook his head. "No, it's okay. Zach shot at you. I figure I can at least talk to you. We just can't call it kidnapping."

"Alright. Let's talk about what happened on the night of July Fourth, then, and the days that followed."

Stewart nodded. He whispered something to himself that I couldn't make out. When he didn't say anything else, I got started.

"You took three women and locked them in a basement room on the night of the fourth to the fifth. Can we agree on that as a premise? I won't call it anything. No labels. Just facts."

Stewart nodded. I kept going.

"I know much of what led to that. What happened next? What did the bunch of you do after putting that padlock on the door?"

Stewart nodded like a bobblehead doll, even as he started talking. "We went back to the beach through the room we'd entered from, and we argued. Well, Robert and Zach argued. I didn't have anything to say. I was crazy scared.

"Robert poked Zach in the chest and asked, 'Now what?' and Zach batted his hand away and said he needed to think, and we'd handle it in the morning. Robert said, '*You* handle it in the morning, it's your mess,' so Zach called him a pussy, and it kept going on like this for a while. In the end, we all went home like Zach said and didn't decide anything else."

"You went straight home?" I asked.

"Yes."

"What did you do once you got there?"

"I was shaken up by what happened, so I took something to help me sleep and slept past noon."

"Where were you that evening, the evening of the fifth?"

"Home. I didn't move all day. My mom was there most of the time, and my dad in the evening after he got home from work. They'll tell you." His head jerked up. "And the cops have my phone. That should prove it, right? Like some GPS thing? They can look things like that up, can't they?" He pointed at the wall as if the evidence locker was right across from where we sat.

I could have told him it wasn't quite as simple as he thought or they made it look on TV, but I didn't answer him. I was the one asking questions. "What about Robert?"

"We chatted on and off. That will be on my phone too."

"Where was he?"

"Home, I think. It sounded like it, anyway. He didn't say anything about being anywhere else."

"Could he have gone back to the house with Zach, help him with the women in the basement since they're both into bashing skulls?"

Stewart winced. He seemed to shrink in size at the thought. He ran his fingers through his hair. Either it was a nervous tick, or he needed time to think of an answer. I waited him out.

"I doubt it," he said. "I hate how Robert is sometimes, especially with Zach—all that violence and stuff. But he was furious at Zach over those women."

"He was mad on the Fourth. That does not mean he was mad on the fifth."

"Maybe they'll let you read our texts. It's hard to remember everything we said. But he was still mad. He was mad at me because I thought we should lay low for a while, not do any Skull and Coins stuff, and he wanted to go out like always. But he was also mad at Zach for taking it too far."

I moved on to the next question, the one every other question had been leading to. "You locked three women in that basement. Zach's mother kept two locked up in her shed. What happened to the third?"

"She escaped," he said. He was no longer looking at me. He was looking at the smooth metallic surface of the table between us. He knew it wasn't true, but he toed the line.

"That's what Zach said," he added. "I was worried about it because she could recognize me."

"She was murdered," I snapped.

Stewart swallowed hard, still avoiding my eyes. "They showed me pictures. It's horrible. But I don't know anything about it. I swear. Maybe Zach lied, and he killed her. I don't know."

"Can you think of anything that could help me figure that out?"

Stewart closed his eyes. Eventually, he shook his head. Then he sat there, head still down, spent. He was jerked back to reality by the noise of my chair scraping against the floor as I stood up.

"Do you think you could put in a good word for me? That I helped?" he asked.

I looked down at him. "When they talk to me, your lawyer, the ASA, and whoever else, I'll tell them the truth. In your case, the truth will help."

I put a reassuring hand on his shoulder. There was no reason to deny him that. A few seconds later, I banged on the door and left the room. Matthew Stewart would be returned to his cell.

I worked the jail security in reverse until I left the building and crossed the parking lot to the CR-V. I called CJ on Bluetooth before I even turned onto the street, not bothering with hello.

"Stewart didn't do it," I said. "Robert Cornell is still a question mark."

"So, maybe him," CJ answered. "Or maybe Zach, as unlikely as it sounded the other day."

"We're not going to solve this case with maybes. Fuck, it could be someone else, someone who's not even on our radar, some crazy shit we haven't thought about yet. Your guess is as good as mine. Either way, I'll need another day away from the office on this case."

"When?" CJ asked. She would be the one juggling her and Courtney's time to make up for it.

"I'll let you know. I need to make a call."

CHAPTER 25

"**When" turned out to be** the next day. Cassie Raymond answered on the first ring when I called. She said I could come anytime. I took her up on it and let CJ know I'd be gone.

Even so, the next day seemed a long way out. I spent half the night pacing my living room. I got in trouble with Amy me for not sharing my frustrations with her. Eventually, I managed a little sleep before getting on the road to Orlando in the morning.

I didn't like having to go. I downright hated the idea of making the Raymonds talk about their dead child. But I had to start somewhere. Much as I loathed to admit it, I didn't think that Tiffany or Zach Skidmore had killed Christine. Robert "don't call me Bobby" Cornell was a lawyered-up black hole. Christine could have had the worst luck since Murphy wrote Murphy's law. She could have been kidnapped by one stranger one day and killed by another the next. Shit happened.

Then again, as Tornero pointed out, there were other possibilities, remote as they sounded. That didn't mean they fit any better. Nothing fit. Nothing made sense. This case didn't add up because I was missing something, a vital piece of the puzzle, maybe several. I had no clue who killed Christine, and it sounded like Tornero and Michaels didn't either.

So, I needed to start from scratch and to do that, I had to start with the victim.

The Raymonds lived on the southern edge of Orlando in a two-story home with beige walls, a paver driveway, and a three-car garage, all ensconced among other houses just like it in a neatly planned, upper-middle-class suburb.

There were few cars in the streets when I got there early in the afternoon. I saw more work trucks tending to lawns and pest control than private vehicles. People were either at work, running errands, or using those big garages for their intended purposes. The CR-V wouldn't look out of place, though. Most residents here spent their money on homes, immaculate lawns, and private schools. Flashy cars were not on the list.

I rang, and Cassie Raymond welcomed me with a firm handshake. She showed me into a house cluttered with too much furniture, too many knickknacks, and too many pictures on the walls. It looked haphazard. Some of it was new, some antique, some light, some dark, some soft and rounded, and some all-hard edges. Had it been less clean, it might have made an episode of *Hoarders*, but everything was spotless.

"We're on the lanai," Cassie said as we crossed the living room. "I have some lemonade and sweet tea waiting for us unless you prefer coffee."

"Coffee would be heaven-sent right about now. Thank you."

"I don't know about heaven-sent, but it is a fresh pot. How do you take it?"

"Black, thanks."

She stepped into the kitchen long enough to pour a mug, which she handed me as we walked to the lanai.

For most of us, a lanai is just Floridian for back patio. Hers was a pool area as wide as the house and nearly fifty feet deep, with a summer kitchen, an in-ground hot tub, and a dedicated dining area. Reggie sat on one of three chairs arranged around a small wrought iron table. He started up when he saw me.

"No need to stand up," I said.

I reached over the pitchers of tea and lemonade to shake his hand. Then I sat down, and Cassie lowered herself into the third chair, folding her arms over her belly.

My instincts are always to get straight to the point, but I am not devoid of humanity. I am not dead inside, not yet anyway. Those people had lost a child. I wasn't going to start interrogating them.

"I feel stupid asking how you're doing," I said instead, "but—how are you?"

A ghost of a smile crossed Reggie's face. "It is not a stupid question," he said. "Most people are afraid to ask. It's not their fault. They don't know what to do. These kinds of things are not supposed to happen, yet it did, right here, close to them. It unsettles them. And to answer your question, I don't know. I can't say I'm okay, but maybe I will be. I started seeing a therapist. He seems to help, or maybe I'm just helping myself by going. It's a process. It sounds like a cliché, but I guess it's true."

"I'm getting help too," Cassie said, smiling at her husband. "It doesn't make it easy, mind you. It may not even make it easier. I try to trust in that process, like Reggie said. And I trust in God and His plan, even when there are times when I want to kick both to the ground and keep kicking until they hurt as badly as I do. Forgive me, Jesus. All we can do is try. I go back to work in another week, just half-days. My therapist thinks it will help to focus on something else for a while each week. I'll try and see."

"And, of course, we have our son," Reggie said. "It would be unfair to him to stop living, and he needs our help figuring out life without his sister just as much as we need help."

The Raymonds were tag-teaming, letting loose some of their emotions for no other reason than I was there to listen. If it hadn't been me, it would have been someone else, a friendly neighbor or the proverbial milkman.

"Mornings are the toughest," Cassie said. "Even though Christine was away at college, she'd send me a good-morning text full of emojis some days. I keep looking at my phone next to my cup of coffee, expecting it to ding and her name to show up on the screen." She choked up as she finished her sentence.

Reggie took over. "Talking helps," he said, "but it hurts too. Suddenly, I realize I'm talking about my daughter in the past tense. It's unbearable. My therapist says it's good, that I have to embrace those feelings because they suck. I'm not so sure. It's tearing up my heart. It's like a little more of me dies with her every time."

It went on like this for a while. I just let Cassie and Reggie talk. They talked about displaying pictures of Christine on the mantel, taking them all down because it looked too much like a shrine, then putting them back up again. They talked about going on walks, sometimes the two of them, sometimes with their son. Reggie talked about trying to write Christine letters, only to stare at a blank page stained with tears.

I had little to offer, but that wasn't my role. If talking was good for them, I'd force myself to be patient for once, to find my compassion and give them time and space to share.

Then talking tapered off, and all eyes were on me.

"I won't sugarcoat it," I said. "The most likely suspects, those closest to the kidnapping, probably didn't kill Christine. I say, 'probably,' but I put them under a microscope as much as I could, and I haven't found anything pointing in their direction." I didn't mention that Robert Cornell was still too much of an unknown. That was for me to deal with. And what I told them was true. Nothing pointed at Cornell, even if nothing pointed away from him either.

The Raymonds didn't ask any questions, didn't probe, so I kept going. "If Christine ran into a random killer as she ran away, we won't know who that is until the cops find a piece of forensic evidence from their canvas, or the killer is caught doing something else, and then tied to Christine's murder. A random act like that is always possible, but it's damn unlikely."

"What, then?" Reggie asked. He was unfazed by my lapse in manners. There was something else in his voice, though I couldn't say what.

It could be harshness or impatience. But most likely, it was fear, fear that we may not find out. He believed the perpetrator would be caught and made to pay for taking Christine from him. That belief could not be shattered without consequences.

"That's why I'm here," I said. "To figure out what we're missing. I want to start by learning more about Christine, who she was, who her friends were, what she liked, what kinds of places she went to. If we assume this isn't random, this isn't an awful fluke, then I need to know her better."

The Raymonds took over once more while I sat back and listened. They talked for a good ninety minutes, taking over from each other, telling stories about their daughter. Even discounting their narrative for the proud-parent syndrome, multiplied by the loss of a child, Christine sounded like quite the woman.

She was well-rounded, both smart and popular.

She played sports because she liked the way it made her feel more than the competition, though she didn't like losing any more than the next athlete. She had her quiet moments—she loved reading biographies of strong women—and her crazy ones. She had a pregnancy scare in high school, which prompted her parents to stop pretending she was still seven and help her be a safer teenager. She had nightmares as a child and big dreams as a young woman, even if she had not yet figured out what major would best help her make them happen.

And then she died, and her dreams died with her, I thought. *And I don't know who did it.*

I didn't know what I expected coming here—probably nothing. This was a fishing expedition, if ever there was one. My bobber refused to budge.

"She stayed friends with Chloe and Ann in college?" I asked.

"She did," Cassie said. "In high school, they were inseparable. And I mean completely inseparable. It's how they met. We all live in the same area."

"Southern suburbs?" I asked.

Cassie chuckled. "Orlando may not be Miami, but it's still a large city. There is more than one high school in the southern suburbs. No, I mean this area—half a dozen communities and the businesses around them. They all went to UF in part so they could stay together. They had different classes and different new friends, but they stayed close."

"Inseparable is right," Reggie said. He pointed to the dining area behind me. "Jill spent many an evening with us right there while our daughters hung out in their high school years. Ann's mom, Jennifer, well, let's just say she's harder to like, a bit prickly. She drives the bus in their house, so we didn't see much of either parent."

Cassie took a breath, then seemed to think better of it.

"You were about to say something," I said.

Cassie pinched her lips, still hesitant.

"Cassie," I said, leaning toward her. "You strike me as the kind of woman who doesn't like to say anything bad about people. That's usually a good quality. And what you're thinking about may have nothing to do with finding who did this. But if there's one thing I've learned in my years investigating crimes, it's that you never know. The craziest thing can lead to something new, and suddenly, you figure it out. It all comes together. You can never tell."

Cassie looked at me and put a hand on her heart as if looking for guidance from within. Then she looked up briefly for guidance from above and started talking.

"Very well," she said. "But when I tell you all this, keep in mind, I am a religious person myself. Christine's death has been hard on my faith, but I still believe in God and that He is good."

"I hear you. I won't forget."

"Thank you. What I was about to say is . . . well, maybe I need to go back a bit. Jennifer Berger was born Catholic. When we met, she attended services at St. James Cathedral, as she had her entire life. As I said, I am religious, but God was even more a part of her life than mine. None of that was of any consequence. We loved Ann as if she were another daughter, and we liked both Jennifer and Bill.

"Then, the summer before the girls' junior year, Jennifer joined a small, evangelical church. Now . . . how do I say this . . . I suppose my overwhelming impression of Jennifer is that she'd always been an unhappy person. But after she changed churches, it got much worse. She became judgmental and nearly hostile. She closed up, and we pretty much didn't see her or Bill at all after that.

"This was hard for me to accept. My religion means a lot to me. It shows me so much love. I couldn't understand Jennifer acting that way. I tried to be happy for her if it gave her some kind of inner peace, but I could tell it was really hard on Ann. I was not exactly surprised when Christine told me Ann had grown a rebellious streak as a college freshman.

"That's what sparked my thoughts. I don't know how rebellious or what that entailed, and I absolutely do not believe it had anything to do with Christine's death, but you asked us about Christine's friends, so . . ."

"I appreciate that you shared. It may be nothing, but it's context. That's always useful."

I'd glimpsed Ann's rebellion from Courtney's dive into her computer—running after boys and the fights with her mom. I now knew it did not erupt out of nowhere. It had been simmering below the surface for a long time. Maybe it did more than simmer since the Raymonds had noticed the strain on Ann.

I followed up with a couple more questions, thanked the Raymonds for their time, and promised to be in touch. I thought over our conversation as I slowly exited the neighborhood. The car crawled over empty streets. If kids were playing in the summer heat, they were in backyard pools.

Cassie had been reluctant to talk about Jennifer and Ann. And she was right. It was probably nothing. But probably did not mean certainly. It gave me a trail to follow—the only trail I had. You didn't catch the big fish without chasing a few red herrings.

Most of Ann's friends would be on summer break, so sending Courtney back to Gainesville would probably be a waste of her time, even if she'd enjoy having the CR-V for another day. Jennifer was unlikely to talk to me since she hadn't when her daughter was missing. We'd talk to Ann and Chloe again, but we could do that by phone.

There was one more thing I could do though, and I might as well make the most out of being here. I stopped the car, looked up an address, and plugged it into the GPS.

CHAPTER 26

I t took me the better part of forty-five minutes driving up the Turnpike, across I-4, and through downtown Orlando to reach St. James Cathedral. It felt like it took me half as long again to find parking. Downtown Orlando was as bad as downtown Miami, and the single row of parking places next to the church were all taken.

St. James was a sprawling stone building with Spanish-tile roofing and the traditional rose window carved into the facade. A priest approached me as soon as I entered. I must have looked out of place. I explained why I was there. He asked me to wait.

The church looked even bigger inside, with a vaulted ceiling high above the nave and rows of stained-glass windows. Varnished pews and varnished wood floors let out a faint smell of polish. I started walking toward the altar, curious about the statues above it, but my greeter soon returned with a studious-looking priest in tow. He introduced the man as Father George, then turned back around, leaving the two of us alone.

"You were asking about Jennifer," Father George asked. He was gentle in manners, slightly stooped, with full yet receding hair. He looked more like a professor than a priest. His brown eyes seemed too big for his face behind rectangular eyeglasses.

"That's right," I said. I explained again who I was and why I was there.

"I will pray for Christine's soul," Father George said, crossing himself. "Poor child. But I don't understand what it has to do with Jennifer."

"Probably nothing. Jennifer's daughter Ann was fast friends with Christine. I'm trying to learn more about Christine, to see her through the eyes of people who knew her, like the Bergers."

"I'm not sure what I can tell you. All are welcome here, but the Bergers left our congregation. Bill and Ann were never as involved as Jennifer in any event, and she joined a different church. It must have been, oh, two or three years ago now."

"Has Jennifer visited since then? Maybe to pay a social visit, see old friends at church, participate in a charity event, anything?"

"No. Her departure was quite abrupt."

"Did she say why she left?"

"She didn't mention Christine, her family, or any of their friends— if that's what you're wondering. In fact, she didn't mention anything at all. One Sunday, she was in church. Three or four days later, the staff received an email saying she had joined that other church and would not be attending mass here anymore."

"Was that out of character?"

"The email part, maybe not. Jennifer was always shy, withdrawn even. Her leaving? Now, that was a shock. She'd been very involved with life here at St. James."

"What can you tell me about her new church?"

"Very little. I'm sorry. I'm not much help. I suppose not knowing is a little odd in and of itself. No matter how many churches there are in Orlando, we tend to know each other."

"What is it called? Where are they?" I asked, pushing.

"Uh, just a second," he replied, pulling his phone out. He mumbled something about looking for Jennifer's long-ago email, then something about church directories, but he eventually looked back at me.

"They call themselves the Holy Church of Sanctuary," he said. "I can give you the address."

I took it. It was better than nothing, and nothing is what this little trip had gotten me. It seemed I had one more stop today.

"Thanks, Father," I said.

"I'm sorry I couldn't be of more help. If you see the Bergers, please send my hellos. I will keep them in my prayers."

I told him I would and made my way back to the car and onto Orlando's crowded streets. I drove until the GPS told me I had reached my destination, its disembodied female voice promising that I had "arrived." If it had not been for modern technology, I would have easily missed the Holy Church of Sanctuary.

I pulled up to an unassuming, square, single-story stucco building with a flat roof. From the street, it might as well have been a warehouse. The parking lot seemed too big for the building's size. I coasted around half a dozen scattered cars and SUVs as I drove toward the structure.

I picked a spot close to the front and walked to the wooden double doors that appeared to be the only entrance to the building. It was hard to think of it as a church, even with the carvings on the door. The left panel had a cross, complete with Jesus crucified upon it. The other panel had two Bible verses carved into it. One read, *For he says to kings, "Thou art wicked" and to princes, "Ye are ungodly." Job 34:18*, and the other, *"Depart from me, you who are cursed, into the eternal fire prepared for the devil." Matthew 25:41.*

Wicked kings and eternal fire, I thought. *How cheerful.*

I pushed down on the lever door handle and tried the door both ways, in and out. It was locked. If the few cars on the lot were any indication, someone had to be inside, but the door wouldn't budge. So much for sanctuary.

I walked around the building. Sure enough, the front door was the only entrance. There were only a few small windows high up on the wall. But there was no shortage of cameras—a set of two on each corner. Upon closer inspection, I also found cameras mounted on the parking lot lights. This was starting to look more like a bank or a bunker than a warehouse, let alone a church.

I got back in the car, started the engine, and let the air conditioning cool me off—or try to. I took a minute to think, the supposed church vaguely menacing across the windshield. This place gave me the creeps, enough to feel tightness in my neck. I cleared my throat and made up my mind.

"Fuck it!" I said to the steering wheel as I put the CR-V in gear. Jennifer Berger may not want to talk to me, and it was getting late, but I owed it to myself to try. I owed it to Christine. Something wasn't right here. It may have nothing to do with her death, but I'll be damned if I was not going to make sure, one way or another.

I headed back south. It took longer this time. I got caught in the gathering swarm of rush-hour traffic. That, and I stopped at a strip mall for a sandwich and a Coke, lingering long enough that Jennifer would be back from work by the time I made it to her house. With my belly full, or at least full enough not to be hangry on top of being pissed off, I drove the last four miles.

I rang the doorbell a little after six. A lock slid, and the door opened. Jennifer Berger took one look at me.

"I don't want to talk to you," she said, starting to close the door.

"Hold on a minute," I asked, raising both hands. "I'm not here to bust your chops. This doesn't need to be a confrontation. A young woman is dead. Do the right thing here. Please."

"The right thing is to trust in the Lord, and after that, the police, but definitely not you," she said through six inches of space between door and doorjamb.

"I'm well aware of how you feel. But Christine's parents have asked me to see what I can do, so I'm gathering information. You may not like me. You may not even like them. But have a little compassion."

"I have plenty of compassion," Jennifer said, her face turning red.

"Enough to give me ten minutes?"

Jennifer pinched her lips but slid between me and the doorjamb, pulling the door shut behind her. She faced me and crossed her arms over her chest.

"What do you want?" she asked.

"Ann and Christine were close. You knew Christine. Tell me about her." I liked starting with open-ended questions. You never knew what people were going to say. Sure enough, I had not anticipated what came out of Jennifer's mouth.

"Christine was wicked," she said, her face turning a shade darker. "The devil takes many forms. Christine and Chloe led my Ann astray, away from the righteous path and into sin and vice."

I thought about the quote about wicked kings on the door of Jennifer's church. Her little speech was wicked enough for a hundred tyrants, and she was just getting started. She uncrossed her arms and jammed a finger toward my chest.

"Christine and Chloe got to Ann when she was pure. She was innocent, and those two spread their evil influence on her. They did the devil's work. They led her to sin and to destruction. They threatened her eternal soul.

"We live in fraught times, Mr. Malone. There is a war being waged, a war between good and evil, and this war is coming to our world. The devil is cunning and deceitful. He does not come to you with horns, a forked tongue, and a tail. He came to my innocent Ann through Christine and Chloe."

"Or maybe Ann grew up from a child into a teenager," I said. "It's never easy on parents, but children grow. They change. They explore this big world we live in."

"It was the devil's work, sir, the devil's. And Christine was his instrument."

"Are you saying Christine deserved to die?"

"She was punished for her sins."

A shiver traveled up and down my spine. I squinted at her. "By you?" I asked.

Tornero had asked if Christine could have been killed by someone at the resort. It seemed impossible then, but now, I wasn't so sure.

"By the Lord," Jennifer replied. "It is the Lord's shining lance that pierced her flesh."

I'd seen my fair share of representations of Jesus or God in my days, no more or less than the next guy. I didn't remember ever seeing a shining lance, let alone large-caliber bullets, but I let that go. I'd get better results by playing along.

"Who did the Lord's work, then?" I asked.

"Does it matter?"

"It matters in this world."

"I answer only to God in the next one."

I took half a step forward, closing what little distance remained between us. "Do you own a gun, Mrs. Berger?"

"Your time is up," Jennifer said. She reached for the door, stepped inside, and locked herself in.

Her math was off. It had been closer to five minutes than ten. I wouldn't get anything else out of her, though, so I turned around. I had a long drive ahead and a longer day waiting for me tomorrow.

CHAPTER 27

"**H**i, Coop," Courtney said when I walked in the next morning. Somehow, she always seemed to arrive before me, chipper as hell, too, no matter the time of day. It was getting annoying—or I was just in a mood. I hadn't had enough coffee yet for cheerful.

"Yeah, hi." I took a few steps and leaned over her desk.

"What's up?" she asked.

"I emailed you my report on yesterday's interviews. Clean it up and put it in the file, will you?"

"Already working on it."

"Thanks. And one more thing. We're throwing you into the deep end on this case, but if you're up to it, I'd like you to call Ann Berger. Interview her about what happened and also about Christine and their friends in general."

Courtney shrugged. "Sure. It can't be worse than talking to Tiffany Skidmore."

"Be honest with her," I said. "Tell her we don't know who killed Christine. Tell her we don't even know if she was the target. That will open the door to ask about Christine's friends and her own, how their families got along, all that jazz."

"Uh, what am I looking for?" Courtney asked.

"Frankly, I don't know. Something that sounds out of the ordinary. Ask general questions and let her talk. If something makes you go 'huh?' make a note of it. Come to think of it, there's no rush, so wait until CJ is available. You can put the call on speaker and put both your intuitions to work."

"That sounds good. Will do. Do you want us to call Chloe too?"

I stared at the desktop while I thought about it. "No. Ann will relate better to you, but Chloe will respond better to me, the guy her grandfather served with. I'll call her."

"Cool."

I made a mental note to call Chloe and stepped into my office. I had other plans for my phone to start the day. I may not have thought Tiffany Skidmore killed Christine, not anymore, but I was not ready to let her off the hook. She was still a person of interest to me. I couldn't quite put it in words, but something in my gut kept going back to her.

From what I heard at Skidmore's bail hearing, some people thought I was obsessed with her. But those people were paid to think that. And regardless, I didn't care. I'd been right to focus on her. I found Chloe and Ann locked up in her garden shed. I thought she was still hiding something now, so I'd keep hammering at her until I'd squeezed all the blood out of that turnip.

Just for shits and giggles, I googled Matt Scheer by searching his job and location without using his name. He showed up at the top of the page. Skidmore's attorney knew a thing or two about search engine optimization—by which I meant he'd hired good people to do that shit for him.

I closed my office door, sat at my desk, and leaned into my chair, putting my feet on my desk. Once comfortable, I dialed Scheer's office on speaker. I looked at the ceiling, a half-smile on my face, waiting for the gatekeeper to answer the phone.

"Law Office of Matthew Scheer, how may I help you?" a female voice answered. She sounded a little like a robot. That wasn't exactly a surprise. There are only so many Courtneys in the world.

"Cooper Malone," I said, "calling for Mr. Scheer."

"Is he expecting your call?"

"I'm pretty sure I'm on his list to call, so we might as well chat now."

"And what is this regarding?"

"Your client, Tiffany Skidmore." I made sure to make the distaste evident in my voice, but I refrained from answering her question with "murder and kidnapping by your scumbag of a client." That might have gone too far and ended the call.

"One moment, please."

The speaker crackled back to life a few moments later with the deep voice belonging to Matt Scheer, Esquire. I remembered it all too well from his antics at Skidmore's court appearance.

"Mr. Malone?" he asked, sounding mildly incredulous.

"That's me."

"Why, what a pleasant surprise!"

"It's a surprise, anyway."

"I'm an eternal optimist."

I swallowed back the urge to tell him that he'd have to be with the kind of clients he represented.

"Is that so?" I asked instead.

"Indeed. Though for all my optimism, you are not on my list to call. You were wrong about that too. You are on my mailing list for a subpoena."

I didn't take the bait—either one. I didn't ask what else I was supposedly wrong about. And I didn't ask about the subpoena. It didn't surprise me that he was smart enough to try taking control of the conversation. I was smart enough not to let him.

"You'll get your chance," I said, wiggling my toes inside my boots. "But maybe we can start with something more productive."

"And what would that be?" He kept his voice engaged, if not cheerful. He probably always did—a learned practice that had become a habit. Even so, he didn't sound too interested.

"I'm not buying that Skidmore doesn't know more than she's saying," I answered. "If the two of you were to sit down with me and the ASA, just the four of us having a chat, talking about hypotheticals and shit the way you guys like, maybe we can make a lot of people a little less miserable, including your client."

"You're deluded if you think my client had anything to do with any of this."

"Her garden shed tells a different story. So do the victims. And so does her son."

"Or that she knows anything about it," Scheer said over me.

I put my feet down and straightened up in my chair. I leaned closer to the speakerphone and tried not to sound exasperated.

"I'll take my chances," I said. "The most it can cost your client is an hour of your time, though that probably doesn't come cheap."

"Is the State Attorney's office even on board with your wild-goose chase?"

"Let's assume they'll show up at the party once you and I agree to play nice."

"That's a big assumption. So is the one that my client will sit down in the same room as you, no matter who else is there."

"Your client is a petulant child. I'll give you that. But I thought it was your job to get past her temper tantrums. All those Google reviews say you're supposedly good at it."

"You seem to think awfully little of Ms. Skidmore and an awful lot of yourself."

"I'm a good judge of character. Now, do you want to talk or not?"

He hesitated a moment before answering. "I think I'll wait until after I depose you."

I stood up, and the chair rolled back against the wall. When I answered, my mouth was inches from the speaker.

"You're not that dumb. Maybe you think I am, so let's clear the air. First, this offer for a friendly chat is on the table until I hang up, not a second longer. After that, *friendly* is over.

"Second, if you don't take advantage of my good mood, you'll be waiting a hell of a long time to talk to me. I'll move to quash your subpoena or refuse to answer based on our confidentiality rules. You'll argue it doesn't create privilege and a bunch of other bullshit. We'll go in front of a judge. That will take a month or two, maybe more. You'll probably win in the end, or maybe not. Maybe we get someone on the bench who likes to ponder what the meaning of 'is' is and gives our regulations a new interpretation."

There was a short silence on the other end while he processed that I could be just as much a pain in the ass as he could. Not that I had much hope it would tilt the balance. He probably thrived on making other people's lives as difficult as possible.

"I'll tell you what," Scheer finally said. "I'll talk to my client. If you can convince the State to send someone with authority, we can meet at, say, four o'clock tomorrow. My office. We can all chat. By all, I mean you, too, Mr. Malone, even after you find out Ms. Skidmore knows nothing."

That had been too easy. He hadn't changed his mind because I was being a jerk. He must have thought of an angle, something I wasn't seeing. Pinning me down to answer a couple of questions early wasn't enough. I drummed my fingers on my desk, thinking furiously—and needlessly. I was committed.

"We'll be there," I said.

I hung up, pulled my chair behind me, sat down, and picked up the headset. It took me longer to reach Assistant State Attorney Dennis Orrin through layers of bureaucracy than to convince him to show up. I told him I'd made his job harder (he didn't disagree) and that I was trying to make up for it, so he was receptive.

"What makes you think she's hiding something?" he asked.

My gut feeling morphed into a few words as I talked to Orrin. "She spent days going through the motions, asking Chloe and Ann to pretend they'd never seen Zach fire his gun. But they weren't going to change their stories. She had to know this. I think there's something more, something we're missing, and she can tell us what that is."

"It's more likely she thought they'd break if she kept them there long enough."

"I don't think so. She'd never be able to make sure they weren't lying to get out."

"Or she may have gone through the motions while trying to figure out what to do with them."

"It's possible but hardly certain. If I'm right and she knows something relevant to Christine's death, I'd like a crack at it."

"I still don't think you're right, but it's just possible enough to be worth the time. I'll join you."

"Thanks," I said. I gave him the particulars of the meeting, then I hung up.

That left damn near a day and a half. I spent some time on the phone with Chloe. She was charming and eager to help, but I didn't learn anything new, not anything useful anyway. I did busy work on other cases, things that didn't take too much brain power as my mind wasn't in it.

Mostly, I got pissed off at waiting too long without moving this case forward. I'd already spent three days away from it. One more was breaking this camel's back. And there was something else. Assuming my instincts were right, it was too much time for Scheer to come up with something sneaky. I was brooding about that too.

At least, I called Amy this time and asked her out instead of brooding alone. I'd learned my lesson. When we'd had a bite to eat and a couple of drinks, I stopped home long enough to grab a change of clothes and a toothbrush before heading to her place for the night.

"You know," she said over her cup of coffee the next morning, a devilish smile brightening her face, "we would have had an extra half hour last night if you kept a couple of T-shirts and a toothbrush here, and vice-versa."

I raised an eyebrow at her. Amy was unlike any woman I'd ever met, but it was a bit early to exchange drawer space, even for her.

"It's practical," she said.

"Uh-huh."

"And . . . I'm confident." Her voice took on a new softness. She put her coffee down.

I looked at her for a long time and realized what she said didn't feel odd. It probably should. I probably should be more cautious. We probably should take it slower. Fuck all that.

"I'm confident too," I said.

"Good," she said. I blinked as her eyes welled. She went on. "That's good. I know we've only been together three weeks and change, but—don't laugh, okay?—this is my longest relationship since college."

"You're kidding, right?" I wasn't exactly a poster boy for long-term relationships, but even I could beat that. And more to the point, I wasn't Amy. The way she looked, the way she loved . . . it seemed impossible.

"No joke," she said. "The bad boys like to fuck me but can't handle that I have a brain. The nice guys respect my mind but are intimidated by my wild side. I don't have patience for either, so no one's lasted this long."

"Fuck, I think I'm feeling ashamed of my gender."

She kept talking over my quip, not to be interrupted. "Remember when you freed Chloe and Ann, and I met you in the Keys, then we came back here, and you dropped me off at work on the bike the next morning?" She sounded nervous, her words tumbling out faster than necessary. Now she stopped, waiting for confirmation that I remembered.

"Of course," I said.

"One of my good friends at the office, Dee, came in right at that moment. Let's just say Dee knows me. Girls talk, you see. She grinned at me and elbowed me in the ribs as you left. She asked, 'Who's *that* bad boy?' and I told her it was the most decent guy I'd ever met. That's when I knew."

She stopped talking, her mouth hanging half open. I did her a solid and responded before she needed to say more, the words surprising me more than her. "I love you too, Amy."

She stood up. She took my coffee from my hand despite knowing how dangerous that was. She straddled my lap and gave me the softest, longest kiss we'd shared, and that was a pretty high bar.

"T-shirts and a toothbrush?" she asked as our lips parted company.

"T-shirts and a toothbrush," I said.

This day was starting right. I had a bad feeling about the rest of it.

CHAPTER 28

"**What the fuck!**"

Flashing blue lights lit up behind me the moment I crossed into Monroe County, and I swore at the dashboard. I don't deny that I tend to treat the speed limit as a suggestion. I did it that afternoon too. But I wasn't going so fast that MCSO should bust my balls over it. I pulled over, tried to find my Zen through gritted teeth, and waited for a bored deputy to ask me if I knew how fast I was going.

I'd kept my mind busy throughout the day by working on other cases. The only news in Christine's was no news. Ann, who was back in Gainesville, was eager to help when Courtney and CJ called her, but she didn't have any helpful information. That meant it was up to me to find something. It was annoying enough having to wait until four in the afternoon for this meeting. I didn't have time for some speed trap bullshit.

I gathered my paperwork and watched a uniformed officer amble along the street to my vehicle. He started walking the minute he stopped behind me.

And Detective Sergeant Brian Michaels leaned in my window and smiled at me. "Good afternoon, sir," he said.

"Yeah, that. Good afternoon, Sergeant. You don't seem surprised to see me."

"No, sir."

"Then I'm guessing you're not here because you pissed some-one off badly enough to be sent to a corner working a radar in the afternoon sun."

"No, sir. Not that I know of."

Michaels was leaning in, one hand on the CR-V's roof, head at window height. He was grinning like an idiot.

"Spit it out, Sergeant," I said.

"Something interesting happened. A criminal complaint was filed against you late yesterday for harassment, trespass, and false imprison-ment. Then, this morning, we received an anonymous tip that you'd be crossing the county line right about this time of day."

I could only laugh. "Let me guess. The tip came from Matt Scheer's office."

"The caller ID was masked, but that is my guess."

I knew Scheer hadn't merely changed his mind on our call yes-terday. He'd come up with something screwy. Now, I knew what. He was trying to make his bogus defense sound better by making the cops investigate me. What better way to paint me as the aggressor and Skidmore as the victim? Forget about the kidnapped women. They didn't matter to him.

Michaels took off his hat, wiped his brow, and put it back on. "How did Mr. Scheer know where and when you'd be?" he asked me.

"He agreed to a meeting at his office with Skidmore, the ASA, and me at four o'clock today."

"You won't make it if I follow protocol."

"Which is?"

"To detain you based on the sworn complaint and question you on the charges therein."

I shook my head. Scheer would know that, of course. He was count-ing on it. He was counting on putting me on the stand at Skidmore's trial and asking if I'd ever been detained for trespassing on his pre-cious client's property and imprisoning her. I'd be forced to say yes, and jurors don't know the difference between detained, indicted, or even convicted.

One point for Scheer. The spotlight would be on me for harassing a kidnapper. He was a sneaky son of a bitch.

"Is that what you're going to do, follow protocol?" I asked Michaels. My neck muscles tensed. He could just be enough of a good soldier.

"Captain Tornero gave me discretion on how to proceed after talking to you. We can't appear to be playing favorites or ignoring a complaint. By the same token, we do not appreciate being played."

I leaned back against the headrest, tapping my fingers against the steering wheel. Traffic zoomed past us, from deafening semis to whispering Teslas.

I turned to him, one hand still on the wheel, raising the other palm. "There's always a chance he'll drop the complaint after our meeting," I offered.

"I don't think Mr. Scheer intends to have that meeting," Michaels said, frowning.

"He'll have to go through the motions if I show up. The ASA's involved."

"That's all he'll do—go through the motions."

"That will be his intent. But you never know what happens once people start talking."

"I suppose that's true." Michaels pouted through his words as if unsure he really believed them.

I pressed on. "That may be reason enough for you to stay your hand in good faith. Wait and see. If there's no movement at the meeting, I'll come and have a chat with you voluntarily. You won't even have to detain me, so you'll have done your duty and taken that word, 'detained,' out of Scheer's quiver at trial."

Michaels slapped the roof of the car and tipped his hat. His pout turned into a smile. "Alright, I like it. I can work with you on that. But I am counting on you to call me right after that meeting, no matter what."

"You have my word."

He straightened and wished me a "You drive safe, now, sir" in his best cop voice. I flipped him off with a grin and accelerated off the shoulder. I even made it to my destination on time.

Scheer's office was located in a large house on a shaded corner lot off US 1. It could have passed for a southern mansion despite sharing the block with a strip mall, complete with its coffee shop, computer repair store, and other indispensable commerce.

I parked on the street, walked to the covered porch running the length of the house, and crossed to a faded front door that had once been some shade of blue. Or maybe gray. It was hard to tell.

Dennis Orrin, the Assistant State Attorney, was already there, sitting on a plain wooden chair the same faded color as the door. It looked uncomfortable as hell. I recognized him from Skidmore's first appearance, but he'd never seen me before.

I extended my hand to him. "Mr. Orrin, I'm Cooper Malone," I said.

He stood, smoothing his suit jacket, and shook my hand. The front-desk person stopped typing when she heard my name. Orrin noticed. It was pretty obvious. He glanced at her, then back at me.

"I'm going to need a minute before we all chat," I said in answer to his unspoken question.

He glared at me. "Are you going to make my job harder again?" He was dead serious.

"I'm hoping to make it easier," I said.

I turned to the front desk, which was nothing more than a distressed wood table painted white, with a phone, a laptop, and a printer on it, haphazardly plugged into an old outlet in the wall. The lady staring at me from behind the desk was fair-skinned and black-haired. She looked younger than she'd sounded on the phone.

"I need to talk to your boss," I said.

She cleared her throat. "You'll actually be in the conference room. I'll see if Mr. Scheer is ready. If you don't mind taking a seat?"

"I do mind," I said and walked past her.

Her chair creaked as she turned around. "No! Sir! Mr. Malone!!"

Scheer's voice came through a closed door to my left. I went that way, ignoring the sounds of protest and indignation behind me, and barged through the entrance to the office from which his voice came. I found Matt Scheer sitting behind a massive desk, a phone pressed to his face, looking the part in suspenders and a crisp, white shirt. His jacket hung from the back of his chair.

He looked up and barked into the phone. "I'll have to call you back." He hung up without waiting for a response.

"You and I need to talk," I said.

A presence behind me made me look over my shoulder. A security guard filled the doorway in his make-believe uniform, a taser on his hip. I wondered if he was there just for me or if Scheer had such shady clients that he required full-time protection.

I ignored Rent-A-Cop and turned to Scheer. "I said 'talk.' If I wanted to beat you up, I'd already be behind your desk."

Scheer waved off the guard. "Thank you, Sam. We'll be all right. And close the door, please."

I started talking before the door was fully closed. "If it's MCSO you were on the phone with, you can save yourself the call back. Your little stunt fizzled."

"I have no idea what you're talking about," Scheer said.

"Oh, cut the bullshit! I don't mind you playing hardball, but don't insult my intelligence."

Scheer spread his hands. "If you play dirty, you've got to expect mud on your face."

I sat down without being asked. "You know, they teach you a couple of things about the law in criminal-justice programs. One is that the system doesn't work because lawyers make sure it doesn't. It's all a game to you guys—who can dream up the cleverest argument, take the jury for the longest ride. That whole thing about searching for the truth is a damn fairy tale. Let me make one thing clear. It wasn't a game for Chloe and Ann—or for Christine."

Scheer wheeled his chair backward as I talked, stretched his legs, and folded his arms over his chest. "If you want to debate rules of evidence and fair trials, I'll bullshit with you when this trial is over. I'll even buy you a beer—if you're not in jail."

"Another thing they teach you," I said, ignoring him, "is that even lawyers must live by a set of rules, not to mention laws. Trying to get the cops to detain a witness smells an awful lot like intimidation. But I'll be happy to debate it over that beer. If you still have a license."

Scheer chuckled. It really was a game to him, and he was enjoying it. "Let me worry about the law, Mr. Malone. But at least you're making this case interesting. I should be thanking you."

"You're welcome. Is your client even here?"

"She's here."

"Are we going to have that meeting then, or are you afraid she'll spill the beans?"

"Do you play basketball, Mr. Malone?"

"What?"

"Basketball."

"No."

"Two on two is the best exercise. I love it. I play every week. We'll meet, the four of us, two on two. It will be good exercise. You're still wasting your time, but we'll play."

"Play" seemed like the right word. It was yet another game to him. I got up, turned on my heels, yanked the door open, left Scheer's office, and went to join Orrin in the lobby. I waved at the security guard standing dutifully outside Scheer's door on the way by.

Orrin was reading some papers, sitting in the same wooden chair he was in when I got there, his reading glasses perched on the tip of his nose, light reflecting on his balding forehead. He looked up at me over the lenses.

"You caused a ruckus," he said.

I sat down next to him in an identical chair. I'd been right. They were uncomfortable as hell.

"It's one of my many talents," I said.

The woman at the front desk must have agreed with that. She shot me a dirty look.

Orrin took his glasses off and turned to me. "Did you make my job harder?" he asked.

"Not this time. Maybe I even helped a little. We have a few minutes to talk it over. Scheer's going to have to explain to his client why we're having this meeting after all."

Orrin squinted at me. As if on cue, Scheer crossed our field of vision, all put together with his suit jacket on, presumably on his way to the conference room.

I told Orrin about Scheer's stunt and my conversation with him. He played with his glasses as I talked, the papers he had been reading lying flat on his lap.

"Witness intimidation requires harassment or threats," he said, talking mostly to himself. "Filing a complaint does not normally rise to that level." He spoke in whispers, conscious that the front desk had ears just a few feet away.

"I'm no lawyer, but I'll argue that the complaint's only purpose was to threaten me."

Orrin grimaced as if he didn't want to fight with me over it, but he didn't see it.

"Not that I care anyway," I continued. "Scheer and I won't be sending each other to jail. He's fighting dirty, and I'm punching back. He probably has little choice. Correct me if I'm wrong, but blaming the victims, or in this case, the PI who found them, is the only strategy he's got."

"You won't hear an argument from me. The evidence against his client is solid. Using you to keep some of it out, maybe gain sympathy for his client, that's a good move."

"It may be, but it's still bullshit." I hated lawyers.

Whatever Orrin was going to say next was drowned out by a ringing phone. The lady up front kept her eyes on me as she said a simple,

"Yes, Mr. Scheer."

She seemed annoyed, hanging up the phone a little too hard, her lips set in a straight line. "If you'll follow me, Mr. Scheer is ready for you."

I was ready for him.

CHAPTER 29

The receptionist stood up behind her table, waiting for us to follow suit.

Orrin picked up his briefcase from the floor, put his papers back in it, and slid his glasses in his jacket's breast pocket. All that done, he stood up, and I stood up behind him. We followed the young lady to the last room on the right.

Skidmore was seated on the far side of the conference table wearing a cream-colored business suit and a pale pink blouse. She had her back to the window, her hair like a helmet and her arms crossed over her chest. She had pushed her chair a foot or two away from the table as if sitting any closer would put her too close to me. She did not move or say a word when we entered.

Scheer reached over the table to shake Orrin's hand, then we all sat down. Scheer was poised, sitting comfortably, his hands folded in front of him like a CEO about to call a board meeting. You wouldn't know his client was facing life in prison. That was the point. He wouldn't want a jury thinking about that all through trial, either, wouldn't want them to think of her as a criminal.

"So, Mr. Malone," he said, "what makes you believe my client has anything to say?"

I dove right in. I was never going to be on friendly terms with that woman. Trying to build a rapport was pointless.

"Your victims tell me you spent your time talking to them through the door," I said, "trying to convince them to change their story, to forget what they saw."

"Mere allegations," Scheer said.

"Sworn testimony," Orrin interjected.

"I don't care what we call it," I said. I drilled a stare into Skidmore's skull. "You're not that dumb. You've made a career out of reading people, selling them million-dollar homes, and figuring out what they like and what they don't, whether they are serious or not. You knew Chloe and Ann weren't going to change their tunes. Or if they did, they'd change it right back. I want to know what this was really about. You tell us, and maybe you'll be helping yourself with Mr. Orrin here."

"Is that why you wanted this meeting?" Sheer asked, raising his voice. "Some harebrained theory? What you think happened does not make sense to you, so you want a bedtime story instead?"

Skidmore must have learned her lesson from her first appearance. She was a statue next to Scheer.

"Except that it did happen," I said, "and it doesn't make sense. Why don't you let your client answer? What are you afraid of, Scheer?"

Scheer raised his hand in front of Skidmore just in case I'd baited her after all. He answered instead. "We are not admitting anything happened. Ms. Skidmore has nothing to say in response to your fantasies. We are done with your questions as they are nothing more than a fishing expedition and up the wrong stream to boot, which means it's time for my questions."

He was already on to his backup plan—a free depo. Even if I'd been willing to play ball beforehand, that came off the table the moment he filed his complaint against me. Either way, his rush to shut his client up told me I was right. I'd just have to find the information a different way.

I started getting up when Skidmore put her hand on her lawyer's shoulder. I sat back down, ass on the edge of my seat, ready to leave if it meant nothing.

Scheer leaned back, and Skidmore whispered something in his ear. Try as I might, I couldn't make out any of it. They talked for a minute like that, cheek to cheek like perverted lovers whispering sweet nothings.

When they were done, Scheer turned to ASA Orrin. "What kind of conversation could we have if Ms. Skidmore had information relevant to the murder of Christine Raymond?"

Orrin leaned back in his chair, looking unconcerned. "If she can help solve a felony, I might be willing to forget about the underlying felony in her case. She does the max on false imprisonment."

I expected something out of *Law & Order*. One side says, "She pleads to this and does that many years," and then the haggling starts. Maybe that's even how it's usually done, and Orrin was enjoying a little poetic justice to back up his move this time around, one felony for another. What did I know? I was never in the room after I found the perp.

Either way, Scheer found no poetry in Orrin's reasoning. "One year," he said.

"One look at the makeshift prison where she kept the victims, and she gets the max in court—and on kidnapping charges no less once ballistics comes back in the Howard case." Orrin said. "This is the best deal she'll get."

Skidmore looked back and forth between the two men like a spectator at a tennis match who tried to understand what was happening but did not know the rules.

"I can't go to prison!" she said, blurting out the words before Scheer could respond.

"Will you give us the room, Dennis?" Scheer asked, dropping to a first-name basis.

That surprised me for a whole second. Those two probably crossed swords often enough to know each other well. They traded insults in court one day and played golf the next—or basketball. That seemed to be Scheer's sport.

Orrin picked up his briefcase. I took my cue and stood up with him.

"Thanks," Scheer said. "Mary Jo will show you to the other conference room."

We left the room. By the time we made it back to the lobby, Mary Jo—as it was evidently her name— was putting the phone down and standing up.

"This way, please," she said, extending her hand. We followed her down the corridor to the left of her desk, past Scheer's office, and into a conference room identical to the one we had just vacated at the other end of the house.

"What's the max on the false imprisonment charge?" I asked Orrin as we sat down. Mary Jo closed the door behind her on the way out.

"Five years."

"And she could get out early on good behavior?"

"She could."

I chewed on that. She'd only kept the girls for a few days, but that was because I found them. The low time wasn't sitting well with me.

"Would she do real time, not tending gardens at Club Fed?" I asked Orrin.

"That's up to the Department of Correction. She'll ask for a minimum-security designation and to be sent to Homestead because it's closest to her family. We'll oppose, but neither of us has much say in it. Security designation is pretty standardized, and location depends on beds available as much as anything else."

We didn't talk much after that. I sulked, and Orrin pulled papers back out of his briefcase, put on his glasses, and started reading, making an occasional note in the margins. I contributed to his hard work by trying not to fidget too much next to him. I didn't even check my email.

There was little I could do to influence whatever deal Skidmore got, but I couldn't help wondering if I'd be okay with it. I'd have her drawn and quartered, but that option wasn't on the table. Five years didn't feel like much for what she did. Then again, what difference did it make if it was one, five, or ten? Prison changes a person. It does it in a year as readily as a decade.

Zach would be in for the duration. Maybe that was punishment enough for a mother. I tried to figure out what Chloe and Ann would want. I thought it would be justice for Christine, finding her killer, even if it meant their captor spent fewer years behind bars. But then again, I wasn't the one trapped in that shed. I couldn't be sure.

Scheer interrupted my thoughts by knocking on the door and walking in with a notepad in hand. He sat in front of Orrin. He gave me a courtesy nod, but I was clearly right. Whatever I thought about Skidmore's punishment, I was a spectator here.

"We are ready to make a proffer," Scheer said. "I've been asked to make it on my client's behalf. You'll be able to ask questions, of course. I just sense she does not want to say anything that sounds remotely like an admission in front of Malone here."

Scheer glanced down at his notepad, waited for Orrin to finish scribbling notes, and continued. "If we have a deal on the nature of subsequent statements or testimony made pursuant to the proffer, she is willing to plead guilty to the false imprisonment charges. Now, about the sentence . . ."

Scheer waited for Orrin to make eye contact. "Come on, Dennis. She got caught in a bad situation. One year is enough to teach her a lesson the hard way."

Orrin put his pen down and pointed a finger at Scheer. "Your client is asking for a lot with a weak hand, and to top it off, she still refuses to take responsibility. First, she blamed it all on Malone. Now, she cries she's a poor, unlucky woman who got caught in the wrong place at the wrong time. She kidnapped two people, Matt."

"What are you offering?" Scheer asked.

"First, she allocutes and takes full responsibility for her actions. Everything, every act, every detail, without deflecting blame. Second, she drops her complaint against Malone and waives a civil action. It's her crime, not his."

Orrin took a breath and dove back in. "Third, she agrees to fifteen or eighteen months. We'll have to consult the gain-time tables and do some math, but I want a sentence that keeps her in jail for twelve months, no matter how well-behaved she is in there. She committed a felony, she does felony time, no blame game, no excuses."

Now it was Scheer who furiously took notes. When he finished, he looked up at Orrin and said, "I'll be back." Then he stood up and left the room, closing the door behind him.

"Is that how it always works?" I asked. "Horse trading? It's not just for TV shows?"

"Same as you did as a cop. You let the smaller fish go easy to catch a bigger one."

"I was never a cop, not really."

"Most PIs are," Orrin said by way of explanation.

"I came from the military."

Orrin nodded with the air of someone for whom something clicked, and the world finally made sense.

After that, we stayed silent for a while, and Orrin returned to his papers. It took longer than I thought it should have, but Scheer eventually returned. He didn't have a notepad with him this time. He just pushed the door open, popped his head in, and said the terms were acceptable and we could reconvene.

Orrin gathered the tools of his trade—papers, glasses, briefcase, and all—then walked past Scheer back to the first conference room.

I went through next, and Scheer fell in lockstep with me. He extended his hand to me as we walked side by side. "No hard feelings, Mr. Malone?"

"That depends on what your client has to say. But if you're talking about your tactics, no, no hard feelings. I may even call you if I'm ever up shit creek." I shook his hand.

Scheer chuckled. "You know where to find me. And I have a big paddle."

We entered the conference room and took our seats. Skidmore hadn't moved, but her eyes were red and her makeup splotchy. The box of Kleenex that once sat on a side table now rested in front of her.

Scheer started telling his client's story—the legalese version, anyway. "Under a plea agreement, Ms. Skidmore may be able to testify to the following: On the night of the fifth to the sixth of July, she became aware that her son Zach had gotten in a fight with three young women. She also learned that in an impetuous act, he had locked them in a house she had listed for sale. She was told that one of the three women had escaped. Acting on that information, she helped Zach move the other two women onto her property."

"The garden shed," Orrin said, looking up from his pen and paper.

"Yes," Scheer said. "In any event, she believes she was followed. She was wrestling with how to end that mess—that is how she viewed the situation—when she received a visit on the evening of the sixth. That person assured Ms. Skidmore that if she kept both women for a few days, her interlocutor would convince one of them to retract her story about Zach, leaving only one to testify against both Zach and the other boys, and her son wouldn't be in trouble."

"Which victim was to be convinced to retract?" Orrin asked.

"Ann Berger."

"Thank you. Go on."

"That's the gist of it."

Orrin looked up. "That does not tie to Ms. Raymond's murder." He was thinking like a lawyer about what he could put before a jury, about what did or did not constitute evidence in court.

I was thinking like an investigator, linking the dots. "But it does," I said. "She's probably right, and she was followed, or her visitor would not have known where Chloe and Ann were. So whoever followed her was at or near the beach house when the girls were moved, right after Christine escaped. And if they were at the beach house right around that time, it's probably because they ended Christine's escape. They murdered her."

"Even if Mr. Malone is right," Orrin said, waving his reading glasses around, "and your client's testimony leads to the identity of Ms. Raymond's killer, her allocution will have to be much more detailed than that. She will have to take full responsibility for every aspect of her actions, including her treatment of the victims after she moved them to her garden shed."

I barely heard him, let alone Scheer's assurances in response or Orrin's reply to that. I was inside my head. What happened the night of Christine's death was becoming clearer. I could picture Jennifer Berger preaching about Chloe and Ann's wickedness, all fire and brimstone—and hate. Especially hate. I could picture her righteousness in making other people suffer. How had she gotten that way? And how . . .?

I spoke up. "How on earth did she say she would convince Ann to change her story? These two are barely talking. She had not convinced Ann of anything in years. Did she tell you that?"

Skidmore nearly jumped from her seat before Scheer could answer for her. "She? It wasn't a *she*. It was some dude!"

"Can you describe him?" Orrin asked.

"Tall, glasses like a windshield. The seventies called and asked for them back . . ."

I stopped listening. I texted Courtney, begging for a picture, any picture of the man in my mind, from social media, his job—wherever God or the devil had put one up.

The others were still talking when Courtney texted me a photo. I thrust my phone in Skidmore's face, interrupting everyone again.

"Him?" I asked.

"Yes, that's him. He looks younger in the picture, but that's him."

I got up, nearly toppling my chair, and powered to the door.

"Malone!" Orrin called back.

"It's Bill Berger," I said without looking back. Then I was gone.

CHAPTER 30

It was too late to head straight to Orlando. By the time I'd get there, no one would answer a friendly knock on the door—or an unfriendly one, for that matter. So, I went home. I could afford to wait a few hours. I'd still reach the Bergers' house long before Orrin could get the ASA in Orlando to act on Skidmore's testimony.

I called Sergeant Michaels on my way home and told him the complaint against me was about to be dropped. I called CJ, too, and filled her in. She asked if I was on my way to Orlando to get Bill Berger. My partner knew me well. I told her I would go in the morning, and we argued about backup. I didn't want any.

"The man is deranged," CJ had said. "He killed once already and conspired to keep his own daughter prisoner. There is no telling what he might do."

"This may all be true, but he's still a suburban dad who's in over his head. I'm pretty sure I can handle him safely. Your time is better spent on our ten other cases than babysitting me."

She hadn't been convinced, but she relented and hung up after telling me to be careful.

I texted Amy next, fessed up that I was sulking tonight, but I needed to leave for Orlando in the middle of the night, so it was better I stayed by myself, and I was okay. She wasn't convinced either, but she let it go. There was a pattern to the people in my life.

Once home, I had a shot of rye. It would long be out of my system by the time I needed all my wits about me, and it took the edge off in the meantime. Then, I sat for a while and worked on quieting my mind.

I needed to know why. I needed to know how. How did Berger get to Christine? Why did he kill her? Sure, he was bitter over his life, over the fights between Jennifer and Ann. He'd even told me he blamed Chloe and Christine, though not as directly or vehemently as Jennifer had. It was a stretch from there to killing.

What went through Berger's mind when he pulled the trigger? When he kept firing his gun again and again? What went through his mind when he got into cahoots with Skidmore? It was enough to drive me crazy, but I couldn't let it. I'd get my answers tomorrow. That's what I needed to focus on. I would get answers. Tomorrow. That was the only way to quiet my screaming brain long enough to sleep.

I opened my door long before dawn the following day, all decked out with my .45 on my hip and the short-nosed .38 in its custom holster in the small of my back, both covered by my overlong polo. Outside, darkness welcomed me like a warm blanket. Orrin could have stopped me if he'd really wanted to, but there were no night-shift cops on my doorstep, no patrol car bathing the house in blue lights. Orrin had one piece of testimony and little proof of anything. Sure, he would get to the bottom of it—eventually. Maybe he wouldn't be heartbroken if I tried it my way first.

I got in the CR-V and started on the long drive up.

With Ann back in Gainesville, Jennifer in a nine-to-five job, and Bill working from home, it wasn't difficult to time my arrival to catch Bill alone—and before local law enforcement was called to detain him.

I parked on their street right around nine in the morning. Jennifer would be at work already. In fact, the whole neighborhood looked deserted. I walked to the house, head on a swivel, ready for anything, but nothing moved. There wasn't even a breeze blowing through the magnolias in the Bergers' front yard, not a footstep echoing down the sidewalk—nothing but a lonely sprinkler down the street watering the lawn at the wrong time of day. Suburban life played itself out in all its languor.

The door was open a crack when I got to the porch. I pushed it with two fingers, and it swiveled noiselessly on its hinges. I stepped in, careful to stay silent. I wasn't worried about being heard. I figured Berger somehow knew I was here, that he knew I'd come and left the door open for me. My silence was meant to help me listen. I didn't want to mask any noise coming from inside.

I walked in, hand hovering by the gun on my hip. I wasn't sure what to expect. Maybe I shouldn't have argued with CJ over backup. I crossed a tiny vestibule—an entryway just big enough for a rug and an umbrella stand. There was no sound but the soft contact of my rubber soles on the tile floor. I took one step into the living room and found myself facing Bill Berger, sitting on a sofa with a gun in his hand.

"Are you armed?" he asked, pointing his weapon at me.

"I am." I cursed myself for not drawing the moment I entered the house. I'd underestimated the crazies, suburban dad or not. You'd think I was a rookie at this shit.

"Remove your gun with two fingers," Berger said. "Two fingers only. And put it on the kitchen island on your way over."

I did as he asked. I lifted my polo, unholstered my .45 with two fingers, and placed it on the giant quartz island separating the kitchen from the living room.

"Sit in that chair," he said, pointing to a loveseat across from him with his gun barrel.

I was halfway there when he told me to stop.

"You want me to sit, or you want me to stop?" I asked.

"Lift your shirt," he said.

I did.

"You pant legs too. You guys always carry a backup piece around the ankle."

I lifted my jeans over my boots, showing nothing but leg. "You watch too much TV."

He pointed to the loveseat again. I'd hoped he'd forgotten. I preferred being on my feet, ready to move. I sat down anyway, staying aware of my surroundings. My automatic was four feet behind me. Berger and his gun sat ten or twelve feet across from me. An orchid and a candle sat on a tray on a coffee table between us.

Berger slumped on the sofa, shoulders drooping, dark circles under his eyes. His white dress shirt was wrinkled, the cuffs unbuttoned. He spoke slowly, like a disinterested high schooler in drama class, making a show of not caring about the lines he was rehearsing.

"I knew you'd show up again after you came to talk to Jennifer the other day. I'd been waiting for you. I even left the door open so you wouldn't have to break the lock."

"I'd have knocked."

"Maybe," he said, sounding as disinterested as ever. "You took longer than I thought."

"Is that the gun you used to kill Christine?" I asked, cutting short our discussion about my timeliness and door manners.

Berger looked down at the weapon, examining it as if he saw it for the first time. "It seems like everyone in this state has one," he said, "so I got one too. It lives in a case under my car seat. Nobody knows I have it, not even Jennifer."

"It's one thing to own a gun. It's another to put a bullet in someone."

Berger cocked his head. "Not really. You know what I found out? I found out how easy it is. You pull the trigger, and the bullet goes. Just like that."

"And somebody dies."

"I really don't care about that. I'm dead too, you see. Her heart stopped beating. So what? It was easy. Bang, bang, bang, bang." He pushed the gun forward with each *bang* as if poking me with the barrel or reliving the way bullets flew with each pull of the trigger.

He sounded like he was in a daze. I wondered if he was on something and immediately dismissed the idea. For all the heaviness about him, his eyes were clear. His gun wasn't wavering.

"You look pretty alive to me," I said.

"Looks can be deceiving," he said in that detached voice like he was speaking someone else's words. "I died inside the moment those girls came into our lives. I just didn't know it then."

"Chloe and Christine?"

"They drove a wedge between Ann and her mom, and I lost them both. You don't know what it's like to lose your family like that. Their bodies were still all around me, but the people I knew were gone. The way Ann started talking to her mom . . . it wasn't her. She was mean, cruel. She did everything she could to provoke and anger her. It was as if creating misery in our house was all she cared about.

"And Jennifer? She just stopped talking. She barely said a word to anyone. She just hid in church. Nothing mattered anymore—not her family, certainly not me—only the church. It was bad enough when it was St. James. But then she joined that . . . that cult. It wasn't even religion anymore. It was all hell and demonic possessions. It was like a bad horror movie, except it was my life. Have you ever lived in a horror movie, and you couldn't say, 'Cut!'? It kept on going and going. I had lost them both. I lost everything."

He kept on talking, and I let him. The more he talked, the better. Maybe if he talked long enough, if he got it all out, he'd put the gun down.

"It would have been easier if they died in some car accident," Berger continued. "Then I could have grieved. I could have let them go. But they didn't. They transformed into monsters. They lived in my house, ate at my table, and brought nothing but their anger with them. I was living through their spirits' deaths every single day."

"Killing Christine wouldn't change that," I said when he trailed off.

"I know that. She didn't give me any choice."

"How's that?"

He leaned in, and his mouth spread into a smile. He windmilled the air with his free hand. He spoke louder. "When they were taken, I thought things would finally change. That's what I'd been waiting for—something to end this cold, inner death that had taken me over. Now, Ann would see how dangerous it was to live the way she did. I would be able to talk some sense into her, into them both—Jennifer too. Everything would go back to the way it was before. I would have my family again.

"Except that the next day, well, Jennifer was holed up in that church on the island, the other parents were all in Reggie's RV, and I was on our cabin's porch. I saw movement by a house near the ocean. I recognized Christine right away. If she was running out, the others would follow. She was ruining everything. I got my gun and ran to meet Christine. I couldn't let her reach the resort. I nearly didn't make it. Damn, that girl was fast. But I got to her. I told her she had to go back. She had to stay wherever they all were."

He ran one hand through his hair, rubbing his scalp, and gesticulated with his gun hand. "She tried to run by me. She screamed for her parents. She said she'd take us to Ann and Chloe. She pointed to the house where they were. I couldn't let her do that.

"I . . . I don't know what happened, really. I was mad, and she wasn't listening. My hand tensed over the gun, and it went off. The bullet made a weird sound when it hit her body, and all of a sudden, I knew what I needed to do. I shot her again. I shot her until the gun went click, click, click, and all the bullets were gone."

His gun barrel dropped as he expended the last of his ammo in his mind. Then he caught himself and gripped the weapon tighter, pointing it straight at me again. He made a fist with his other hand. "It was so easy! Man, it was such an elegant solution. People were still shooting some fireworks even though it was the day after the Fourth. No one heard the gun. I dumped Christine in the ocean, and voila. I couldn't believe my luck. I could make it all work out again."

I didn't move. I stayed still on the stupid loveseat. My back sweated against the cushion. I couldn't let him see any reaction. I couldn't antagonize him. I had to keep him talking. It wouldn't take much for him to do to me what he did to Christine.

"Then you followed Skidmore and made sure Ann wouldn't get out, not until you decided she could," I said.

"Is that the woman's name? I never asked. I laid in wait by the house Christine had come from. When I didn't see anyone else come out, I took my car and drove to the front. There was a black SUV in the driveway. Two people with guns were walking Ann and Chloe toward it. I followed them. People really don't pay attention, you know. You must have an easy job.

"Once I knew where Ann was being taken, I returned to the resort and tried to figure out what to do next. I went back the next evening to talk to the woman in the SUV. I needed Ann to stew for a few days, so she'd be ready to listen. That way, I'd get her and Jennifer back."

He extended his arm. Having the gun six inches closer to my chest must have made a difference to him. "I had a chance to get my family back, and you ruined everything."

"Were you hoping Jennifer would convince the others not to hire me? You didn't play along with her all that hard."

Berger grinned. "I'm a smart man, Mr. Malone. I played both sides. Jennifer has to be good for something. If she could keep you out of the way, great. But I didn't care that much. I didn't think you'd find them, not that quickly. Too damn bad. Now, I might have to kill you."

The man was gone. Maybe he had it right—he was dead inside. His life had gone off the rails so badly it had changed him, driven him to insanity. Maybe, long ago, he could have done something about it—get counseling, become firmer with Ann or Jennifer, or even get a divorce. No one will ever know if, in another world where Bill Berger made different choices leading to that fateful Fourth of July, Christine still lived.

In this world, Bill had done nothing—nothing but wait and slowly descend into madness. And once he'd fired his gun, the gun became the object of his deliverance. He lived in a world so far away from reality that there was no reasoning with him. My only chance out of this was to play along.

"Why don't you come with me?" I asked. "We'll explain everything. Family comes first. I get it. Others will too. People will understand."

"No, they won't. But that's okay. I have enough money squirreled away. I can go somewhere no one will find me and wait for my own heart to stop. I only need to decide whether I need to shoot you first so I can be left in peace."

I closed my eyes for an instant. I needed to find an answer that would fit into his demented world and keep him from shooting me.

"People will understand," I said. "I understand. I've seen losses like this before—soldiers coming home to nothing, a world that's empty for them. I've seen them die inside, the way you have, and just wait for the body to catch up. I can give closure to Christine's parents with what I have. I don't need to chase you down. If you kill me, though, other people will."

Berger stood. He moved slowly as if every movement was an effort. He wasn't hurt, not that I could see, not physically. It was a different kind of hurt, one that made him unpredictable.

He kept his gun pointed at me, finger on the trigger. He moved silently, tracing a semi-circle, giving my seat a wide berth. He reached the kitchen island and took my gun.

I turned around in the loveseat, keeping my eyes on him. I stayed seated, like he'd said, with my feet flat on the floor.

Berger rounded the island. He was about to disappear down the hallway toward the garage when he said, "Eh, fuck it."

Those three words saved my life. Before he was done speaking, I launched myself off the loveseat, diving forward and sideways, staying low. His shot went through the back of the loveseat and sailed over my head as I dove behind the coffee table.

He roared and fired two more shots, putting another hole in the furniture and breaking a window. Then he ran.

I ran too, but I didn't run after him. He only had one way to go, and I planned on being there to give him a warm welcome. I ran toward the front door. I pulled my .38 revolver from its holster at the small of my back, the one Berger's half-ass search had missed when he asked me to lift my shirt but never had me turn around.

I hadn't closed the front door when I came in. Now, I pushed past it and headed straight out, sprinting toward the end of the driveway.

Berger was already gunning his Edge out of the garage. The door wasn't up all the way, but he kept accelerating and took out the lower panel. He'd moved quicker than I'd thought.

I was level with his front bumper. I lifted my gun over my head and sprayed six shots into the hood. I needed to get lucky. A 38-caliber bullet from a short barrel was likely to bounce off the engine block. Even if it damaged something, it wouldn't stop the car there and then unless I hit something critical like the electrical system, all while firing blind. One bullet had zero chance to seduce lady luck all by itself. I fired all six rounds. Maybe, just maybe, one of them would be the proverbial silver bullet.

As the last slug left the barrel, I made for the ground and rolled to the side until I reached a tree. I crouched behind the trunk, moving without thinking, each action coming to me automatically. Point the gun up. Drop the shells. Pull the speed loader from the holster's pouch. Slam six new bullets in.

Only once I flicked my wrist, locking in the cylinder, did I realize this was all happening to the tune of the most beautiful sound in the world—silence. The engine had stopped.

I straightened up and chanced a look around the tree just as Berger flung his car door open. He emerged with both guns in front of him, one in each hand, roaring and firing like he was starring in a Tarantino movie. And he kept firing, shooting wild, blind with rage and pain. If he didn't hit me, he'd end up hurting someone else.

I dove to the ground in a forward roll impressive enough to make a gymnast envious. At least, it looked that good in my head. All that mattered was that Berger's bullets flew high.

I landed in a crouch, aimed, and fired a clean double tap, just as I'd trained to do those many years ago. Berger took both to the chest.

Bill Berger's body slackened, held up at first by the Edge's back door. Blood spread onto his shirt. The guns fell to his side, clattering on the pavement. His lifeless body slid down the side of the Ford, leaving nothing but his crumpled form on the ground and a bright red streak on the side of his car.

Just like that, it was over.

CHAPTER 31

checked Bill Berger's body for a pulse. There was none. Straightening up, I looked down at what was left of the man. Maybe it had been too easy a death for what he did, for Reggie's and Cassie's suffering, for the life Christine never got to live. Or maybe not. Who was I to say? Bill had suffered his own kind of torture for years. He'd lost his humanity, little by little. The day he pulled the trigger and killed Christine, the last shreds of it vanished.

I holstered my weapon and called 911. I identified myself and told the responder the scene was secured, but they'd need to roll in the medical examiner. The cops showed up with lights, sirens, and screeching tires anyway. I greeted them with empty hands, arms wide to my side, and most of them calmed down quickly.

The uniformed officer who first talked to me was a young kid who had trouble taking the story down. The detective who showed up ten minutes later was easier to work with. I gave him a report in cop-speak. He took it down, shook my hand, bagged my gun, and asked me to wait there.

There were a lot of statements and a lot of waiting after that. I tried not to dwell on the nature of life. A drunk hooligan fired his gun in the air on the Fourth of July and set in motion a chain of events that left three people dead and countless lives shattered. I didn't dwell but committed their names to memory: Pamela Howard, Christine Raymond, and Bill Berger.

Yes, Bill too.

I used the time to make some calls. I fessed up to CJ that she'd been right. Backup might not have been the worst thing in the world. I told Amy we caught Christine's killer, but gunfire may have been involved. She was thrilled about part one, not so happy about part two.

I gave Tornero and Orrin a courtesy call. Tornero reminded me I was a pain in the ass. He didn't gloat about being right. It had been someone on the resort. And Orrin did not say anything at all. He wasn't about to admit on an open line that I'd made his job easier.

I went to the Raymonds' house as soon as I was free to go. I had to tell them that someone they'd once considered a friend had killed their daughter out of some senseless, monstrous delusion. I could only do that in person.

I'd given my share of bad news in my career. This case was bound to be worse than most, and it was. I told the Raymonds everything I knew. When I was done, they were sitting on an overstuffed sofa, heads down, holding hands. Cassie wept openly. Reggie had run out of tears. They tried to thank me, talk to me, but words could not pass through choked-out throats.

I couldn't blame them. What was the point? Was that even closure, or just breaking two hearts into smaller pieces? I put a hand on Reggie's shoulders and rose to leave them to their grief. Cassie caught up with me before I put my hand on the door. She hugged me and managed to whisper, "Thank you. God bless you." And she meant all of it.

I got back on the road after that. I needed to talk to Chloe and Ann, too, but that could wait a day, and it would be easier taking Courtney with me, someone the ladies could relate to better. It still wouldn't be an easy conversation. To Ann, I was the guy who killed her dad, who had killed her best friend. That wasn't a reason to delay, but it had been a long day.

It was dark by the time I got home. Amy's purple Wrangler was parked in the driveway, Amy leaning against the tailgate. I angled the headlights away from her face, killed the engine, and got out of the car.

"What's wrong?" I asked. Her million-dollar smile had lost all its zeros. She wasn't smiling at all.

We walked to each other. She tried to say something, swallowed the words back, then hit my chest with her fists and kept at it. About four or five blows in, she croaked, "You asshole."

"Okay, I'm an asshole," I said matter-of-factly, giving her space to explain.

She punched me harder, just once, then put her forehead to my chest, her blond hair falling on either side like a protective curtain. Once she started talking, the words came tumbling from her mouth like a dam had broken.

"One month, Coop," she said. "One month, and you've been shot at and punched and ambushed, and God knows what else. You made me fall in love with you, and I even told you I loved you, and I hadn't said that to anyone since I was young and stupid and naive. You can't do that, you asshole! You can't make me love you and then go get yourself killed."

I took her fists in my hands and held them close to my heart. She looked up at me, eyes rimmed with tears.

"I could tell you I've pulled my gun more often in the past four weeks than the four years before," I said. "It'd be true, but it wouldn't change a thing. And now that we've solved two murder cases, we'll likely have more violent crimes referred to us. It's a small world. Word gets around."

Amy laughed in spite of herself. "Is that supposed to make me feel better?"

"It's supposed to show you I'll never lie to you. Never did, never will. What I do is risky. I can't promise you that nothing bad will ever happen. But the risks I take are calculated. They're calculated to stay within the universe of what I know how to handle. I'm not reckless. Even when it looks like I'm going full speed ahead and damn the torpedoes like a bonehead, I'm not reckless."

She nodded, a single tear trickling down her cheek, and buried her head back into my chest. The weight of her distress squeezed my heart, but she was breathing more softly now. It was time to take her inside and lift her out of her dark mood like she'd done for me so many times, like only we could do for one another. But first, I wrapped my arms around her. I kept her close and whispered in her ear.

"I'm not going anywhere."

ACKNOWLEDGEMENTS

It may be my name on the cover, but this book would not exist without the love and support of so many friends and family members, not to mention publishers, editors, and all the others who added their touch along the way.

It starts with you, Penny, because without you, not only would this book not be in print, but it wouldn't mean a thing regardless. You are my life, my happiness, my inspiration to be a better person and a better writer.

My parents are a constant source of love and support.

I could rattle off two dozen names, but we all mute the TV when they do that at the Oscars, and I'd forget someone anyway, so I won't even try. I am filled with gratitude for all those who have helped me in small ways and big, for every kind word and every minute spent for my benefit. And because I can't help it, I'll give a quick extra tip of the hat to Nick, my (younger) oldest and dearest friend, Lauren, who keeps my mind and joints fluid, Josh, who truly gets Coop, Jon for his keen eye, Emily, who called me tautological, and Cocoa, wise beyond her years and with an infectious enthusiasm.

Last but not least, books are a business, and my thanks go to all the people who toil in it, from paper mill workers to big rig drivers, those behind keyboards or the wheels of delivery trucks. I am in your debt.

DON'T MISS COOP'S NEXT ADVENTURE

A good girl gone wild. Two bullets to her chest.

She had secrets. Is it what got her killed? Or is something more sinister lurking in the underbelly of glitzy Miami?

Coop takes the case despite knowing danger awaits from the start. How deep into the darkness will he, CJ, and Courtney—now a fully-fledged private investigator—need to go to find a killer?